Sue Williams is a science and travel writer and a chartered accountant who also holds a PhD in marine biology. Her articles have been published in a range of magazines and on 'The Science Show' on ABC Radio National. Sue lives in Melbourne with her husband. *Murder with the Lot* is her first book.

SUE WILLIAMS

MURDER WITH THE LOT

TEXT PUBLISHING MELBOURNE AUSTRALIA

textpublishing.com.au

The Text Publishing Company
Swann House
22 William Street
Melbourne Victoria 3000
Australia

First published by The Text Publishing Company, 2013

Cover design by WH Chong
Page design by Text

Printed in Australia by Griffin Press an Accredited ISO AS/NZS 14001:2004 Environmental Management System printer

National Library of Australia Cataloguing-in-Publication entry : (pbk)
Author: Williams, Sue I.
Title: Murder with the lot / by Sue Williams.
ISBN: 9781922079787 (pbk.)
ISBN: 9781921961984 (ebook)
Subjects: Detective and mystery stories.
Dewey Number: A823.4

For Ross

If I wanted to hide somewhere there's no way I'd choose Rusty Bore. A hundred and forty-seven residents and every single one of them is watching. No one here forgets a thing. Especially your mistakes.

It was a normal Friday evening in December, or so it seemed. I was auto-cleaning my spotless counter, considering putting up my row of knitted Santas in the window, when Madison Watkins arrived and tied up her ferrets out the front. I don't permit animals in my shop, particularly not the frenzied, hissing kind. The doorbell jangled as Madison sashayed in.

'The usual, thanks Cass.' She slipped into one of my white plastic chairs and crossed her long legs.

I dropped her dim sims in the oil, gave her the welcome smile.

Madison is an overflowing-looking girl, fond of green eyeshadow and clothes that strain to contain. She's not what you'd call fat, more a person that stores her weight in the right places. Sometimes I allow myself to toy with the idea that I still look a bit like Madison. I was runner-up Chiko Chick 1983, after all. Dim the lights and I could be Madison with twenty years' more wisdom and experience. And two adult sons; some extra smile lines; supplementary stretch marks.

She picked up a copy of *Truckin' Life* from the pile on the plastic table. 'You've gotta get better reading material in here,' she said. 'Something with a few hunky blokes.'

Maybe that meant she'd split up with Logan. Maybe he was back in jail. Since she broke up with Brad, Madison had been steadily working her way through the local dropkicks.

'I'll bring in a few copies of *Cleo*,' she said. 'You should read the article about settling for Mr Reasonably OK. It'll help you understand why you're single.' She sighed. 'It's your standards, Cass. They're too high.'

I straightened up my pile of white paper, ready for precision wrapping. Reasonably OK didn't sound exactly tempting. But it was true I could probably find space in my life for a nice fella, someone who made me laugh.

'I mean, I know forty-five is getting pretty old, but...'

'I'm in my prime.' I tried not to bristle. I had to admit it was a drawn-out and alone type of prime since Piero died, what, one year, ten months and fifteen days ago. I met Piero when I was seventeen. And fell pregnant shortly after. Piero had a ferocity of fertility that was bloody well uncalled for.

'Course,' she said quickly. 'And you still look terrific. Really.' She gave me an appraising stare. 'You could use a bit more makeup maybe. And a better hair cut. But you've got bones, and the voice isn't bad. Blokes love that molasses-over-gravel thing.' She uncrossed and recrossed her legs. 'You know today's forty-plus woman is having miles more orgasms than ever before? Saw that in *Cleo*.' She paused. 'You only get so many orgasms before you die.'

I shook her order in the oil.

'Hey, I've just had a brainwave.' She threw aside the magazine. 'What about Vern? You two have got a lot in common. His shop, your shop.'

Vern's general store and my place constitute the CBD of Rusty Bore, along with a row of three galvanised-steel silos. It's a town endowed with a royal flush of used-to-haves since the school, the pub and even the op shop closed down.

'And Vern fancies you. He's motivated. Definitely.' Madison stood up and walked over to my counter, all fired up. She put her arms up on the glass top, bangles jingling.

'Uh huh.' I'd experienced Madison's brainwaves before. First up there was Ben, the McKenzies' Landcare volunteer: tall, tousle-haired and divorced. I'll admit I didn't mind the way he wore his shirts unbuttoned and his jeans tight. But Ben wasn't sure. He stopped at a very inconvenient time to tell me so, a serious case of lustus interruptus. He could be gay, he said, or maybe bi; he needed more experience to figure it all out.

Next was Will, sixty-two, soon-to-be-retired wheat farmer, on his own since Bronwyn died of dementia. Will had looked into my eyes and asked if I had Alzheimer's in the family, then spent the evening sobbing into his chocolate and hazelnut terrine.

'Reckon you need someone a little younger,' Madison

had said, lining up Adam, saggy-stomached computer sales rep from Mildura. Adam got down on his knee in the foyer of the Deakin cinema on our first date and asked me to marry him. Turned out he was already married. In three states. And a territory.

Finally, in desperation, she suggested Showbag. But even Madison knew there was no way that could ever work, not after what happened that time at Vern's.

To be fair, it was Madison who told me about the blindfold speed dating night in Muddy Soak. That was a night with some real potential. I got talking, blindfold on of course, to a bloke with a gentle voice. He managed to make me laugh before the three minutes was up. He reached across the table and touched my hand, ignoring the signal bell to move on to his next date. But then the fire alarm went off, sprinklers gushing water, people stampeding everywhere. My chair got knocked over and I ended up on the floor. By the time I got my blindfold off, the bloke had gone. I had no idea of what he looked like; hadn't even got his name.

'Look, Madison, it's nice you care...'

'Standards,' she wagged a finger. 'You're as bad as Tamie. She's picky too.'

'Tamie?'

She pointed at the six ferrets squirming on their leads outside. One was sitting alone, away from the others, staring at the road. The wind whipped some leaves against the shop window. Clouds stained the colour of rust were building in the sky, a dust storm on its way.

I hooked up Madison's dim sims to drain. I don't suppose anyone likes being compared with a ferret, especially one that's a failure at the basic pursuit of ferreting.

4

But was it possible Madison had a point? Was I being picky? There was nothing really wrong with Vern. He was mostly intact. It was just...

'Thing is, Madison, just because the fella's motivated doesn't mean I am.'

'Well, think about it. Vern's not a bad bloke. I bet he'd stick by you. Not like...um.'

'Not like who?'

'Oh you know. Half the men around.' She rubbed her face.

I wrapped up her order in fresh white paper.

'So, um, Brad around?' Madison cupped her chin in her hands and tried to look casual.

Brad's my youngest, a certified organic vegetarian and friend of the earth, albeit with a weakness for the smell of frying bacon. He's six foot one, straight black hair, exact spit of Piero. I just hope he doesn't have the hyperactive fertility as well.

'Abseiling the Hume Dam wall at the minute. Putting up a banner.'

'Oh? What's the banner say?'

'Save the Murray.' I'd tripped over that banner enough times, laid out for days along my hallway, held down by piles of old *Australian Geographic*s and *Chain Reaction*s. Before he left, Brad had borrowed another hundred bucks and was now categorically overdue the parental pep-talk. The one that mentions getting a job that pays some bills. And moving himself and those magazines out of my place. Trouble was, I liked having Brad around, and not just because he reminded me of Piero. I'd have to do it though. It's not good for a boy to grow up viewing his mother as a slush fund.

'Brad's got so much passion,' said Madison with a sigh. 'Anyway, think about Vern. Seriously. Chicks like us need to get realistic.'

Chicks like us? I handed over her order. Maybe a woman my age couldn't afford to be too picky, but Madison needed to raise her standards, not lower them. Madison could have almost anyone. Especially if she ditched the ferrets.

Not long after Madison left, trailing ferrets, the dust-storm hit. All living creatures fled the street as the red waves of wind ripped through town. The shop roof shuddered, corrugated iron screeching overhead. Within minutes the street was shrouded in a red–brown haze and Best Street's solitary streetlight clicked on. My nose tingled as the air filled with the dust storm's distinctive burning smell. I galloped around the shop, armed with towels and rags, plugging up every tiny gap. But the hot, gritty air still swirled into every crevice you might imagine and a few you'd rather not.

My doorbell jangled and I looked up, thinking it was Madison returning, taking cover from the dust.

It wasn't Madison. A young fella in a grey suit. He was kind of oily looking, but then I operate in a permanent atmosphere of oil so I couldn't hold that against him. And I know better than to turn away a customer based on looks.

'Yeah, burger with the lot and chips.' He flicked a look at my door. 'And make it quick.'

Quick? Superior fast food takes time. I pride myself on quality chips; crisp on the outside, fluffy in the middle. And a top-notch burger with the lot requires precision stacking. With unhurried and steady hands. Comfort food's been in my family for generations. I plonked his patty and onions onto the grill, then turned back round to give him the glare.

'Oh, no onions,' he said. 'Or beetroot or egg. And I hate pineapple.' Another glance at the door.

A burger without the lot, in fact. I scraped his onions off the grill. Dumped his chips into a basket and lowered it into the oil. I kept up the glare.

Skinny and slope-shouldered, he was holding tight to a briefcase, a scruffy-looking number with one of those combination locks near the handle. There were gold letters next to the lock that I couldn't quite make out. His suit was torn, the sleeve shredded and bloodstained.

He looked like an accountant who'd been shoved backwards through his ledger. Or maybe he was a crook, a grubby white-collar kind. He didn't let go of the case. He didn't put it on the floor near his feet. He didn't put it on the table while he waited for his order. He gripped it in a white-knuckled hand and darted glances out my window.

From his ripped-up sleeve, three drips of blood splashed on my floor.

'You all right? Need a bandage?' I said.

'Nah. It's...nothing.' He didn't sound too convinced of that.

'I'll phone the doctor for you.' There's no doctor in Rusty Bore but the hospital in Hustle is only forty clicks away.

'No!' His voice was sharp. He limped over to the door, peering up and down the road. 'Anyone been in looking for me?'

I stared. 'Not unless you're called Minimum Chips.' I

tried a little smile to ease the tension.

'You're sure? No one's been in after me?' His voice was high.

My skin prickled.

'I need somewhere quiet to stay for a while.' The sleeve dripped more blood in my doorway.

I wiped the sweat from my hands onto my floral apron. Maybe I should phone Dean. Leading Senior Constable Dean Tuplin. My eldest. Only a senior constable at the moment, but on a career trajectory. I didn't like to bother Dean without good cause, though. Not in view of that slight fiasco regarding Ernie.

'So I can write my book. I've got to do it straight away,' he said.

I gave his chips a little shake, put the basket back into the oil.

'I can pay all right.' He walked over, flipping open his wallet with the bloodied hand, still holding onto his case with the other. Inside the wallet was a photo of him with a girl, their heads close and cosy. Nice-looking girl. Maybe he had hidden talents under the unfortunate weaselly exterior.

He laid the wallet on my counter, slipped out a pile of shiny one-hundred-buck notes. His wallet was thick with them. 'How much?'

I hooked up his order to drain and did some rapid thinking. There was Ernie's old shack up at the lake. Ernie could do with the money, it would help him pay for his care now he's in the home. 'What's your name, anyway?'

'Clarence...Brown.'

'Where you from?'

'Ah...Melbourne. Looking for a sea-change.'

We're approximately four hundred kilometres from the sea, but coming here would be a change all right. A million acres of wheat stubble. Good long stretches of red dirt. One salt lake. Shimmering.

I turned around and flipped his burger, laid out some bacon on the grill, turned back to face him. 'What you do in Melbourne?' I probably didn't need to know that. But around here grilling a stranger for their secrets is better than a holiday.

He gave me a glassy look. 'I'm...an accountant.'

Aha! But what kind of book would an accountant want to write? Some kind of textbook, maybe? Without delay, though? How urgent could an accounting textbook be? I kept my gaze fixed on Clarence. There was something about him that made me think of the time a huntsman spider found its way down my neck. The bristly soles of its too-many hairy feet against my skin. Ernie wouldn't want any trouble.

'And I don't want some journalist getting all the credit.' His voice was low, fierce. 'This book's gunna be a bestseller. Then they'll see.' He gave me a look that meant it.

'Who'll see what?'

He shrugged, staring at the floor. *Mumble, something, mumble, Muddy Soak.*

I stacked up Clarence's burger then wrapped his order and put it on the counter. He handed me a wad of hundred-dollar notes. I counted them. Jesus. Five thousand dollars. For a place without electricity? I paused a tick. Well, what harm could he do to the place? It was pretty much a wreck. Ernie would be bloody happy to see the money, he'd be giving me one of his smelly-breath cackles when I took it up to him. And Ernie's been good to me ever since I was a kid.

'It's up by Perry Lake. Make sure you keep the gate shut.' I handed Clarence the key.

'Thanks. And...just keep it to yourself...where I am,' he whispered. Another drop of blood splashed onto the floor.

I woke the next morning as a car pulled up outside. Very early, just on dawn. I don't like being woken by the sound of early-morning cars. Sometimes it's followed by the sounds of smashing glass and of me yelling at kids to leave my bloody windows alone and bugger off.

I live in the weatherboard house behind the shop, it's just me. And Brad, when he's not away, tying up banners to save rivers, trees, birds or blue-tongue lizards.

I got up, pulled on my dressing gown and peered out of the window. The sky was slashed with jet trails tinted orange by the sunrise. I grabbed the sawn-off star picket I keep beside my bed. Bustled up the hallway, firmly dressing-gowned and star-picketed, ready for rodent kids.

But it wasn't a rodent-kid kind of car. It was a clean-looking white car, a late-model Commodore. A dark-haired man in sunglasses sat at the wheel. He darted a look at my shop window, flicked out some chewing gum, then drove off. I went around the place, checking all my windows, my door, the till. All seemed intact. I grabbed my handbag. Check. It still contained Ernie's wad, his five grand.

After breakfast I checked the bag again and headed out. I'd get Taylah to lock the money in the safe at the home, then I'd bank it for Ernie on Monday. I glanced at my watch. Nine o'clock. If I made it quick I'd be back before opening time.

My sky-blue Toyota Corolla might, like myself, be past its heyday, but it's still a goer. The lock on the driver's door was broken since someone tried to break in a couple of months back. I'd have to ask Brad to fix it, somehow get him galvanised. I sighed. Another pep-talk.

I got in the car from the passenger's side, squeezing myself over the handbrake and gearstick into the driver's seat.

I drove along Best Street, which some argue is Rusty Bore's only street, illogically in my view since we've also got Second Avenue. I headed past the closed hardware shop, its dusty windows covered in graffiti. Past the old town hall, Rusty Bore's own leaning tower of Pisa, propped up along one side with steel girders. Me and Piero danced at discos there in the early eighties. Him in his green Miller shirt, me in a silky white dress and long pearls from the op shop, deep into my Ultravox phase. It was there, out the back, that I first encountered Piero's overactive fertility.

Piero would have known what to say to Brad. Thing is, the boy needs a skill, something practical to earn a living. What Brad hasn't realised is that while everyone wants the planet saved, kind of, no one actually wants to pay for it. Still, he's building important retail expertise in my shop. I hope.

'How can you do it, Mum?' he'd asked on his first day, when I got him to cut up a couple of fresh yellowbelly. 'See their eyes? The way they look at you, full of blame?'

'You just cut off the heads and pop them quick into the bin,' I said. 'Why would you need to look into their eyes? You're not asking them out on a date.'

Really, if I faced facts, it was more than possible Brad wasn't going to make it as a top takeaway monopolist. Not that my monopoly was doing all that well these days, in any case. No, the survival of the Rusty Bore Takeaway was entirely dependent on low overheads.

Of course it was all different back when Piero and I set up our place nearly thirty years ago. Back then we still had rain and the full attention of the attendees of the annual show. *Rusty Bore—Original home of the Mallee Farm Days*, proclaims the weathered yellow sign at the entrance to the town. It's pretty sad our only claim to fame is what we used to have. We lost the Farm Days to Hustle back in '91.

I passed the row of three steel silos shimmering in the heat and took the turn onto the highway, heading south. The sun was already a hot glare in a polished blue sky.

They were good little eaters, those Farm Days visitors. They came from all over the country to look at the agricultural machinery on offer. It's hungry work, people used to tell me, looking eagerly at our lunchtime specials board. I could understand. I'd have been starving too after a morning of climbing around tillage and seeding machinery, nodding my head thoughtfully as I considered belt grain conveyors, chaser bins and land rollers. Even the Federal National Party member for the Mallee used to come in for a feed.

What would I say if I got the chance to update that welcome sign? *Home to a row of wheat silos and derelict railway sidings* might be fair but it doesn't have the upbeat tone I'd be looking for. We've got the Murray Matlock Dryland Tank Museum up the road, of course, with its array of old header parts, remains of a blacksmith's shop and an extensive bottle collection. They've even got a website. Although I don't think it gets a lot of hits.

Acres of greying wheat stubble drifted on by. A little dust devil whirled over the paddocks beyond.

A clammy twenty minutes later I was in Hustle, parking outside the squat apricot-brick building of the Garden of the Gods Extended Care Nursing Home. I struggled out of the car and crunched my way across the gravel car park.

Sophia was coming out the front door. 'Ah, Cassie, my little *bambina*.'

I'm not Sophia's bambina but she's Piero's mother and I don't argue with Sophia. Never, not even now Piero's dead. At ninety, Sophia still dresses with more flamboyance than anyone I've ever met. She describes herself as a geriatric starlet. A couple of art galleries have put on shows of her clothes.

Today she was wearing an emerald green shirt, huge flared pants and a chunky gold necklace. Ronnie, her second husband, is in the room next to Ernie's.

'Poor Ronnie,' she sighed. 'He move back ten more years, now he thinks we're in 1973. He keep asking when we gonna go see Mr Whitlam. I tell him next week, all set for lunch in Canberra. How's he, your Mr Jefferson?'

'I've got great news for Ernie.' I told her about Clarence and the rent. 'Writer bloke. Fella handed over five grand.'

'You joking. What is he like, this rich man?'

'Young fella. Dark hair, bit oily looking.'

She looked thoughtful. 'Not that young man the other man he's lookin' for?'

I stood still. 'What other man?'

'I don't remember now who tell me. Perhaps Vern. He knows many things.'

That shop of Vern's is just an elaborate device for sucking news out of the veins of anyone passing by.

'A man, he was askin' in the Sheep Dip roadhouse. Not very friendly, Vern say. He have a gun.'

My skin chilled. 'Gun?'

'Yes. Underneath his jacket, Vern say. And there was something about his eye, it was, you know, really off.' She gestured vaguely at her own eyes, bright unexpected blue behind huge flying-saucer glasses.

'Looking for the young fella, why?'

She leaned forward, lowered her voice. 'Mildura Mafia, most probably.'

'The fella looking say that?'

'*Omertà*, Cassie.' She nodded significantly. 'These men do not break their code of silence. Don't you watch the movies, *cara*?'

Suddenly, Ernie's five grand felt very heavy in my handbag.

'But I must not keep you,' said Sophia. 'Is new-stock morning in the Op Shop. I'm lookin' for some nice thing to wear to Laura's deb.' She bustled off to her car.

Clarence was a normal customer, just slightly injured and carrying a lot of cash. Course he was. What was it he'd said? *Keep it to yourself...where I am.*

No way I was giving Ernie Mafia money. I turned around and strode back to my car.

'Dean?' I spoke into the mobile. 'Got someone you better check on, pronto. Bloke by the name of Clarence Brown. Possible Mafia type. Says he's a writer from Melbourne.'

'Really.' Dean's voice didn't have quite the sense of urgency I was looking for.

I explained about Clarence's blood, his mysterious book, the mean bloke at Sheep Dip looking for him. 'We don't want a gangster battle breaking out in Rusty Bore.'

'Gangsters. Right. Mum, why are you so sure he's a criminal?'

'I'm not sure, that's the point. That's why you need to check up on him.'

He sighed. 'This is the fourth time in the last two years you've asked me to check up on someone. And on each occasion they turned out to be completely normal law-abiding people. One of them was the mayor of Randall.'

'No one more devious than a politician, everybody knows that.'

'Look,' his voice softened. 'I'll try my best to get over tonight for a cuppa. I know you're lonely. But I can't go looking into people's personal details, not unless there's an actual crime I'm investigating. Reasonable grounds for suspicion, at least.'

'I've just explained all that. I've definitely got reasonable grounds.'

'Mum. *I've* got to have the reasonable grounds, not you.' He hung up.

Great, thanks Dean. I spent a moment drumming my fingers on the steering wheel. Time for a change of plan.

In fact it was obvious. Clarence could have his five grand back. I started the car. Yes; I'd tell him the place was double-booked. Big rush on Christmas tourists. I took the turn onto the highway, wound down my window to get some breeze.

I swerved, dodging a rabbit on the road. It was embarrassing I'd taken that money in the first place. I hadn't even asked for references. How bloody hopeless was that? Ernie didn't need Mafia fellas stamping around the home.

But would Clarence be the type of bloke to just accept his eviction without an argument? Did he have a gun? I shivered, despite the heat. No one would hear a shot at Ernie's place. Nothing around but miles of mallee scrub. Maybe I should have brought along my star picket. The car shook as a truck carrying irrigation pipes thundered past.

There was a car parked by the roadside ahead. Silver Mercedes, no rust, no dust. A girl was walking around the car holding out a mobile. Looking for a signal. She had honey blonde hair and wore a floaty apricot dress. She'd be lost, headed for one of the fancy river towns up by the Murray. Or broken down. There was nothing for her here, not unless she was in the market for a silo.

I pulled over, struggled out over the handbrake and strolled across to the Mercedes. 'Need some help?'

She was young, anywhere from thirteen to eighteen. Her face had that perilous blend of innocence and over-confidence, a girl her parents would never stop worrying about. For the first time I was glad I'd only had sons.

'Yes. I must have like mixed up the directions,' she said, a too-bright smile.

Something about her nagged at my memory.

'I told you not to rely on that stupid GPS.' There was a woman in the driver's seat. Map spread out over the steering wheel, its edges crumpled in her white-knuckled hands. Lines chiselled around her eyes and mouth, age spots on her hands. She was wearing a gold knit dress.

'Where you headed?'

'We're fine, thank you.' The woman's voice was glacial. 'Get back in the car, Aurora.'

'Just a second. She might have seen him.' The girl fiddled in her apricot-coloured handbag, exact match with her dress. She held out a photo. Her wooden bracelet, sculpted into waves, clunked against her bag.

'Oh, for God's sake. This...person won't know anything. Get back in the car.'

I took the photo. Two people. The girl standing in front of me, and Clarence. I'd seen the same photo in his wallet. 'Yeah, I've seen him. Friend of yours?'

Aurora stiffened. 'He's my brother.'

This girl had a brother with Mafia connections? Did she know it? Jesus, wasn't it a family thing? What about her?

'We need to find him. Nanna's really worried. About what he's going to do. It's kind of urgent,' said Aurora.

'Urgent how? If he's just writing a book?'

The woman flung the crumpled map aside and shoved the car door open. She stepped out, a tiny woman, an angry sunbird in gold heels. 'Book? What's your involvement in this? Are you hiding Clarence? How dare you.'

'Why would I be hiding him?'

She compressed her lips, then looked at the girl. 'I should have sent Ravi. I simply don't have time to deal with this, with people of this...ilk.'

'Now you listen here. Clarence is, as far as I am aware, staying in Mr Ernie Jefferson's shack, which is fifty kilometres that way.' I pointed one firm finger to the north. 'And as the agent for that property, I require him to leave the premises immediately. Leave the district, in fact. We don't tolerate criminal types around here.'

'Criminal types?' The woman's voice had gone up an octave.

'Nanna.' Aurora gripped the older woman's arm.

The sunbird sucked in a breath.

I fossicked in my handbag, found Clarence's wad of money and held it out. 'Here. Take his stupid money. We don't want your kind around here. Now on your way.'

She frowned, pushed the money back, then put her hand into her bag. A bag easily big enough to hold a gun. I swallowed.

The hand came back out and she held out something

small. 'My card. Mona Hocking-Lee. Look, we seem to have got off to rather a poor start...'

I took it. *Managing Director, Balance Neutral.* No mention of the Mildura Mafia. But then they probably wouldn't put *Cosa Nostra Enterprises (North-West Division)* on their cards. An address in Muddy Soak.

'What's Balance Neutral?' Some kind of neutralising business? Hit-women maybe?

'I run a group of environmental organisations. Carbon offsets. Bird protection charities. But I'm not here on business. I'm here to talk some sense into my grandson. Before he does something stupid.' She glanced at Aurora.

'What kind of stupid? I'm not letting Ernie's shack out to the Mafia. I don't care whether they're tree-huggers or not.'

'Mafia?' Mona's voice was tight. She ran a hand across her forehead. 'Aurora, you didn't say anything about Mafia. You little idiot.' She got into the driver's seat. 'Get in the car. Quickly.'

Aurora folded her arms. 'I don't see why I'm getting the blame. I did the right thing, told you about his phone call. I'm not responsible for his like completely immature behaviour.'

Mona snapped me a look. 'What exactly did he tell you about the book?'

'Not a lot,' I said. 'It'll be a bestseller. That's it. How an accounting textbook could be a bestseller beats me, but what would I know?'

She sat up straight like a piano teacher, handbag in a death-grip on her lap. 'Accounting textbook? Is that what he said?'

'Well, no, not exactly.'

'No way it's some textbook, Nanna. He said we'd all be sorry.'

'Sorry for what?' I said.

Mona held up a hand. 'Oh, for God's sake. We're wasting time here. I really must talk to Clarence. This property, it's north of here? Get in the damn car, Aurora.'

Aurora scurried around the Mercedes and got in the passenger side.

'Thank you, Mrs...' Mona said, starting the car. She reached to close the driver's door.

I grabbed the door, held it open. 'Tuplin. Cass Tuplin. Of the Rusty Bore Takeaway. Best Street, Rusty Bore. Not so fast, though. You should contact the police if you're worried. In fact, my son...'

'No, no; no need to involve the police.' Her face had a hunted expression.

'Right, well, I'll come with you. I need to evict your grandson.'

'Ah, we really mustn't detain you, Mrs Tuplin. This is a family matter and I'm sure it won't take long.' Mona's tone was firm. 'I'll return your keys later today, I promise.'

'Hang on, what about this five grand? I don't want to carry all this around.'

'Yes, yes, we'll sort it out then.' She batted me away with a hand. 'I'm sure I can trust you with it.'

She stomped on the accelerator. The car jerked forward, ripping the door out of my hand, and she slammed it shut. The Mercedes tore off in a cloud of dust.

Mona didn't come into the shop that afternoon. She didn't pop around that evening, or even phone. I spent Saturday night fretting about that woman and Clarence and his five grand. In my distraction I burned Edna Rawson's snapper and chips.

'Acrylamide, Cass—carcinogens.' Edna waved her walking stick at the fryer. 'Millions of the bastards everywhere.' I stared at the blackened snapper in my basket. I never burn an order.

A bad night's sleep, tossing around, worrying about the money, the Mafia, the whole rental debacle. At dawn I decided I'd had enough. I rolled out of bed, got dressed and picked up my handbag. Check. I stood in the doorway of my bedroom, uncertain for a tick, then grabbed the sawn-off star picket from beside my bed. I headed out to my car.

The horizon was turning pale lemon as I took the turn

onto the highway, past the row of silos, black silhouettes against the sky.

I'd make a quick call in to Ernie's shack to return the rent. A polite request for them to be on their way, and life would go back to normal.

But what if they got violent? Come on, I whispered, Mona drives a Mercedes. And she's a grandmother. Hardly likely to get violent. I wound down the window and sucked in a deep lungful of dawn air.

I swerved for an early-morning kangaroo. The clouds were turning pale pink, blood-red wisps near the horizon. The twisted multi-trunks of the mallee gums were visible now, like long, pale necks above nests of fallen bark and leaves.

I passed the turning for Perry Lake. The gate was open. Shit, I really should put a padlock on that gate. I slowed the car and pulled over. Perry Lake's part of Ernie's place, a kilometre of so south of the shack. The lake was mined for salt once. It was long abandoned by the time my sister Helen and I used to come here, a wonderland of dereliction for a kid. Now it's become a spot for four-wheel-drives, trail bikes and joy riders, a free camping spot for cash-strapped grey nomads and a general dumping ground. I don't mind the campers, it's all the crap—the broken bottles, discarded tyres, cars and rusting fridges—that bothers me. I'd told Clarence to keep the bloody gate shut.

I turned onto the sandy track towards the lake, the track twisting through the spinifex and clumps of scrappy native pines. I should get Brad in here with his environmental whatsits, they could clean up the place, maybe turn it into a national park, like that Pink Lakes park over to the west. Perry Lake was just as good as that damn place. We've got miles of pink water; a long shore of pink sand with a rim of blinding, salty white. Visitors could marvel at the colour of the water and learn about the algae that cause it. Kids could play beach cricket while Dad burned their sausages on the barbie.

The lake smelled salty and faintly rotting, like the sea. There were fresh tyre marks in the sand. Muffled noises came from somewhere near the lake. Then a dull popping sound. A firecracker? A gun shot?

Maybe I should call Dean. I tapped the steering wheel. No, not after yesterday. It'd just be trespassers, and they were my problem, not his. And I had my star picket on the back seat.

I drove around the piles of decaying cars and fridges and the dumped sheets of rusted corrugated iron. A gust of wind buffeted the car. Brown clouds were building in the sky, more dust on its way. The lake appeared, clouds reflected in its pink–brown surface. The pink sand was crimson in the morning light. I scanned the perimeter of the lake. No strange cars in sight. But there was something over there. Yes, by the edge of the lake, a shape. A shape that didn't look right.

I stopped the car. Swiftly performing the exit manoeuvre over the handbrake to the passenger side, I leapt out and grabbed my star picket. I crunched my way across the sand, avoiding the squishy mauve clumps of glasswort, to the edge of the lake. The wind tugged at my dress. Grains of sand blew against my legs.

The shape beside the water was a woman. Her white fingers were curled up like claws. She was wearing a gold knit dress. There was a hole in her forehead, fringed with blood. More blood had pooled onto the sand.

Something had taken her eyes. I turned away, leaned over my star picket and threw up.

'Dean. Quick,' I said into my phone. 'There's a dead woman.' The reception wasn't real flash. Dean's voice came back a series of meaningless syllables, unconnected 'aps' and 'ets'. Still, he'd be speeding down the highway in a jiff, siren on full whack, strong jaw jutting out, like the cops in the midday movie.

The wind gusted, hot, hard breaths against my face. A posse of hungry-looking ravens stood near the woman.

'At Perry Lake,' I bellowed. More jumbled noises from the other end. I walked around, trying for better reception. I tried not to step in the uneven footprints around the body.

'A dead woman. It's that Clarence's grandmother, Mona Hocking-Lee. I told you that fella was trouble. You hear me, Dean? It's your mother.'

'What?' Dean finally connected his syllables. 'Is that you, Mum? What do you mean, you're dead?'

'No, *I'm* not dead.' For God's sake. 'It's your mother, me, *calling*. To report a body.'

Choppy bits of his voice. '...you're sure, really sure?'

'Sure of what?' I snapped. 'There's a dead bloody woman. Here in front of me. Hurry up and get here.'

The ravens edged closer to the body.

Dean's voice was back. 'What makes...think she's dead?'

Jesus, Dean. 'Because it's obvious.'

'It's just that there was that other time. You know, when you thought Ernie was dead.' Dean was coming through loud and clear now that it suited him.

'What's that got to do with it? No need to bring that up.'

Can't anyone ever make a little mistake around here? Ernie had looked dead. He smelled it too. And how could anyone sleep that deeply with their neck twisted in that position?

'I'll phone for the ambos,' said Dean.

'She doesn't need the ambulance. She's dead. There's a bullet hole in her forehead.'

I waved the cawing ravens away and bent over to peer at her face. A cloud of flies rose to greet me. I moved back quickly.

'And something's ripped out her eyes, ravens probably. Ernie still had his eyes.'

'I'm on my way.' Dean's voice was grim. 'You wait there.'

'You want me to phone Homicide?'

'No, that's my job. Just wait there, I'm not phoning anyone until I've seen things for myself. And Mum?'

He paused.

'Don't go touching anything.' He hung up.

What, am I an idiot? I know about not tampering with a crime scene. I scuffed some sand over my little pile of spew.

The grey-brown clouds were thickening in the sky, the wind gusting around my face. I put my phone back in my bag. My stomach moved uneasily. Maybe I was going to be sick again.

All right, Cass. Think of something cheerful. Homicide would be up from Melbourne, probably send in a team. A whole big team to investigate. Possibly a full-scale task-force. How many people in a taskforce? Stressful work for them. They'd need comfort food. Maybe I could set up a delivery service. My stomach moved again. No, the thought of food wasn't helping.

Leaning on my star picket, I settled in to wait. I'll admit I felt a sense of anticipation. Here I was, at Dean's crime scene, his first actual murder. Had to be murder, surely, who'd come all the way out to Perry Lake to shoot herself? Poor old Mona. I hoped it had been over quickly.

Whipped-up sand stung my legs. I glanced up at the sky. The storm was almost here now, a huge wall of rusty cloud approaching from the north. I'd have to take shelter in my car. I didn't fancy hanging around out here, filling up my lungs and eyes with grit. But by the time Dean arrived, Mona would probably be covered over with sand and dust. What was left of her, that is, after the ravens had their go. I clapped them away, my dress billowing in the wind. I'd have to take a quick look around now, so I could describe everything to him in detail.

Mona's body was six feet from the lake's edge. Grains of sand were gathering in her brittle-looking hair. No gun in her hand. Two gold bracelets. A gold watch. Not a robbery then, they hadn't killed her for her jewellery.

Heaps of footprints and gouged-up pink sand all around her. Something glinted in one of the footprints. Using my hanky, I picked it up, turned it over. A key. Silvery, small and ordinary, it looked like the key you'd buy with a padlock at any hardware shop. So where was the padlock?

I dropped the key into my bag.

I walked around, the dust-laden wind tugging at my dress and hair. I put my hand over my nose and mouth. Thunder rumbled overhead. No tyre tracks visible. So the murderer hadn't driven here. Jesus, the murderer! I glanced around. He could still be here, waiting invisibly in the shade of the native pines. Or behind the piles of rubbish, the cars, anywhere. Dean would be ages, Hustle's at least an hour away, and he's not one to hurry unless he has a reason. Surely he'd consider this a reason?

A twig snapped. I whirled around. Was that a dark shape, among the trees? The hairs on my forearms stood up, all on their own, with no assistance from me.

I started scurrying towards the car but soon realised I'd left my run too late. The storm wall of dust hit me hard. The sun disappeared and the place went dark like someone had snapped off the light. Sand carried from miles away whipped up in stinging slaps against my face, lacing my eyes with grit. I cupped a hand over my eyes, trying to shield them.

My star picket in one hand, I groped around in the rust-coloured fog, blinking painfully. Where was the car? Where was anything? I stubbed my toe on a rock, it rolled over with a shallow-water splash. Water. I was at the lake's edge, so the car must be the other way. I turned and blundered around some more. I tripped, stubbed my toe on another rock. Another splash. Cass, you bloody fool, you're going around in circles. Sour-flavoured panic rose up in my throat. Stay calm, I whispered. Just find some shelter and wait this out. Where? Where? Come on, think.

I knelt on the sand and held my dress up over my face. In different circumstances I'd find it hilarious to be in this position with my dress over my head. Sand scoured my arms and legs, crunched nastily between my teeth. I coughed up a gobbet of grit. My sister Helen used to pull her dress up like this when she was a kid. When any stranger came to visit.

Helen and I used to play cubby house in the old corrugated iron shed out here by the lake. A ruin left over from the mining days. Probably some poor bastard's house, probably raised six kids in it. The shed. Yes. It was by the water. I just needed to follow the edge of the lake.

The mud was deep, black and stinky underneath the pink crust. Still holding my dress up over my face, I waded along the lake's edge, my shoes full of the stinking squelch. At least my feet were protected from the wind, they weren't stinging with sandpaper burn. Finally the shed loomed up on my right. I slipped in through the doorway, let go of my dress and slumped against a wall, panting. The relief from the scouring sand-wind combination was like an instant balm.

The wind blew sand in through the doorway, the broken window and every crack. I stepped away from the wall and hunkered down in the corner furthest from the door. The light was dimmer here, but near my feet I could see a few loose strands of coloured wire, left over from the days when I'd wound them into a bracelet for Helen. The place smelled stale. I wiped my stinging eyes. Ran my tongue over my teeth. I was looking forward to a drink of water and a shower, maybe even a long cool bath.

I stared at Helen's old bracelet wires, the wind buffeting the hut, while I worried about what to do. That snapping twig. Maybe it was just a kangaroo. Surely murderers don't hang around after the event, snapping twigs, waiting to be found.

Dean would be here any minute. Surely. The dust storm would have covered up those footprints, though. I squeezed my eyes shut, trying to remember what they'd looked like. I should have taken a photo on my phone.

Red dust crept in around the doorway. So when had Mona died? Last time I saw her was yesterday morning when I'd come across her and Aurora along the road.

So she must have been killed sometime between Saturday morning and Sunday at—I glanced at my watch—seven-thirty. That would help Dean determine time of death. Homicide would be impressed. It'd be a chance for me to make it up to Dean. Maybe it'd help him get over that stupid business with Ernie.

A moaning sound from outside. I jumped, then peered out through the cracked window, into the moving sea of dust. Endless rust-brown shadows out there, any one of them could be a murderer.

A tapping noise. I whirled around. A man stood in the doorway, rapping at the jamb with a skinny hand. I shrank back into my corner, star picket clutched in a shaky fist.

He stood there, his long white hair and ragged beard whipping around his face, a frayed check shirt flapping against his bony frame. He looked like Burke, or maybe Wills, one of those lost explorers from Australia's past. A gaunt-looking fella on an expedition headed straight for doom. He shambled in and a large black dog followed him.

I eyed him as he sat on the floor opposite me. He set down an esky and made room next to him for the dog. The hut filled with a sour, unwashed smell. The dog had unfriendly eyes and big jaws designed for killing things. It kept its unblinking gaze on my face.

The man shook sand and dust from his hair and rubbed it out of his beard with knobbly fingers. 'Good morning.' He smiled a smile that didn't reach his eyes. 'Invigorating wind.'

No gun that I could see. 'Yep,' I croaked. 'She's windy all right.'

He closed his eyes, leaned back against the creaking wall, one arm resting on the esky.

'Ah, you know you're trespassing?' I said. 'This is actually private property.' I firmed my grip on the star picket.

He opened his eyes. 'Oh? I saw the gate was open and...'

'You didn't open it?'

'Oh no, no.' He straightened up, smoothed down his shirt. 'I'm a birdwatcher. This looks like excellent scarlet-chested parrot country. And a good spot for Major Mitchell cockatoos. A pleasant little place, in fact.' He gestured at the dust storm raging outside.

A birdwatcher without binoculars.

'Why don't we get better acquainted, you and I? I'm Noel. You'll soon find I'm no trouble.'

It sounded more like a threat than an invitation.

'Where you from?' I said.

'Oh, I rove,' he waved a hand in a regal way. 'I'm not into ties. And Bubbles loves to travel.' He looked at the dog. 'We have a van that we call home.'

The dog made slopping sounds, licking dust from around its mouth. It kept its death-stare fixed on me.

'So,' I cleared my throat. 'You stay here last night, Noel?'

He froze. 'Possibly. I can't recall at the moment.'

'Just wondering if you heard anything.'

'What kind of thing?'

'Gunshots. Screaming, maybe.'

He stared. 'Gunshots? Do you mean hunters?'

'There's a dead woman by the lake. Shot in the head. Didn't you see her? I've phoned the police. They're on their way. Be here any minute.'

'The police?' He glanced around.

'So, did you? See or hear anything?' I persisted.

'No, no. Look, this is nothing to do with me.' He stood up. 'I think I'll take a rain check on those scarlet-chesteds. Shame.'

'You'd better give me your mobile number. The police might have some questions. Noel...what was the surname?'

'Ah...I don't have a mobile. I really must get on.' He picked up his esky, cradling it to his chest. He moved to the doorway, his long white hair waving, Medusa-like, around his face. 'I could do without police harassment, actually. I don't want Bubbles upset. Not in her condition.' Clutching the esky like a new-born baby, he charged off into a whirling blast of dust, the dog thumping along heavily behind him.

Well, anyone could see the bloke was up to something iffy. Who could see a bird in all this? And where the hell was Dean? I pulled out my phone from my handbag. No signal.

I popped my head out of the doorway and looked around. The lake was a pink–brown blur. The wind was dropping, dust hurtling at a slower pace. At some point soon the wind would be running out of dust to blow. I tied my hanky over my nose and mouth, grabbed my handbag and star picket and headed out.

Noel was walking along a track behind the hut, through the native pines. Every now and then he looked behind him. I kept well back, darting into the scrub. He reached a white van parked under a tree. A white HiAce, it looked like, broken side mirror.

Crouching behind a scrappy shrub, I watched him get in. The van started and, with some crunching of gears, turned and headed along the track towards the highway. Before it disappeared, I grabbed a pen from my bag and wrote down his rego on the back of an old docket from Vern's shop. Dean would thank me for that later.

Twenty minutes later, back at the hut, I heard a car engine over the wind. I poked my head out. A police van. It stopped way back along the track I'd driven in on, and the driver got out. Dean at last. I'd never been so pleased to see his neat blue uniform. The wind dropped and the sun suddenly came out now Dean was here, like he'd arranged it all. Evidence of the dust storm lay all around, red streaks over pink sand. I marched towards him.

Dean crunched across the sand. 'Hi, Mum.' He leaned in and pecked my cheek, like he was calling in for a cuppa on a normal day. 'Where's this body, then?' He stared at me with those confident brown–black eyes.

'Listen, there's a whole long history to tell you. There's a weird fella calls himself Noel. A birdwatcher without binoculars. And his awful dog, killer dog I'd say. I took down the bloke's rego for you.'

'Mum, I'm not in the mood for a mound of drivel. I've

got a heap of paperwork waiting at the station. Is there a body, or isn't there?'

'Course there is.' I rummaged through my handbag. Three used tissues, some sticky-looking Butter Menthols, a creased copy of the *Pocket Guide to Elves and Fairies* for Dean's youngest, must have been in there for years.

'Where is it?'

'Hang on,' I said. 'You'll need this rego, I'm sure of it.' Out fluttered the docket, finally. 'Here,' I tucked it into Dean's shirt pocket and tapped his chest. 'You'll need that later. Now. The body. It's over near the lake. Let's go.'

We crunched our way along the gravel track, over the dune, the mallee gums clinging low on the stained pink sand.

I was almost skipping along, now that Dean was here. I started imagining myself on the front page of the *Hustle Post*. I might even be on the telly, once the taskforce arrived. I'd have to nip out quickly and get a new outfit.

'Want me to call for back up?' I said. 'I could call Bendigo on your radio. Reckon I can handle a police radio.'

'No, Mum!' You could have cut an arm off with his tone. '*I'm* the police officer. That means *I* handle the policing. All of it.'

We passed my car, covered in red dust, parked where I'd found the body. Only a few hours ago, but it felt like centuries.

'She's over there.' I pointed to the edge of the lake. Endless pink-tinged brown water, the sand covered with streaks of red dust. Trees to the left. Husking cars and fridges. More trees beyond the rubbish. No ravens.

No body.

What? I looked again. No mounded body-like shape, covered in dust or sand.

Dean looked grim. Piero used to set his jaw like that when I pointed out he was cutting the chips too thick.

'It's Ernie Jefferson all over again.' Dean's voice was low.

'Listen. It's not something anyone could misunderstand,' I said. 'Her eyes were gone. There was no mistaking it. She was dead. Definitely. He must have moved her.'

'Only Ernie was actually *there*,' Dean continued as if I hadn't spoken. 'Not dead; but he was there, I'll give you that.'

Dean drilled through me with those black-clay eyes. It's not something I'd admit in public, but Dean's stare can be a touch unnerving.

No one's ever died from a stare, I told myself. 'Hold on Dean and think. Why would I drive out here and make up this story?' I tried for a firm, unhurt, commanding-mother tone.

'If this was the first time, Mum, I might believe it. You heard of the boy who cried wolf?'

Well, of course I had, I read it to him when he was a little tacker.

'Wasting police time is a serious matter.' Dean's voice oozed official-sounding disapproval.

The body must be here somewhere. I walked back and forth, Aboriginal-tracker style, staring at the sand. Surely there'd be marks if she'd been dragged away. She was so small though, anyone could have slung her, like a gold-knit sack, over a shoulder. There'd be footprints. I kept staring at the pink sand until my eyes were blurred. Nothing. The dust storm had fixed all that.

The colour hit my cheeks. How dare this woman get herself shot. And let her body disappear. How bloody careless was that? I kicked uselessly at the sand.

Dean crossed his arms and stared off into the distance, like he needed to be alone, far far away from his parent.

'I know it looks bad, but you've got to believe me.' It sounded unconvincing, even to me.

He swung away, stomping towards my car and I draggled along behind him like a ticked-off kid.

'Right.' Dean flung open my car door. 'Straight home, Mum. And you need to eat something. You know how you get when your blood sugar's low.'

He crunched over to his van and got in, slamming the door. Then he drove away.

Dean's damned lucky I'm not sensitive. And blood sugar? Kids. Why would you have them? You just end up surrounded by people who don't believe you. Still, he'd thank me later when the body turned up. I marched over to the rubbish heap and searched through the dumped cars, all through their torn-up interiors and rusting boots, crawling underneath each one to look.

Zippo. No signs of digging. I opened up every one of the seventeen stinky discarded fridges, in case she'd been shoved inside. Nothing.

Stretching my aching back, I sat down on the sand a minute. The sun was out properly now, dust clouds completely cleared. I would have been willing to shoot someone myself for a strong cup of tea and a couple of Panadol.

I brushed the sand from my oil-stained dress. Maybe Clarence and Mona had had a big fight about his book.

But who shoots his nanna over a book she doesn't like? Shooting seems a bit uncalled for.

I stood up. When Mona's body turned up, it wouldn't look good for Dean that he'd ignored me. I'd have to do something to prove the truth to him. There was that five grand, of course. Maybe it was stolen money. I'd show it to Dean once he cooled down. Pop into the station with a plate of sausage rolls to help him digest the facts.

I looked at my watch. Ten o'clock. I'd better get home, wash this dust off and open the shop.

I was walking back to the car when something tucked in a narrow gap behind a disused fridge caught my eye. I sidled closer. It was brown; looked like leather. Briefcase-shaped. I reached in and tugged. The case was jammed tight against the freezer. I struggled, pulling, puffing. Finally, with a tearing noise, it came out. Yep. Brown leather briefcase, slightly torn. Across the top, in gold looping curls, *Pittering and Son*. I tried opening it. It was locked.

I started feeling happier once I got back into my car. I'd get the shop open, then later on when things got quiet I'd find a crowbar or something to crank open the briefcase. Although...I sat there a moment. Maybe I should check on Ernie's shack first. There was that girl, Aurora, I'd like to know she was OK. And Clarence of course.

I steamed along the bitumen, breeze blowing in through my window. Ernie's place should have been fixed up or pulled down years ago, but since he's been in the home, he hasn't had the marbles required to renovate, or even detonate. He still understands money though. There'd be a lot of Ernie's smelly-breath cackles when I finally gave him Clarence's five grand. No point in returning it to

Clarence now. It was way too late to send these people off before they made trouble. Might be best if I didn't tell Ernie that his tenant was a suspected murderer with potential Mafia links.

At the turn-off to the shack—close by Perry Lake, only a k or so of desperate mallee scrub away—I stopped. Peered through the windscreen down the track and past the mailbox, a beaten-up old kerosene drum. A white car was parked outside the place.

I firmed my grip on the steering wheel and pressed the accelerator, heading towards the shack. My breath pounded out in between teeth-rattles as the car bounced over the corrugations.

The shack came into view, front verandah all sagging in the middle. Its lacy wrought-iron edging had been pretty once, now it was rusted and forlorn. Broken red bricks lay in a messy heap on the roof where the chimney used to stand.

I pulled up out the front. Next to the shack was a row of four cars, all squeezed in tight. A black Lexus at the front, Mona's silver Mercedes, a beat-up orange ute in the middle, and at the end of the row, the white car I'd seen from the road. Clarence had a heap of visitors. So much for quiet time to write his book.

A flock of corellas shrieked their way across the sky. An insect hum. No other sounds in the miles of mallee scrub around. Gangland types wouldn't be interested in this place. Course not. Would they? My legs started trembling, like they do when I stand near the edge of something high. Get a grip, I whispered. All I needed to do was knock on that door and check Aurora was alive. I've got my sawn-off star picket, after all. Although it wouldn't be much use against a gun.

There was a movement at the shack window.

I grabbed Brad's spare binoculars from my glove box, held them up, scanning the shack. A man was moving around the bedroom. He had his back to me. I could make out blond hair, a leather jacket. I moved the binoculars to view the other window at the front. Nothing. I scanned back to the first window. The bloke had gone.

Crunching-over-gravel noises. I put down the binoculars. My stomach gave a turn. Two men in leather jackets, strolling. A confident kind of stroll, like fellas who know they're in charge of the planet. One was a stumpy-looking fella, in his forties maybe. The other one was younger, leaner, and a foot taller than anyone I'd ever seen. He had a half-closed eye, like there was something wrong with it.

They were coming towards my car.

I started the car and turned it fast, wheels spinning in the dirt. The men coughed, covered with my spray of dust. I drove quick-smart out of there, skimming over the corrugations on the track, my foot heavy on the pedal.

My tyres screeched on the bitumen as I turned the car out onto the highway. I realised the panting sounds I could hear were coming from my mouth.

I looked in my rearview mirror. One white car, coming up behind. I pushed my foot down. The little engine whined. Like me, my vehicle's never been in a car chase but unlike me she seemed willing. I rocketed along that dead straight road heading to Rusty Bore.

As the mallee gums flashed by I fumbled for my phone to call Dean. A police siren behind me. Dean? But glancing into the mirror I saw it was the white car from Ernie's place, blue lights flashing in the front grille. They caught up, effortlessly it seemed, pulling out beside me.

The passenger signalled for me to pull over.

The car parked ahead and the front doors opened with a pair of clicks. The tall man got out first, his calf-length leather coat flapping around him in the wind. That'd have to be a two-cow coat, I thought, he must have been close to seven foot. His half-shut eye looked sleepy.

The stumpy older-looking man followed him, limping. His leather coat was shorter, it only reached his thighs. He had messy hair and a haze of stubble, like a general tidy-up hadn't been his main concern when he'd got up today. He had the build of a fella that eats like he means it. Smiling, he gave me a little wave.

The tall man came around to my window, held up a police ID. I wound down the window. 'Senior Sergeant Dale Monaghan.' He didn't introduce the other man. 'Step out of the car, please.'

I held my hand out of the window to shake his. He didn't take it.

'Step out of the car,' he repeated.

I heaved myself ignobly over the handbrake.

'Can I see some identification?'

'Oh, you won't be needing that,' I smiled. 'I'm Mrs Cass Tuplin.' I waited for the surname to sink in.

It didn't seem to.

'Mother of Senior Constable Dean Tuplin,' I said. '*Leading* Senior Constable Tuplin. Our local officer. No doubt you've been working with him.'

If he had, he wasn't letting on. 'Your driving licence, please.'

While Monaghan studied my licence, I wondered whether I should mention Mona's body. Maybe Dean had come to his senses and phoned CIU. But CIU was in

Bendigo, at least three hours away. No way they would have got here yet. Shut up, I told myself. I didn't want Dean in trouble.

Then I remembered what Sophia had said, about a fella at Sheep Dip, looking for someone. A mean fella, with a bung eye. Must be this cop, surely. How many strange men with off eyes could there be wandering around the Mallee?

Monaghan handed back my licence.

'So what brings you fellas here?' I asked in my brightest tone. 'Up from Bendigo?'

'I'll be the one asking the questions,' said Monaghan. 'Now, perhaps you'd like to tell me why you were breaking the speed limit. And what, exactly, you were doing at that property.'

'And why you left in such a hurry,' said the other man, scratching a stubbly cheek. He gave me a smile.

Where had I heard his voice?

Monaghan gave him a nasty look, a look that said, *Back off mate, I'm in charge.*

I drew myself up to my full five feet and two inches, 'That property is owned by Mr Ernie Jefferson. As his agent, I am perfectly entitled to attend the property. Especially if I have reason to believe the tenant may be under police investigation. And,' I was on a roll, 'might I ask if you have a warrant to search the house? I don't recall the police advising me they would be visiting the premises.'

Monaghan looked off-balance. 'I see,' his tone was one degree friendlier. 'So why did you drive off in such a hurry?'

'Well, wouldn't you? Two scary-looking men marched out of the house towards me. How was I meant to know you were police officers?' I patted down my hair. I must have looked a sight, after the dust storm and crawling around those cars and stinking fridges in search of Mona.

'Can you tell me anything about Clarence Hocking-Lee's whereabouts, Mrs Tuplin?'

'Hocking-Lee? The only Clarence I know told me his surname was Brown. And I haven't seen him since Friday,' I said, truthfully.

'And his relatives? Any idea where they might be?' He squinted at me with his good eye.

I didn't care to go into the whereabouts of Mona. 'I'm sorry, officer. I'd like to find them as much as you. Especially if he's in trouble with the police.'

He handed me his card. And with my promise that I'd call him right away if I heard from Clarence or anyone who knew him, he let me go. Without a speeding ticket.

Showered and freshly dressed in an outfit not covered with oil stains, I opened the shop. A quiet afternoon. At four o'clock I put up the *Back in 10 minutes* sign and headed out.

I walked along Best Street, flicking flies. A flock of galahs, noisy pink, shrieked from the scraggy native pines lining the road. Fifty steps later I was outside Vern's shop, rusty corrugated iron flapping above walls flaking yellow paint.

Vern's a blow-in. Only moved here twenty years ago. He stocks the full range from Neapolitan ice cream to header parts.

His grey-muzzled kelpie cross, Boofa, came trotting out and took a leak on the phone booth. That's Vern's strategic advantage, the phone booth. And the petrol bowser; the mobile library stop; his post office licence; his agency for the Commonwealth Bank. These are points he makes often. Vern doesn't need to play Monopoly, he's got Rusty Bore.

I walked up the three wooden steps to his shop. Vern was lying in his hammock on the front verandah, notebook tucked under an arm, his only arm. He was dressed in a white singlet and blue shorts that were too small on him.

'Ha. You come to tell me we should merge, have ya? At bloody last.' He laughed, a sound like a tractor firing up. 'Economies of scale, Cass. And no one could ever say you're not a fine figure of a woman.' His eyes swept up and down my body.

While it's nice to be appreciated, I'm used to having the run of my own place. And I'm no snob, but Vern's not really my type. Too much debt and not enough arms.

'Don't know how you manage, Cass. You really gotta diversify.'

'Don't you worry about me. I'm getting by. Now listen,' I said. 'I could do with your help. Couple of things. I'd be grateful.'

'Grateful.' He tugged at the crotch of his shorts.

'First, I need some information. About the young fella I rented Ernie's shack out to. I'm now thinking that might have been an error of judgment. Clarence, he said his name was.'

'Young fella.' Vern stood up, opened his notebook on the hammock and flicked through the pages. He took a chewed-up pen from the pocket of his shorts and ticked something on the page. 'Yep, yep. Come in at ten past six Friday. Bought one heap of food. Cleared me right out of Tim Tams. Driving a flash car, Lexus. Black. Got his rego here.' He scratched his chest with the pen.

49

'What's this I hear about a Mafia fella looking for him?' I kept my voice casual.

'Hold on, not finished with the young fella yet.' He licked his thumb, then turned the page. 'Saw him drive out towards Perry Lake. Out on my hammock, I was, taking in the air. Watching these two blue-tongues. The male, he was going for it, biting her all over, but she just kept scuttling away, wouldn't let him settle on her. Poor fella. Not an easy life for the male...'

I interrupted. 'And the Mafia fella?'

'You mean the bloke was in the Sheep Dip roadhouse? That come from Craig, not sure who he got it from, maybe that Canadian backpacker kid helping at the McKenzies' place, the one all the girls go mad for. Dunno what they see in him. Perfectly respectable mature blokes available here in Rusty Bore.' He sucked in a breath. 'Where was I?'

'Craig.'

'Yep, yep. Craig said the story is the fella had a gun tucked under his coat. Said he needed to find some young bloke urgently that had nicked his property.'

'Could the fella looking have been a cop? Plain-clothes?'

Vern shrugged and scratched his head, thoughtful.

'Clarence told me not to tell anyone where he is. Sounds suspicious, doesn't it?'

Vern shrugged again and made a note in his book.

'Also, Vern, I need a crowbar or something.'

'Outta crowbars. Sell you a top-notch pinch-bar, though.'

I got back to find a red minibus outside my place. A dreadlocked bloke sat in the driver's seat. He gave me a cheery wave and a smile full of the straightest, whitest teeth I'd ever seen. The bus door slid open and Brad stepped down, a girl stepping out behind him. She wore a white T-shirt and tattered yellow skirt. Bare feet. And a prominent stomach-bump.

Brad gave me a kiss, then turned and waved as the minibus drove away. Turning back, he said, 'This is Claire. She's, um, going to have a baby.'

'I see. Hello, Claire,' I said, putting down my pinch-bar. There was a gust of chilly wind. 'You been abseiling dam walls too?' It wasn't the question that was at the top of my mind but I could hardly say, 'Hello, whose baby?'

'Oh, no. I'm not too good with heights.' She laughed, a nice laugh.

'Claire needs to eat,' said Brad. 'You're staying for dinner. Isn't she, Mum?' It wasn't a question.

'Course.' How many months? Looked like the baby could arrive any day. 'Where you from, Claire?'

'Perth. I'm over visiting some relatives.'

Where was Brad nine months ago? 'Oh? In Albury-Wodonga?'

'Ah, no. Around here, actually.'

When exactly was that Men of the Trees thing he did in WA? 'And you met Brad...recently?'

'Jesus, Mum. Let Claire eat before you launch into the full interrogation,' said Brad. 'Got any bacon? And what are you doing with a pinch-bar?'

'Long story,' I said. 'I'll tell you inside.'

Over dinner, eggs, tomatoes and bacon, I filled in Brad. Selectively. I told him about Clarence, Noel the bird-watcher without binoculars and the cops at Ernie's place. Claire listened quietly.

'Noel?' said Brad, looking thoughtful. 'There's a bloke called Noel emailed my blog last week. He was after regent parrot spots.'

'You, ah, related to any police, Claire?' I said, putting down my fork. Might not be a good idea to go into the bit about Mona being dead, not if Claire had big-wig police connections. I didn't want Dean in trouble.

She glanced at Brad.

'Why do you ask, Mum?'

'Well, Dean doesn't need any more hiccups in his career.'

Brad stared at me. 'What have you done this time?'

Now or never. I explained about Mona's body and her disappearance.

Brad put his hand over mine. 'Mum. Look. Are you really sure she was dead? I mean *really* really? You remember, um, Ernie...'

'There's no need to go over all that again. Can't anyone around here ever make one tiny error?'

'OK, OK,' he said, taking back his hand.

'Anyway, long story short, I need to get this briefcase open.' I shoved the pinch-bar into the case and heaved a bit.

'If Clarence is under police investigation, the case could be important evidence,' said Claire.

'Yeah,' said Brad. 'You should take it in to Dean. Could be anything in there. A gun. A bomb. Anything.'

I stopped. 'Nah. Clarence didn't look the bombing type.'

'What's the bombing type?' said Brad.

Good question. Bearded, maybe? Although I'm not against a bearded person. Those Hells Angels, for instance, they make big orders when they drop by. A rare event, unfortunately for my profit margins. Noel had a beard though.

I held the case to my ear. It wasn't ticking. I fiddled again with the pinch-bar. No go.

'Dean's not exactly talking to me at the moment,' I said. 'Best if I leave him alone while he gets over things. I'll take this up to Ernie tomorrow. He's always been good with locks.'

On Mondays I close the shop. I drive up to Hustle and visit Ernie in the home. We sit ourselves down in front of the midday movie, him with a rustling bag of mini Cherry Ripes, me with a strong cuppa and some Panadol. You need an adequate supply of Panadol to get through an afternoon with Ernie. Even on a normal Monday.

Today, Ernie didn't look pleased to see me. I'd slept in after the weekend's excitement and then got stuck forever behind a road train. The movie had already started when I hurried into his room, puffing.

'Shh,' said Ernie, as I took a seat. 'There's your cuppa. Probably cold now.' He pointed at the table beside the Christmas tree, then turned back to stare at the TV. He rustled through a bag of Cherry Ripes with his brown-splodged hands.

We watch the movie in his room, since he doesn't like the communal lounge. 'Full of people who've lost their marbles,' he says. He spends a lot of time in his room, when he isn't lurking on his walker by the roses. He goes out there to smoke. The staff discourage smoking, but he's eighty-seven, there's no point him giving it up now.

I sat clutching Clarence's briefcase in my lap.

It looked like today was one of Ernie's good days. He lets his marbles come and go, sometimes I think it's intentional. On his good days he acts as if he's the one doing the favour when I come to visit, as though he's humouring a lonely woman with no friends. In fact, there's a lot of places I could go on Mondays if I had the time.

I sipped my tea. The movie today was *The Lady in the Lake*, oddly enough. Wait until Ernie heard about the lady in Perry Lake. I fidgeted, looking around at his posters. I'd helped him put them up when he moved in. Battered-looking pictures of pin-up girls from World War Two. 'Didn't see all the bosoms in those days. Left a lot to the imagination,' he'd snickered.

I didn't want to know about Ernie's imagination but I guess those posters help distract him from the decor in the home. The lighting throughout is yellow, like the decorator thought people in the twilight of their lives wouldn't be able to cope with the brightness of white light. The walls are lined with pastel paintings of flowers. It can't be easy finding a style that keeps everyone's minds off funerals, and within a reasonable budget.

At the first ad break, Ernie looked at me sternly, his yellowed moustache quivering, the light reflected in his glasses. 'What time you call this, hey? And why have you got a briefcase?'

'Bit of a rigmarole, Ernie. Can you get it open?'

'Give it here.' He looked it over. 'Simple enough

mechanism, two levers. I'll need a paperclip.' He snapped his old-bone fingers.

While the movie started again and Ernie settled back into it, I searched his room for a paperclip. Nothing. I headed out to Reception where Taylah was busy on the phone, winding a strand of long dark hair around a pen. I stood at the desk and waited. It's not easy for Taylah to manage all her work when so much of her time is occupied with phone calls to her friends.

Behind her a TV screen flickered Jerry Springer.

'Nooo,' Taylah's voice was low and breathy. 'I don't *believe* it.' Some moist clicking while she worked her Spearmint Extra.

'Taylah?' I said.

She held up a hand. The phone system shrieked as a call came in. 'Hold a tick, Moisy.' Taylah pressed a button. 'Hello, Garden of the Gods Extended Care, can you hold a moment?'

She looked at me. 'Can you believe it, Cass? Everyone's going. Almost everyone. To Muddy Soak. To the inaugural Muddy Soak Christmas Fringe Festival.'

Muddy Soak is a swish type of place despite the name, casually bestowed by an explorer, who may not have fully grasped the marketing potential to be squeezed from a town's name. It used to have an Aboriginal name but no one remembers it.

Two hours south, it's a place unfairly endowed with the world's largest mallee stump and permanent above-ground water. The water, Brad tells me, is visited by an unusual number of rare migratory birds. Birds that are followed by people keen on watching them and keen on comfort food when they've finished watching for the day.

Exactly the type of person we could do with attracting to Rusty Bore. And now they have a bloody Christmas fringe festival as well.

'Terrific,' I said. 'What's a Christmas fringe festival?' A CWA event, a charming share-fest of home-crafted fringes?

'Plays,' she said. 'Installations, street theatre, performance art. All that. You want Moisy to get you tickets? You should go. You being such an old acting buff and everything.'

'I watch the midday movie, Taylah. I wouldn't call myself an acting buff.' Although...Muddy Soak. Maybe it was worth a thought. I might run into that nice fella from the blindfold speed dating. Although, really, I had Buckley's of finding him since I didn't know his name or even what he looked like.

'You could like take Mr Jefferson,' said Taylah. 'He'd love it. It's being hosted by that drama group, you know the one. The one where the fella handcuffed himself to the rail. You know. That grain train smash. Fella in the fabulous dress, um, Pearson. No.'

'I'm just after a paperclip, Taylah.'

'Not Pearson. Phillips. No, that's not it either.' She ferreted around her desk, then held out a handful of paperclips. 'Pittering. That's it. Someone Pittering.'

Paperclips in a frozen hand, I stood, gaping. 'Oh?'

But the phone was going off. Taylah waved me away.

I headed back to Ernie's room. He was staring at the movie, briefcase open in his lap.

'Got her unlocked, no thanks to you,' he held up a piece of wire. 'Pulled it out the back of the TV. Lot of irrelevant wires in there. Now shut up and shoosh.'

The TV was still working and Ernie didn't appear

to be electrocuted, although after the last time I wasn't sure I'd be able to tell. He held onto the case and said he wouldn't let me take it until the movie finished. I fidgeted and worried about Pittering and his son, grain trains, men in dresses and their connection, if any, to Mona's death.

Ernie tsked. 'Will you flamin' well concentrate.'

It's times like these I realise I'm too good to Ernie. But he looked out for me when I was young. Looked after me and Helen after Mum died. He helped me set up the shop as well. Even made sure Piero stuck by me through my pregnancy with Dean. There were a lot of extraneous women interested in Piero, not to mention his fertility. I huffed a bit to myself and tried my best to sit still.

As the credits rolled, Ernie finally relented. 'Here you go.' He smirked as he handed it over. I grabbed it and looked inside. Nothing. What? It couldn't be empty; I scrabbled through the pockets. Nothing.

'I think you'd better tell me what's going on,' said Ernie.

After I'd explained, he gave me an intent look. 'Course, there was that time when you thought *I* was dead, so I can understand Dean's point of view.' He looked out the window for a moment, blinking.

In the pause, I stared at the crocheted cover on his teapot that Mrs Watkins had made for him. She makes him little gifts, saying someone as brave as our Napoleon deserves his comforts at his time of life. It's unclear how she formed the view that Ernie's a dead French general.

'Found this key near her body,' I said.

'I don't hold it against you, not really,' he said, still staring out the window.

'I'm sorry, Ernie, I didn't mean it. Anyway, the key.' I

grabbed it from my handbag, using my hanky, held it out.

He looked at it, turned back to the window. 'And I've told you a thousand times to put a padlock on that flamin' gate.'

'You ever heard of a Pittering or a son?' I said.

'He one of the Pitterlines, the harness makers?' said Ernie, finally looking at me.

'Pitter*ing*, Ernie. And I meant this century.'

He glared. 'Fella by the name of Albert. His son ran off to the Northern Territory with the Hustle grocer. Owed me sixty dollars, the bastard.'

Before Ernie could slide full-tilt into a past-injustice rant, I said, 'He have any relatives? Fellas keen on dresses? Anyone that killed themselves?'

He grunted. 'His cousin Andy was the undertaker. Depressing job, but he never killed himself. Not that I recall.'

Maybe we were still talking about the Pitterlines or the 1950s, or both. 'And more recently? Any Pitterings involved in drama groups?' Would being in a drama group get you down?

'Drama group? Not the Pitterlines I knew.'

'Any connection with Muddy Soak?'

'The Soak? That bastard was the last criminal in Muddy Soak. The very last.'

'Who?'

He glared at me. 'You're not listening, are you? Hugo Pitterline, who took off with my money. In 1988. No crime in Muddy Soak since then.'

'None at all?'

'Nup. Crime free for over twenty years. Probably should have a festival.'

'Not one single crime?'

'Nope.'

'How's that possible?'

He heaved himself to his feet. 'Look, I don't have time to sit here all day explaining local history to you. I've got things to do. Off you go now, run along.'

I headed home, fairly demoralised with the key-slash-briefcase situation. I parked the car, unstuck my thighs from the driver's seat, squeezed out over the handbrake through the passenger side and walked into my kitchen. I made myself a cuppa. Sitting at the table, I sipped, staring at the briefcase. I opened it and rootled around the pockets one more time. Nothing. Closing it, I held it up. It felt too heavy to be empty. I shook it from side to side. Something moved around inside. I opened it again.

There was a long slit in the inside fabric. I reached inside the slit. Books. *The Art of Writing Memoir*. Then, *The Big Sleep*. One more, *Death of a Lake*, by Arthur Upfield.

I phoned Taylah. 'I'll take that ticket for the Christmas Fringe Festival.'

'And one for Mr Jefferson?'

'Yep. Thanks. You know,' I tried to sound casual, 'that drama fella who died, whatsisname...Pittering. Did he have a son? Or a father, maybe?'

There were some moist breathing sounds while she adjusted her chewing gum. 'Well, everyone has a father, don't they? It's just, like, biology. I mean maybe those sperm donor children, you could *argue* that they don't, but in reality...'

'I meant as in Pittering and Son.'

'Oh. You mean the accounting firm in Muddy Soak.'

Dean turned up as I put down the phone. He usually comes by on a Monday, for some fruitcake and a cuppa. On a normal Monday. Today he knocked on the shop door instead of coming around to the house. So not a tea and fruitcake visit. I shoved the briefcase into the kitchen cupboard and headed into the shop.

Sure enough, Dean didn't want a cuppa. No fruitcake either. 'Where have you been? I tried to call. There's been a couple of break-ins,' he said.

He didn't think I'd done them, surely? Stop, I told myself, this is just paranoia. It was that hidden briefcase weighing on my mind. 'I was visiting Ernie, of course.'

'Two house robberies. People around here really need to learn to lock their doors.' He flicked through his notebook. 'Cash and jewellery taken. I thought I'd better warn you, in case you're next. They seem to be targeting old ladies.'

Old? 'I'm in my prime.'

A moody look from those brown–black eyes.

I considered telling him about the briefcase. Maybe I'd be in trouble for tampering with important evidence. Although, technically, it wasn't me who'd opened the case.

That part was Ernie, and his fingerprints would be all over it. I opened my mouth to tell him, but Dean spoke before I had the chance.

'Mum. About all that silly business yesterday.' He took off his hat, put it on the table.

I gave him a relieved smile, Dean's not a bad lad, he'd thought it over and he was ready to apologise. Maybe Sergeant Monaghan had been up to see him and set him straight on a few facts.

'We all know you've got an active imagination.' He took my hand. His was dry and warm. 'Nothing wrong with an imagination.' He smiled as if I was six years old. 'And around here, it's important to be able to keep yourself entertained. Especially now so many people have moved away. I'd worry less about you if you had more social life. You could always join the Hustle CWA. Or get involved in that new historical society.'

I tried a casual laugh. 'Don't you worry, Dean. I've got plenty to keep me busy. There's Brad. And Ernie. And the shop, of course.'

He continued. 'And I know business is slow. It can't be easy managing. If you need my help, you'll ask, won't you? Financial, anything.' He paused. 'The thing is...' He took his hand away and wiped some sweat from his forehead, put his hand back on mine, a little stickier this time. 'It's...'

'Yes?' I smiled encouragingly. It's never been easy for Dean to dismount and apologise.

'Well, I have to warn you. If you do anything like that again...' He let go of my hand.

I suddenly didn't like where we were headed. 'Well, what?'

'I'll have to arrest you for wasting police time.'

'Dean. Son.' I held up my hand to stop him interrupting. 'Listen. You're missing important data. That poor dead Mona is out there somewhere, and, more importantly, so's her killer.'

'Mum!' He spat out the word, as though he didn't like how it felt against his tongue. 'I'm not taking any more of your bullshit.' He stood up and stamped over to the doorway. 'I bloody will, I'm telling you. Next time I'll arrest you.' And he left, slamming the door.

Brad met me at the kitchen door. 'I'm off to Madison's. She needs emergency dim sims for the ferrets. Thérèse has been unwell.'

'The ferrets? But I thought you said those animals are a menace?' Irreconcilable differences is what split up Brad and Madison. He's into banners, native wildlife, birds; she's into introduced predators.

'I haven't actually declared a formal policy position on ferrets, Mum.'

'So...you and Madison?'

He shrugged.

'But what about Claire?'

'Claire's resting in the spare room. In case you hadn't noticed, she's pregnant.' He slammed the door.

Jesus, Brad. What did he think he was doing with all these poor girls? Should I warn Madison? And Claire? Should a person be expected to warn girls off her own son? I really needed to give Brad that parental pep-talk. I'd have to galvanise myself. I'd do it soon. I would. And then he'd be moving out, far away, in search of a proper job.

I sighed, staring out the window, at my dried-up

backyard, at the struggling pepper tree friendless and alone, its red-fading-to-pink berries carpeting the dust. Piero and I were proud of this place way back when we'd set up. He planted General MacArthur roses around the fence. Piero loved those roses. I scattered his ashes under them, he would have wanted that. But these days the place just looked parched and tired.

I got up, had a quick, unsatisfying rootle through the briefcase, in case I'd missed something the first forty times I'd looked. No go. I put it back.

A car pulled up on my gravel driveway. Brad must have forgotten something. I heard a car door open then close. Footsteps crunched over the gravel and a face appeared at the window. It wasn't Brad. It was yet another visitor, in a week full of them: the tousled-looking fella. The assistant cop who'd pulled me up yesterday, who'd stood behind Sergeant Monaghan. He was on his own, no Monaghan in sight. He seemed a bit old to be the assistant.

I opened the door.

'Afternoon.' He smiled.

He wore a leather jacket over a creased white shirt. His jeans were dusty. His front teeth overlapped a bit, an endearing kind of overlap.

'Sorry to bother you. I didn't realise you'd be closed. I was hoping for a feed of fish and chips.' He eyed me hungrily. 'And maybe a couple of Chiko Rolls?'

There was definitely something about that voice. Where had I heard it? I never like to turn away a customer, so I led him into the shop. He sat and I started up the burner. 'It'll take a tick for things to heat up.'

He had wide blue eyes, like a baby's. Wide eyes, but somehow disappointed, like the baby's figured out way too early that life's not all it's cracked up to be.

I scooped up some chips and put them in the basket. 'I didn't catch your name yesterday.'

'Terry.' He stifled a yawn.

Maybe he'd spent the night in the car, with Monaghan beside him, snoring, taking up all the space. Maybe Monaghan was a brutal boss. That weepy eye might make him ratty.

'Sergeant Terry, is it?' I put his fish and Chiko Rolls into another basket and set it in the sizzling oil.

'Just call me Terry.' He twisted a ring around his little finger. No wedding band, although that never tells you. 'Nice place you've got here, Mrs Tuplin.'

I smiled. Terry's a name I've always liked. 'Call me Cass.'

'Um...' he said, 'probably sounds stupid, but there's something about your voice, it sounds familiar.' He gave me the endearing overlap-tooth smile.

Muddy Soak, Terry was from Muddy Soak.

'Blindfold speed dating!' We both said it at the same time.

'Yeah, I was sorry I lost you after that fire alarm went off,' he said. 'I waited around outside for ages. Trouble was...'

'You didn't know what I looked like. Yep, me too.'

We had a silent little moment while his order hissed in the oil.

'Look.' He leaned forward in his chair. 'You weren't, ah, holding back on anything yesterday, were you? You look like a smart sort of woman, Cass. A woman who notices things.'

A *smart sort of woman*. I didn't mind that. I slipped an

extra Chiko Roll in his order, courtesy of the management.

I'd bet Terry wouldn't mind hearing about a briefcase. He wouldn't go on about arresting helpful people. And he didn't have Dean's glued-on glare. Terry had quite nice eyes. I snuck another look as I shook his basket. Those eyes were a faded, comfortable kind of blue. He had a thickish lower lip, tender looking, like it could be nice to kiss.

Pull your-bloody-self together, Cass.

Trouble was, how could I tell him about the briefcase without going into the finer points about Mona's body? I didn't want Dean in trouble for botching up the job.

'If I knew anything, I'd tell you.' I smiled as I fibbed. 'What I do know is that Clarence paid a suspiciously large sum of rent.'

I served Terry's order on a plate at the table. The poor fella deserved to sit and eat properly, instead of filling up his car with the smell of fish. And he looked like he could do with some company.

'Yeah. He's one of the Muddy Soak Hocking-Lees,' said Terry. 'No shortage of cash in that family.'

'So Brown isn't his real name?'

'Told you that, did he? Nope, he's a Hocking-Lee. And Clarence is his grandma's grandson, all right. Although he's not up to the atonement stage just yet,' he said.

'Oh? Mona got something to atone for?'

'You haven't heard of her? Heard of Kota though, I bet.'

'Um. Course.' Who the hell was Coata?

'Mona was never prosecuted for that.'

'Uh-huh. Why was that exactly?' I carried on with my auto-wiping of the counter.

Terry was a bloke who ate with sincerity. I've always

67

liked a fella who knows how to appreciate a plate of chips.

'Well, the CEO was convicted, finally, last year. He got two years. Mona was the major shareholder, said she didn't know about the safety standards. Or lack of.' He ate another chip. 'The company paid out compensation. Didn't bring anyone back, of course. Or their farmland. Soon after, Mona set up all her environmental charities.'

He must have seen the confusion on my face. 'Kota,' he said. 'You know, that gas leak in India. Killed thousands of people.'

Ah, *Kota*. 'Yep, yep,' I said. 'So what's Clarence got to atone for?'

But Terry was eating with some concentration. Polishing off his chips, he leaned back in the chair and put his hands behind his head. 'You're lucky, you know, running your own show. I've always fancied a little takeaway shop.' He had that dreamy I've-just-eaten look. 'By the sea, somewhere I could fish. In the evenings, I'd do a bit of wood-carving, listen to the waves hissing up the shore.' He sighed. 'You can tire of big-town life. Especially in a life like mine. Especially at the moment.'

I nodded. Let Terry keep his dream. No need to give him any depressing little communiqués on how those wood-carving evenings would be spent standing over a trough of boiling oil six nights a week. 'Yep, she's a dream life. Couldn't ask for more.'

A pause.

'Terry, why are you looking for Clarence? What's he done? Did he do something to that Pittering fella?'

He looked at his watch. 'Listen, I've got to go. But...' he paused.

He ripped off a piece of chip paper and wrote something

down. 'My mobile number. Call me if you remember anything. Anything at all. Any time.' His warm hand brushed mine as I took the paper. He hurried over to the door.

'Did Clarence...kill him?'

Terry turned and stared at me. It was hard to work out his expression. Scared, maybe? He moved suddenly, as if trying to jolt himself awake.

'No, no. There's been no crime in Muddy Soak for more than twenty years.' He laughed, a forced kind of laugh, then shot out the door.

I guess for cops, a crime-free town would have to get pretty tedious.

Googling *Mona Hocking-Lee, Muddy Soak*, I found her house. Hocking Hall. A huge tycoon-style house with an excess of turrets and iron lacework verandahs. Sculptures in the garden, fountains spouting out of lions' mouths. Built with gold-rush money, I'd guess. Acres of green lawns, lawns that would suck up a heap of Muddy Soak's copious supplies of water. It was certainly a step up from Ernie's shack.

Brad arrived back from Madison's, his hair more ruffled than usual.

'Windy out there?' I asked. It didn't look windy. A raven sat in the pepper tree, cawing its long drawn-out call.

'No.'

'Listen, Brad. You know anything about Kota?'

'You mean the Kota gas leak? In India?'

'Yeah.'

'Killed thirty thousand and poisoned a hundred

thousand hectares of farmland. Still poisoned now, after nearly thirty years. Maybe it will be forever. Bastards,' he summed up.

'That Mona Hocking-Lee was connected to it. You know that?'

His eyes widened. 'Connected how?'

'Major shareholder.'

'In Argon Chemical?'

'You reckon anyone would want to kill her because of that?' I said.

'Kill her? Like who? Half of India, you mean?'

'Well, maybe one of your environmental whatsit friends.'

He swung away. 'Jesus, Mum. What sort of people do you think I hang around with? Murderers? I've never heard anything so offensive.'

'I'm not saying *you'd* do it, son. But maybe someone with...strong feelings?'

'Mum. Listen to yourself. Anyway, how's Claire?'

I'd forgotten Claire.

He sighed. 'I bet you haven't even offered her a cuppa. I'll go see how she's doing,' he started off down the hallway.

'Brad?'

He turned and looked at me.

'You've got to do the right thing by Claire. It's not on, you know...to...'

'What?'

'Uh, you know. The baby.'

He looked puzzled. 'Listen, the baby's not mine. No way.'

'Well, how can you be sure?'

'Mum.' He put his hands on my shoulders, gazed into my eyes. 'There's certain things you have to do to make a baby. You know, the birds and the bees?' He waltzed off down the hall.

Just after tea the phone rang. 'Look here.' It was Ernie. 'What's this about you renting my place out to Mafia types? And then embezzling the filthy money? I've a mind to phone Dean and get him to lock you up.'

Oh shit. With everything that had happened, I'd forgotten to give Ernie his five grand.

'Ronnie told me what you've been up to. He was having a smoke with me, no harm in that, out by the roses. It was while that Madison Watkins was in visiting her grandmother, she's had all the fluid drained off her lungs, and she brought in those bloody awful ferrets. Now.' He paused. 'You listening?'

'Yep,' I said, busy searching for Ernie's point.

'I don't know why the home lets them in. They tell me not to smoke, but they'll let in a horde of vicious, sharp-teethed animals. I could hear them screeching from my room. Had to turn off my hearing aid. I couldn't listen to the wireless. I've got no flamin' idea whether Kippy Tiani won at Horsham.' He paused. 'Anyway. Where was I?'

'Search me, Ernie.'

'Christ, can't you keep track of anything? Boot him out.'

'Boot who out?'

'The Mafioso bloke.'

'Well, I tried. I'm sorry, but...'

'And after all I've bloody done for you, Cassandra Ariadne.'

Ernie's the only person that uses the catastrophe of

my full name. And my sister Helen when I've pissed her off. Yep, I got saddled with Cassandra Ariadne and she scored Helen. Dad and his great ideas. He'd raced out and got the christening cup engraved before Mum had a chance to stop him. Or so she always said.

'Yep, Ernie.' There didn't seem much else to say.

'What do you mean *hic* "yep"?' Ernie hiccups when he gets worked up. If you don't move in quick and calm him, he starts vomiting. If you're in the same room, you need to be agile.

'I meant yep, I'll boot him out. I'll go up there right now and sort it out. And,' I looked at Brad, who'd come in and was shaking his head. 'Brad's checking now to see who won at Horsham.' I handed Brad the phone before he could tell me not to.

'Reckon it must've been Flathead Phil,' Brad was saying as I left. 'Hang on, sorry, wrong race, it was Glendale Wastrel. Is that the dog you backed?'

I chewed my lip as I drove. The road ahead was still glassy in the heat. Taking a clammy hand off the steering wheel, I wound down my window to get some breeze. Would Clarence even be there? Unlikely. Terry and Sergeant Monaghan were looking for him. He would have cleared off, surely. Still, I had to try, for Ernie's sake. And maybe I could find out something useful while I was there. Something Terry might appreciate.

I arrived at the turning to the shack. The shadows of the mallee gums were at full stretch as the light drained from the day. I started thinking about what I'd say to Clarence and what he might say back. No one would hear a shot out here. I shivered, despite the heat. Maybe

I should have brought Brad along for some support. Or at least my star picket.

I pulled up outside the shack, my wheels whisking up the dust. Clarence's black Lexus and Mona's silver Mercedes were still here. Surely Clarence must be around somewhere. It's not as if the bus comes past on the hour. Nearest bus stop is fifty k up the road, a once-a-day job to Melbourne via Hustle, Trawilda and Sheep Dip.

I got out, crunching over the dried tufts of grass to the front door, then knocked, waiting on the skew-whiff verandah. I jumped as the warning call of a willie wagtail stabbed the air. No sounds from inside the shack. No reassuring smells of dinner cooking. No lights on, although that wasn't surprising since Ernie never got around to connecting the power. He was always the sort of bloke who preferred a kero lamp.

I peered in through the window. Dark inside. I went back to the door, turned the handle: peered into the dim hallway. I waited a moment for my eyes to adjust to the murk and stepped forward, bits of plaster crunching underfoot. 'Hello? Anybody in?' My voice had more than a hint of quaver. I jumped as something banged above. A bit of rusted corrugated iron on the roof come loose. The whole place was coming loose.

I tiptoed into the front bedroom. The room looked like it had been hit by a meteorite. Clothes strewn across the floor. A suitcase turned inside out, long gashes cut into it. The other bedroom wasn't any better. There were dresses piled on the bed, some ripped apart. High heeled shoes lay scattered around the room.

I walked down the hall to the kitchen. Knocked-over chairs, smashed-up plates and glasses. I sighed. The place would take a shit load of tidying up. I really should have got references. I stopped by the back door. It had been ripped half off its hinges. Three round holes in the wall. Bullet holes?

I peered out at the mallee scrub, the soil purple in the dusk. The buzzing of the cicadas was fading as the heat bled from the day. The sky was dark blue, last light a smudge of buttermilk on the horizon. I tiptoed outside.

I paused by the row of parked cars, dim shapes in the gloom. I grabbed the torch from my glove box. Strode over to Clarence's car, shone the torch in through his car windows. The foot wells were filled with drifts of takeaway food wrappers and drink containers. The doors and boot were locked.

The door of Mona's Mercedes was unlocked. Soft leather seats, no takeaway wrappers. I rootled around the glove box. One Mercedes manual, a handful of parking tickets and a couple of letters from the infringements court. I peered underneath the seats. Nothing. I closed the door with a quiet thud. The boot was locked. Stepping back from the car, I bumped into Ernie's old water tank and slipped in a wet patch below the tap.

Hang on. There was another car parked here yesterday. The silver Mercedes, Clarence's Lexus, the undercover police car—a white commodore—and another, fourth car. Yes, four cars. What had the other one looked like? I screwed up my eyes while I tried to remember. Orange. A beat-up orange ute. Who did that belong to? And where had it gone?

I stared through the dim at Ernie's shed. Maybe the ute was parked in there.

Ernie's shed has never been an orderly, pine-shelved

establishment, it's more a piled-up-with-dusty-old-sinks-and-handy-bits-of-piping type of spot. It had an overpowering smell of oil, with a hint of something nastier underneath. I shone my torch around. No utes. Down the end was the old tin bath that Ernie called his bathroom. It had a new-looking tarp draped over it.

A sound. A light, scuffling sound, possibly a rodent sound. I swung the torch around. I'm not wild about being near rats, especially in the dark. I shone the torchlight along the floor. No rats. I moved slowly towards the bath, then heard a sob. Rats don't sob in my experience. I waved my torch wildly all around.

'Who's there?' I said in my boldest ragged whisper. I waited, holding my breath. Silence. I stared at the tarp. When had that arrived? Ernie's been in the home for the past year, he doesn't go out tarp-shopping. Not to my knowledge, anyway. I whipped the tarp from off the bath.

I sucked in a quick frantic breath. There was a woman's body in the bath. She lay there in her gold knit dress, her eyeless face grey in the torchlight. The smell hit the back of my throat. I gagged.

There was another sound, behind me. I swung around. A girl's face looked back at me in the torchlight, blonde hair ragged around her face. She put her hand up to her eyes, turned and ran out of the shed, lugging a water bottle in one hand. I charged out after her.

'Aurora,' I shouted, waving the torch at the cars, the track, the trees.

But she was gone.

I'd learned my lesson about phoning Dean. This time I fished out the bit of chip paper from my bag and called Terry.

'I'll be there right away.' His voice was bleak.

He didn't ask any pointless questions like if I was sure she was dead.

Terry hadn't said how long 'right away' would take but he was coming from the Muddy Soak police station, about two hours south of Ernie's. It was possible he might do it a little quicker than that in the circumstances.

I waited at the doorway of Ernie's shed, the wind gusting, hauling at my hair and dress, with a whingey, fractious sound. My torch flickered a few times, then went out. I found myself wishing I'd never heard of Clarence or his relatives. There were a lot more interesting things I could be doing. Like scrubbing out my fryers or Jexing down my sinks.

I leapt in the air as my phone rang.

'Where are you?' Brad.

'Ernie's. Something's...come up. I'll be a little while.'

'Come on, Mum, it's dark. You need to come home. This Clarence bloke could be dangerous.' He hung up.

Brad had a point, but I knew I had to wait near Mona.

I wasn't turning my back on her body. Not this time.

Then, from the shack, a shriek. I jumped, my heart jack-hammering in my chest. The shriek ended in a nasty muffled sound.

I spent a hectic moment panicking. Was it Aurora being killed? If I went in, I could be next. Should I jump in my car, get right out of here? But then the murderer might follow me and kill us all.

I inched towards the shack, stepping as quietly as I could over all the brittle, crispy leaves. At least the raging wind might fill the murderer's ears, distract him from my crunching.

The full moon came out, lighting up the place. I shrank into the shadow, until the moon slid behind another cloud.

Feeling my way along the shack wall, trying not to pant, I found the door. I paused, listening, my ears on high alert. I wished I'd paid more attention to Brad's briefings on screaming-woman owls. Maybe their scream ends in a muffled sound, as if a hand was placed over the owl's beak. Wouldn't it be terrific to find it was just an owl. A lost, bedraggled owl, longing to get home.

I edged along the dark hallway, full of the sad, musty smell of a place empty too long. A scratching sound. I froze, held my breath. Whack. Something hit my leg. Soft, but also sharp. Something way bigger than a rat. I shrieked, kicking, trying to shake it off. It just gripped on harder. A shaft of moonlight shone through the window. I looked down. A cat was clinging to my leg. It stared at me with huge eyes, hissed, then scampered off. I let out a lungful of pent-up breath.

I headed down the hall, retracing my steps towards the back door, almost jaunty with relief. It was just the cat, that noise. A yowling cat. No one shrieking. I needed to Jif out my ears. I turned into the kitchen doorway.

There was a shadow lurking by the door.

I screamed as I leapt back into the hall. The shadowy maniac screamed back. Then it rushed outside, dragging a clanking bag. It was a smallish kind of maniac, I realised, as I followed it outside. A maniac with long blonde hair.

I galloped after her, to see her race to my car and yank at the driver's door, then open the back door, fling in the bag and scramble in over the back seat. She drove off.

I stood, shouting, but Aurora was gone, belting my little Corolla down Ernie's track at top speed.

I scuffed back to the shed, cursing. There was a good long wait, which gave me the chance to review in detail exactly how stupid I felt, how I should have stayed at home, how I should have turned Clarence away that night he'd first arrived. Then eventually headlights appeared on Ernie's track. A car pulled up in front of me, dazzling and skidding in the gravel.

Two men jumped out. Monaghan strode towards me, Terry following. In the headlights, they cast long skinny shadows across the shed. Terry gave me an anxious smile. Monaghan's off-looking, half-shut eye was oozing. Maybe it did that when he was stressed.

'Mrs Tuplin.' Monaghan sounded impatient.

'In there.' I pointed at the shed.

Terry went inside but Monaghan stayed put in front of me. He barked out a bunch of questions. What was I doing here? Where exactly had I seen Aurora? What had she said, where had she gone? And had I seen Clarence?

'And tell me, Mrs Tuplin, why do you continually snoop around this property?'

I explained about Ernie's phone call, his worry about the tenant. Aurora and her water bottle. My stolen car.

Another set of headlights appeared on Ernie's track. We stood, watching the lights approach. It was Brad, with Claire in the passenger seat. He pulled up behind Monaghan's car. Brad gave his horn a couple of parps, as if I hadn't seen him. They stayed sitting in the car.

'And how many more of your family do you expect to call in here tonight?'

I wasn't keen on Sergeant Monaghan's tone. I might have to mention it to Victoria Police. I imagined they'd have standards about police officers' tones.

Terry came out of the shed, looked at Monaghan and shook his head. 'I think we should let Cass go home now.' Terry put a hand on Monaghan's arm. 'We'll discuss all this with her later.'

Monaghan shook off his hand and gave him an angry look. 'Mrs Tuplin needs to answer my questions.' His voice was a hiss. 'It's a serious offence to withhold evidence.'

'Is there anything else you'd like to tell us, Cass?' Terry's voice was low.

I probably could have told them about yesterday, how this wasn't the first time I'd found Mona in her present state. I probably could have told them about the briefcase. And about the key in my bag. But I was worried for Dean. I wondered why they hadn't sent him, it would have been quicker, surely. Maybe it was one of those turf-pissing type of contests; they didn't trust Dean to do a proper job.

I came close to telling Terry, though. He walked me

to Brad's car, linking his arm in mine like Piero used to do. The air had cooled and I liked Terry's warmth by my side, although he held my arm more firmly than Piero would have.

'Go home, Cass.' He almost pushed me into the car. 'I'll call around and talk to you later. When we've finished here.'

'Talk to you later' could have meant a lot of things. I'd imagined a cosy formal statement given one-to-one, over a late-night hot chocolate, in my kitchen. You never know where a hot chocolate might lead when the circumstances are right. But Terry didn't want hot chocolate. And he brought Monaghan along, so any possible circumstances scurried on and out.

Monaghan swept into my kitchen in that two-cow coat and gave me a bad-mannered glare. Terry drooped along behind him looking like a ticked-off pup. It probably wasn't easy working for a bloke like Monaghan. Terry had a black eye, his cheek below it was red and puffy.

'Cuppa? Tim Tam?' I invited them to sit. Terry moved towards the table, but Monaghan just kept walking, striding up and down the room. Back and forth he paced, like some enraged, endangered panther shut up in its cage. His coat made a heavy swishing sound as he thumped along my floor. The eye was oozing bad. He should get some drops for it, I thought. Whitey's, the chemist up in Hustle would have something; I might suggest that to him later. When the timing was right.

Terry sat beside me in a doleful heap, staring at the floor. Things weren't going well with the investigation, then. No sign of Clarence, I was guessing. At least they had Mona's body now, thanks to me. Forensics would be at Ernie's place any minute, jabbing Mona with their tweezers, finding important hairs. Possibly they were there already. I might have to get the burners on. No doubt they'd need a feed.

Dean would be there too, helping out. He wouldn't have had time to call and let me know. They'd need to know what kind of gun the bullet came from. Dean could be good at that, he's methodical. I bet Forensics would want methodical. Another potential career path for him.

Monaghan stopped mid-march and glared. 'You're a foolish woman, Mrs Tuplin,' he snapped out. 'But I suppose plenty of other people have told you that.'

I bristled. This man had no business coming into my house and insulting me. And after all I'd done. Terry stared at the floor, like he had an appointment with a fault line due to split open at his feet.

'Do you make a habit of phoning the police with stupid lies? Telling them you've found a body?'

I stared at Monaghan a tick. And then I understood. Not a blissful type of understanding. Monaghan swished his coat and stamped out. Terry followed, turning briefly to give me a sad look.

How could a body just keep on disappearing?

Next morning, Brad announced he was heading out. 'Claire needs a lift to Hustle. She's visiting some people there.'

'Oh? Anyone I know?'

'Um.' He glanced at Claire. He bit his lip.

'It's, ah, some research. To do with my family history,' said Claire.

'Claire, does your family in Perth know you're here? Do you want to call them?'

'My mother's…ah, she's not really interested.'

'Oh?' I said.

'Um, she joined this cult…'

'Right. Does she know you're expecting?'

'Not really. She's pretty occupied.' Claire shrugged.

I looked at her, worried.

Claire must have seen my expression. 'It's OK, Mrs Tuplin. I'm fine.'

A pause.

'Thing is, I could do with your help in the shop today, Bradley.' I adopted a brisk tone. 'I've got things I need to do.' Like find my car. Maybe Vern could help. He was bound to have something useful in that notebook.

'Can you lend me fifty bucks, Mum?'

'Brad. Listen, we need to have a little talk about money.'

'It's just a loan. I'll pay you back.'

'When?'

He glanced at Claire. 'Well, when I can. You know I don't get paid for what I do.'

'I know. That's the problem. Look, all the passion in the world isn't going to pay the bills, son. You need to get yourself a job.'

'And who exactly is going to employ me? Activism doesn't make the most attractive CV. Or my police history. Anyway, you should think of the money you give me as an investment.'

'In what?'

'In a better world, Mum. In the environment. In the continuation of our species into the future. And it'll help to compensate for what you're doing in the shop. I've told you enough times about flake and snapper. You have to stop selling stuff that's overfished. Seriously.'

Claire nodded, staring at me with those pale blue eyes, so pale they made me think of polar ice shelves melting.

'You have to get out of this business,' said Brad. 'It's not sustainable. You've got to move on from all this pre-climate-change thinking.'

I really had to talk to the boy properly when I got a minute. It was time he made a few decisions about life. Especially if that was his baby.

'This shop provides a vital service, Bradley. And every job has its crappy side,' I said.

'Oh yeah? So what if you were, say, a marine biologist? Studying live fish, instead of cutting up dead ones? What'd be the crappy side of that?'

I thought a tick. Piero would have known what to say to these sorts of questions. He was always good with Brad. It was Piero who'd got him started on environmental goings-on in the first place. Nursing injured ex-racing blue-tongue lizards, back when Brad was nine.

'Well, there'd be a lot of sand rubbing around in your togs. That'd have to get annoying, day after day.'

Brad humphed and walked out.

I started shredding some cabbage for the coleslaw. One thing was clear. Brad definitely wasn't going to make it as any kind of takeaway monopolist.

Rae tramped through to my freezers, boxes of frozen flake, whiting and snapper stacked in her sinewy arms. Tall and wide, she's a woman that could shovel out a mallee gum without assistance.

'Couple of cops in the district asking questions, Rae.' I side-stepped out of her way.

'Drugs, is it? Cops snapped down on that meth lab at Weerimilla, after their silos closed. Kill a town and the dropkicks move right in.' She thumped the boxes into my freezer.

'Dunno. No mention of drugs. They're after a fella called Clarence Hocking-Lee. Done something suss, sounds like.'

'Not that little shit from Muddy Soak?'

'You know him?'

She laughed, a sound more like a throat being cleared. 'Bastard crashed my van, trying to nick it. Full of crays. Special delivery for Stefano's in Mildura.'

'But I thought Muddy Soak was crime free? Since 1980-something-something.'

'Yeah. This was in Hustle. That kid'll soon bugger up the record for Muddy Soak though.'

'And his nanna, Mona Hocking-Lee? What's she like?'

'Yeah, she's all right. Paid for the repairs to my van, no mucking around. Can't be easy for the woman. Raised those two grandkids on her own.'

'What about their parents?'

'Dead.' Rae wiped her ruddy face.

'Oh? How?'

'What's this, some sorta Hocking-Lee inquisition? S'pose you're doing this for Dean. His career, huh?'

'Yep. Could be a good little opportunity for him. Just need to get him galvanised.'

'Well, Ford Hocking-Lee, that was Mona's son, he died in a car crash. His wife died in it as well. Ages ago, have to be getting on for fifteen years. Mona raised those two grandkids like they were her own. Shame Clarence turned out the way he did. He's one fella they should chuck to the bloody chook house.'

A beat-up Holden pulled up outside the shop. Jill McKenzie got out, followed by her four kids. I hurried over to the door. 'Good to see you, Jill. You got a minute? I need to ask a favour.'

She strode in, towing the kids behind her. Jill's a lean, brown-armed, horse-breaker type of woman with short blonde hair, worn just below her ears and cut in savage swipes. She doesn't often come into town. There's not much point when you can't afford to buy anything.

The kids stood in a row beside their mother, a row of appealing fair-haired tykes, aged from five to thirteen. A bit like a row of von Trapps stepped out from their movie, although dustier, thinner and without the singing.

Jill and Stu McKenzie have had it pretty hard, not that it's something we discuss. Their farm's too small to scratch out a living even on twelve inches of rain, and we haven't had twelve inches since I don't remember. Vern reckons the corporate farm up the road is waiting for them to bail, keen to expand its portfolio.

I piled up my largest basket with flake and potato cakes and lowered it into the oil. 'Thanks for coming in. I've got some fish and potato cakes need using up today, they won't keep. Would you kiddies help me eat some leftovers? Be grateful if you would.'

I got the row of quick blond nods I was after, before Jill had a chance to speak. The McKenzies aren't people who'd accept anything resembling charity.

'And Brad mentioned when he was stocktaking there were some ice creams needed using up. On the house, of course.' I jigged the basket in the oil. 'We can't charge for leftovers.'

'Thank you.' Jill looked at me through black-lashed, curtained eyes that never gave anything away.

The kids rounded up some chairs and they all sat down at my plastic table.

'And there's a nice bowl of coleslaw needs eating up, if there's any volunteers.'

No crazed delight for the coleslaw.

'So what's been happening in town?' said Jill.

'Not much.' Well, apart from the odd murder getting no attention from the police. 'Some visitors from Muddy Soak. The Hocking-Lees.'

The tykes were eating their potato cakes with some concentration.

'That old bitch Mona Hocking-Lee was here?' said Jill.

I stared at her like the proverbial mullet, post-stunning. Mona had been in Rusty Bore less than forty-eight hours before she died, but clearly that had been enough time to get up Jill's sunburnt nose.

'Yeah, think that was her name,' I said carefully. 'You know her?'

'Don't you watch TV?' Jill put down her fish. 'She was on *Australian Story*. S'pose you would have missed it,' she looked around the shop, 'working here in the evenings. I'll tell you, she's one misguided do-gooder, that woman. She single-handedly suspended drought relief from the Ramsay Fund.'

'Oh?'

'Yeah. She made this big donation to them. Then asked to see how they spent the money. Wasn't satisfied with what they told her, now they're being investigated. While that happens, they've frozen payments. So no drought relief from them.'

'There's still government money though, isn't there? For people who need it?' I said.

'Yeah, but the Ramsay Fund paid out faster than the bureaucrats. Melanie Fanshaw at the council kept telling everyone to apply. I mean, I don't want anyone's handouts.' Her voice was fierce. 'But it's what kept Adrian going. For a while. Adrian, well, you know what happened.' She

90

glanced quickly at the kids, but they were too busy with their food to notice. 'It was just after the fund froze its payments.' Her voice was low.

I knew about Stu's brother Adrian, that's the kind of news that travels at warp speed. And poor old Dean had been first with it. He'd called in to Adrian's place after seeing his sheep on the road. No answer at the front door. No answer at the back. And then Dean saw the old sugar gum and what was hanging from it.

Adrian was always good with knots.

'If Stu had his way that Mona Hocking-Lee would disappear,' said Jill.

I stared. 'Have another potato cake.' She obviously didn't know. Or she was a bloody good actress. Stu wasn't a violent bloke, was he? He was built of cast-iron muscle and fond of snug-fitting black T-shirts but that didn't mean he'd shoot a woman in the head.

'She should've kept her mouth shut.' Jill's voice was flat. 'You can't keep rats out of a granary.' Her face looked tired, like she'd been breaking in horses since before breakfast.

Jill and the kids ate their ice creams, then left. I started auto-wiping the spotless counter while I worried about Stu. Adrian's funeral had been at the cemetery, a kilometre out of town. A plume of orange-red dust had followed the procession of cars and utes. When I offered Stu my condolences, he gripped my hand and said, in a quiet voice, 'Justice comes to us all.'

Justice? Was that really what he'd said? Would Stu kill? Nah, surely not the type. But what is the killing type?

Brad got back just after lunch. He'd left Claire visiting her relatives. 'Mind the shop,' I said and headed out to Vern's. Maybe Vern had seen Aurora. Maybe he could help me find my car.

Boofa was out, as usual, sniffing the air. We walked together, the heat rising from the footpath, heading past the closed hardware shop, the ex-op shop and the long-closed pub. Next to the collapsing town hall were two bewildered-looking sheep, glancing around as if they were wondering how to get back into their paddock.

Vern was out in his hammock as usual, notebook in his lap. He was scratching his arm stump. A lizard scuttled across the road.

'Cass Tuplin, my favourite bloody woman in this entire town,' Vern put aside his notebook. 'You been thinking over my merger proposal, haven't you?'

A big grin stretched across his face. 'You've come to

tell me *yes*. I can see it in your eyes.'

'Vern. Look, I appreciate your interest, I really do. Flattering, in fact. But, well, I'm just not...ah, you know, Piero's a hard act to follow. I don't mean any offence by that.'

Vern's smile faded. He blinked, looked down at Boofa and stroked his head. Boofa looked up at him with dark liquid eyes; he's a lovely dog. He won Best Dog in Ute at the Deni Ute Muster five years ago. 'Yeah,' Vern's voice was gruff. 'Well, people aren't always exactly what they seem on first sighting. And even later on. Thing is, you can miss things about a person. Important things.'

I'd hurt his feelings. I stood there, unsure of what to say next.

A van pulled up outside Vern's. A familiar white van, with a broken side-mirror, driven by a man with wild white hair and a beard. Noel opened the door and stepped out.

I was pleased to see Bubbles was staying in the van. She pressed her nose against the window and growled, a throaty sound the colour of tar. Boofa gave a startled yelp and ran away.

Noel didn't say anything, just headed into the shop. Vern picked up his notebook and followed him inside. I hoofed along behind Vern.

It was dim and musty inside Vern's shop. The overhead fan fluttered the Australian flag he keeps beside his till. I suppose that little flag reminds Vern of where he lives, although I'm not sure why he'd need reminding. There's nothing wrong with his memory.

Noel drifted around the shelves, shopping basket in one hand. He put six tins of spaghetti, two tins of milk powder, a jar of coffee, seven tins of dog food, a hacksaw and a pack of moist-wipes in the basket. I stood with Vern up the front, pretending to chat.

At the till Vern had a go at some extraction tête-à-tête but Noel wasn't co-operating. He smiled in a distant way, offering no answers to Vern's line-up of probing questions, then paid in cash and left. We followed him outside and stood watching him execute a six-point turn with a lot of gear crunching. Finally, he drove away.

Vern made a note in his book and said, 'Northerly direction. Could be headed to Perry Lake. Just a working hypothesis, of course.' He made a minor adjustment to his groin.

Back in my shop, I pondered on those moist-wipes. Without being sexist, there's not a lot of fellas in my acquaintance that would think to buy a moist-wipe. And Noel didn't strike me as a moist-wipe type of man.

Three regulars came in for potato cakes. I cooked and served, pondering some more. I considered phoning Terry. But I couldn't give him the full picture regarding Noel without mentioning finding Mona the first time, which would make Dean look bad. There were a lot of secrets I was keeping. I wasn't used to keeping secrets, not other people's anyway. The whole point of knowing someone's secret is so you can talk it over with someone else.

'Listen, Brad. Noel bought a pack of suspicious moist-wipes. I need to borrow your car so I can follow him.'

Brad looked up from the chopping board, wiped his hands on his apron.

'He headed out towards Perry Lake,' I said.

Brad sighed, as though he'd had a long day dealing

with a wearying queue of imbeciles. 'Mum. What's a moist-wipe?'

'Well, exactly. That's what I'm saying.'

'What? If there's something suspicious about Noel, then phone Dean. You can't go following people just because they bought some tissues.'

'Really? What about all the poking around you do online, stalking your environmental rapist types?'

'That's just browsing the internet. It's not actually getting in a car and following someone.'

That's one of Brad's problems; he lets himself get too bound up by all these random made-up rules.

'Anyway, Mum, I'm just saying you should phone Dean. Tell him about your car.'

'Maybe you should phone him. He might believe you,' I said.

'The less I have to do with Dean the better.'

'What's that mean?'

'You know.' Brad sighed. 'Look, those arrests weren't my fault. Someone has to stand up for the river. Not that Dean has any idea about that.'

'Bradley. Son. He's just...worried about you, like we all are, about your...direction in life.' Your lack of direction.

'Yeah, whatever. I'm not phoning. Anyway, he'll have to believe you. Your car's obviously gone. Just leave out all the other stuff. Don't mention anything weird like moist-wipes. He already thinks you're off your head.'

Thanks son.

'Dean?' I put him on speakerphone so Brad could listen too.

I gave a neat little summary about my car, leaving out the bit about Mona's latest disappearance. No point in distracting him with things he might not wish to hear.

There was a pause.

I'll admit I didn't handle what happened in that pause with quite optimal effect. It's possible I may have mentioned Noel. And his moist-wipes.

Brad mouthed, 'No,' tried to grab the phone, tried to end the call.

I pushed him away. Brad had his line of reasoning, I know, but there wasn't any point in hanging up. Dean had heard the words and would want to know.

Silence at the other end.

'And Mona's body could be in my car boot, Dean. Every chance of that.'

I've never liked a silence. And there were too many things I wasn't meant to mention. I was a person on confidentiality overload.

'It has a jail term, Mum.' Dean's voice sounded strangled. It was clear he wasn't referring to the possession of a pack of moist-wipes.

'Jail term? Look, I'm just trying to bloody help out here...'

'That's it. I've had enough. I'm coming around to arrest you. Now.' He slammed down the phone.

I turned to Brad, who was holding his head in his hands.

Oh, for God's sake. I kicked the phone table, stubbed my toe.

'I'm going out,' I told Brad in my coldest voice. 'In your car. Don't you worry, Bradley, Dean won't arrest you. Tell him you tried to stop me. Tell him I fought you off.'

I sailed out with as much dignity as I could.

I headed off in Brad's tiny car towards Perry Lake. I don't travel that way too often, not these days. A million years ago Piero and I used to drive along this road on our day off. We'd come along here in the early morning light. He'd bring his camera, Piero always had his camera. Some of his photos were published in magazines. We'd head along this road and watch the sun rise, its glow a pink glaze over the rows of slashed wheat. Piero would take endless shots of backlit fields. We were going to travel all around Australia. While I gazed at the pink sky, I'd think about all those places we'd be going. I'd get that lifting feeling in my chest. The one that says: this is life, and you know, it's not too bad.

I belted along the road in Brad's shaking car, hot air blasting through the vents, drying my tears. Yep, that lifting feeling; I hadn't felt it in a while.

Slowing down, I peered, blinking, at Ernie's shack. No

sign of Noel's van. Then, ahead, by the side of the road, I caught sight of my car.

I parked behind it, got out and looked around. No Aurora. My keys were in the ignition, where I'd left them. I checked through the car. No bloodstains or hacked-up slashes on the seats. No Mona in the boot.

'Brad?' I said into my phone.

'Mum! I was just about to call you.' He sounded suspiciously cheerful. 'Perfect timing. Dean's just arrived. Look, I've explained about your car. It's all straightened out. I'll put him on.'

I won't bore you with the details of that drab-as-a-bastard phone call, of how hard I tried to explain that, yes, my car really had been stolen, only briefly, but yes, it really had; how the disapproval oozed from Dean's deep voice, over Brad's groaning noises in the background.

Any normal cop would have been relieved my car had turned up.

'I don't like this, Mum, but you're really leaving me with little choice. You're either doing this deliberately, in which case I have to arrest you. Or,' he paused.

'Or what?'

'You need help. In which case I have to get you to a doctor.'

'Come on, son. Don't be so bloody ridiculous. You know, your father would have known to forgive a little mistake,' I said. 'He knew mistakes can happen. And someday soon, Dean, you're going to find out you've made one or two yourself.' I hung up.

I wasn't waiting around to be arrested or strapped down and subjected to some painful mental probe. I had serious matters to sort out. Noel and his moist-wipes. I tried starting my car. No go. Out of petrol.

I got back into Brad's car and steamed along the bitumen. It was true, what I'd said about Piero, how he knew about mistakes. Dean was a bit of a mistake himself, not that I'd ever tell him that. He stopped a whole lot of things from happening in our lives, Piero's and mine. Especially mine.

Motherhood's a special joy, of course. But sometimes joy's not everything it's cracked up to be.

I took the turn and drove along the track to Perry Lake, winding among the spinifex and buloke pines. Bingo. Noel's van was parked beside the track, in the shade. Grabbing Brad's binoculars, I scanned the place. No sign of Noel. No sign of Bubbles either. I crept up to the van, peered in through the window of the sliding door, cupped my hands around my face to shade my eyes. The van was full of shelves and was surprisingly tidy. Maybe I'd been wrong, maybe Noel was a moist-wipe type of person after all.

On the lower shelf was a small fridge, a carton of food and a cardboard box filled with scrunched-up newspaper. Above them, a bag of clothing and a plastic crate piled with ropes and leather belts with metal spikes attached. Next to the belts another glint of metal caught my atten-tion. A small curved saw, like a short, toothed scimitar. Not that I've had in-depth experience with scimitars. So was Noel some kind of bondage freak? A grey S&M nomad?

I stepped back, wiping the sweat from the back of my neck. I fanned my dress. There wasn't a sound anywhere, the only things moving were the ants swarming around the leaves at my feet. Everything else had shut up shop in the heat. The salt around Perry Lake shimmered in the distance.

The moist-wipe question wasn't resolved, not exactly, but I wasn't keen to stick around. And I didn't want to run into Bubbles. I moved towards Brad's car.

Hearing a sharp cry behind me, I whirled around. There it was again, way over in the trees, beyond the van. I skulked towards the van, hunching down beside it, like a cop in one of those hostage-liberation operations. Holding up Brad's binoculars, I scanned through the trees, my eyes adjusting to the gloom. Two people were standing in a clearing, a heap of shopping bags on the ground between them. A black dog stood with them, not obviously attacking anyone. I ticked the people off my list: one tall skinny bloke with wild white hair and a beard; one girl with messy blonde hair and a floaty apricot dress. The dress was looking the worse for wear. They were standing near a third person, who was handcuffed to a tree. He was a smaller, weaselly bloke in a torn grey suit. Clarence.

So were they all into some bondage thing? Is that why Clarence had said his book would be a bestseller, did it involve peculiar porn? Clarence jiggled his leg, cried out again. Well, anyone could have told him bondage would be a problem in the Mallee. Clarence and his cuffs had met up with a crowd of bull ants.

Bubbles looked my way, sniffed the air. She stiffened, then took off; coming towards me. Long, heavy strides, faster than a bolting horse. She barked, strangled gargles, sounding more like an unhinged mother bear than any normal dog. I scurried towards Brad's car with his binoculars swinging heavily around my neck, her galloping thumps closing in behind me. I could feel the dog's hot breath against my legs, hear her teeth clacking as she took empty snapping bites near my feet.

I made it to the car, grabbed the door and flung it open. I was mid-leap when Bubbles got my leg. She clamped on and shook it, like she was planning on worrying it right off. I screamed and held onto the car door, then turned and whacked her with Brad's binoculars. They cracked against her head. She fell back with a whimper and I jumped inside the car and slammed the door. Then I screamed some more.

I checked my throbbing leg and saw it was oozing blood onto the floor. I sucked in a deep breath. Started the car with a shaky hand.

Bubbles raised herself off the ground. She hurled herself at the window with a heavy thump, all black hair and teeth and slobber. My hands shook harder. Most of me was shaking as the car lurched forward and shot out of there, dust swirling in a thick red cloud behind it.

Racing home, I passed Dean's divvy van coming the other way. He pulled sharpish off the road, gravel flying, then turned and followed me. I sped up. I didn't have time to be arrested. The blood from my leg was seeping onto Brad's floor. Dean could wait until I put some disinfectant on it.

Dean surged behind, tailgating. I sped up until the engine whined. He pulled out beside me, waved wildly, wound down his window, shouted to pull over. I ignored him. I knew he wouldn't turn his siren on. He wouldn't want anyone to see him heartlessly pursuing his injured mother in a high-speed chase. He tucked back in behind and followed me home.

Finally, I pulled into my driveway and stopped the car, Dean's car sliding in after me. I limped in through the back door in my tattered dress, a good chunk of it flapping bloodily around my leg. I stared straight ahead, my most dignified look.

'Jesus, Mum. What happened?' Brad's face turned white.

I half-collapsed into a chair. Dean walked in behind me, glowering and sat down.

Feeling faint, I gabbled out a brief summary, Noel, Bubbles, the bite. Best to fill Brad in before I passed out.

Brad dabbed some Dettol neat onto my leg. It stung like hell and I kicked a bit. He had a few things to say along the lines of *don't-you-bloody-kick-me* while he dabbed, interspersed with a hissing mini-rant to Dean, *you-should-bloody-do-something-about-this-instead-of-leaving-everything-to-me.*

I wouldn't have minded a word with them about all that weird stuff in Noel's van, the spikes, the mini-scimitar and Clarence's handcuffs, but I wasn't feeling entirely well.

While Brad wiped my leg and went on with his rant to Dean, I shut my eyes. I tried picturing Miss Marple and her nephew, Raymond. Raymond wasn't one to go on; he was the supportive type. The kind that might thank a person for finding Clarence and Aurora and for short-circuiting a huge police operation to locate her car. He'd listen politely to her description of a mini-scimitar; maybe he'd look it up in some reference book. He might even give his mature female relative, at risk of swooning any minute from a painful dog bite, a little spot of sympathy.

Dean sat in silence through Brad's tirade, arms folded across his chest, then said, 'You'd better take her to Casualty in Hustle.' His voice was low.

Hard to say why they were acting as if I wasn't there. Surely I was pretty noticeable since I was bleeding all over the floor.

'Dog bites can be nasty,' said Dean. 'She could end up with an infection.'

Infection? I tensed up. What diseases do dogs carry? Into my head they all surged, in one big, unwelcome crowd. Brucellosis. Diarrhoea. Tetanus. Rabies.

Dean stood up. 'I'm heading out to have a word with this Noel.'

Well, *finally*. 'And Clarence was in handcuffs,' I said. 'They're probably making some weird illegal porn.'

Dean looked at Brad. 'While you're there, you'd better,' he gave a little nod, one of those nods that are meant to be all hush-hush-significant, 'get her head checked out as well.' He strode out to his car.

I struggled into the passenger seat of Brad's car, careful of the leg. Despite the pain and nausea, I felt surprisingly at peace. Dean was onto this moist-wipe business now, he'd sort it out. And he'd been almost sympathetic, worrying about a possible infection. I rustled up a smile and gave him a wave as he drove away.

'You know anything about the signs of rabies, Brad?' I snapped on my seatbelt. I was pretty sure there was foam involved. At the mouth. Was that awful dog foaming at the mouth? All I could recall was teeth.

'No rabies in Australia, Mum. There's lyssavirus, but that's in bats.'

'Could it pass to a human through a bat-bitten dog?'

'Dunno. Possibly.' He got in the car. Turning the ignition, he started up a briefing on lyssavirus, how long it takes to incubate, all the convulsions and delirium, how long you take to die. 'In atrocious pain, probably.'

I stared out the window, trying not to think of all the ways a dog might meet an infected bat, of the reasons the bat might bite the dog. An angry bat; a hungry bat. A bat could have a lot of reasons.

A road train overtook us, the blast of air juddering against the car.

Brad started up on his favourite desert rant, the one where he lists the two hundred endangered Mallee species. 'The place is dying, Mum.' He thumped the steering wheel. 'Once the last desperate hangers-on have left it'll just turn into one big empty salt plain.'

Did he consider me one of those hangers-on? I knew I wasn't going anywhere. It's the potential of the place that gets to you. What it could be, if it rained.

We crossed a dry river bed. A kestrel landed in a paddock, its feet extended. Maybe the weather was getting to Brad. It was headache weather, oppressive, like it wants to rain but can't remember how.

I told Brad about the weird stuff in Noel's van, those spikes and the mini-scimitar, Clarence and his handcuffs. 'So what's Noel up to with that lot?'

Brad looked at me, his face had a worn-down expression, like he'd packed on some extra years today. 'Well, it's obvious,' he said. 'You've got a choice of three.' He gave me a little list:

One, the mini-scimitar was an actual mini-scimitar, used for slashing unarmoured opponents either mounted or on foot.

Two, the spikes were used for tree climbing and the mini-scimitar was some sort of handsaw used by an arborist for pruning trees, or maybe by a scientist collecting tree samples.

Three, they could all be tools used for some weird sex game.

Options one and three were fairly unappealing. Option two seemed too sensible for Noel somehow; too law-abiding. Anyway, not much call for an arborist around here.

'And surely a reputable scientist type of person wouldn't look so scruffy,' I said. 'He'd drive a natty car provided by the uni, neat logo down the side, not that rusting van.'

He snorted. 'You met many scientists, Mum?' Then he shrugged. 'Look, he's probably an environmentalist. He'll be doing something useful for the planet, maybe bird research.'

'Without binoculars? And what's an environmentalist doing with handcuffs?'

A long wait and three injections later, I was declared dog-infection-free. Leaving the hospital, I spotted a parked ute, dusty orange in Hustle's main street. Terry got out and started limping along the street, staring at the footpath.

'Terry,' I called out. He turned. He still had that bruise on his cheek.

'What happened to your leg, Cass?'

'Oh, a minor accident,' I waved a careless hand. 'I see you've got them, then?'

He gazed at me, an intent type of gazing. Like there was nothing else around to see. I didn't mind it at all. I moved a little closer.

'Sorry?' he said.

'Clarence and Aurora. I see you've got their ute. From Ernie's shack.'

Terry expelled his breath. 'Wow. You're one observant woman.'

I smiled.

Brad folded his arms and stared at the road, suddenly fascinated by the bitumen.

'Nah, that ute's mine. Had it years,' said Terry. 'Your little Corolla out of action?' He was looking at Brad's car.

I explained about the vandalised lock.

He stood closer. I could feel his warmth. 'You need your vehicle fixed, Cass. A woman needs good access to her vehicle. Want me to fix it?' He looked into my face and smiled. What would he be like to kiss?

I was out of breath and words for a moment. *Pull yourself together, Cass.* 'That'd be terrific. Suit you to pop over sometime?'

Terry nodded, glanced at his watch. 'I can swing over tomorrow night. OK?'

I nodded. He turned and limped away.

'I just haven't had the time, Mum. Anyway, it'll give you a chance to see him again. You fancy that bloke, don't you.'

'What a peculiar thing to say, Bradley.' I folded my arms, stared at the wall behind him. It featured a colourful mural of the Mallee Farm Days. Tractors, smiling children. No mention of how Hustle stole those Days from Rusty Bore, of course.

'Yes, you do. And it's about time you started seeing someone. Just don't go making a fool of yourself.'

'Seeing someone? As if I could find the time. No, my interest in Terry is purely Mona-related.'

His mouth twitched.

'Yep, I'm like one of those Mexican whiptail lizards you're always on about. She doesn't have time for males, remember? She has her little lizard kids without him.

Some special bio-whatever-genesis.'

'Parthenogenesis.'

'That's me. Partho-woman.'

'I'm sure you needed Dad for us.'

'Your father was different, Brad.'

'OK. Sorry I brought it up.' He got back into the car. I limped over, got in, shut the door.

Brad started the car and looked over. 'You'll be careful, won't you?'

Brad, the big expert on life. He started the car, hunched over the steering wheel, staring ahead, not speaking. Not one single update on extinctions, not even as we passed the miles of shimmering salt. He was like one of those Alaskan caterpillars he's told me about, all frozen and inert in winter, before they bound into life in spring. He'll be right, I told myself, Brad'll spring to life. When he's ready.

With the worry about rabies-related foam no longer hanging over me, I could focus properly on the Mona business. 'I need your help tomorrow, Brad. We'll close the shop.'

'What?'

'We're going to Muddy Soak.'

'Muddy Soak? Listen, you need to stay at home and look after that leg, Mum. Anyway, we can't close the shop. There'll be customers queuing all along the footpath.'

I liked his optimism. I couldn't remember when we last had an actual queue, possibly not since we lost the Farm Days.

'Good point. OK, you can mind the shop. Don't worry, I'll be fine on my own. I've got a plan. I'll head to Hocking Hall. Return the briefcase, ask some questions.'

'Jesus. Just take that briefcase to Sergeant Monaghan.'

'I'm not taking anything to Monaghan. He was bloody rude. If he wants the case, he can ask. Politely.'

His hands tightened on the steering wheel. 'Mum. Can't you just be a normal mother for a change? You've got to stop putting yourself in dangerous situations. You don't want to run into that dog again. This time it might kill you.'

'Don't you worry, son, I'll be staying right away from Bubbles. Look, that briefcase is important, I'm sure of it.'

We passed a row of dead kangaroos hanging from a fence.

'And anyway,' I said, 'life is full of danger. I mean, a person could die any old day at home, from something completely uninteresting. Heart failure, heat stress, a stroke or anything, just while she's cooking fish. Having done not a single thing with her life. No one wants to look back on all this and think, I should have done more, I could have done more, now, do they?'

'When?' he said.

'When what?'

'When would this nameless person be thinking that? After she's had the stroke?'

'Yes, quite possibly,' I said. 'On her deathbed, waiting for the second, decisive stroke. Anyway, my point is...' I paused while I fossicked for my point, '...I'm doing this for the populace of Rusty Bore.'

'Well, I just hope they're grateful to you, Mum.'

Near the road, a flock of little corellas sat on a bore-water pump. They dipped their heads up and down, drinking from a spurting leak.

'So, what questions you planning on asking at Hocking Hall?' he said.

'I'm considering that at the minute. Making a list. Happy to hear suggestions.'

'You going to talk to Mona Hocking-Lee's sister?'

'Yep, probably.' Stripes of golden wheat stubble flashed by. What sister?

'Her name's Alexandra.'

'I know, yep. I'll be talking to her.'

Brad stopped to decant some petrol into my car, still sitting by the road near Ernie's shack.

'Alexandra's got an antiques shop, in the main street of Muddy Soak,' Brad said.

'Course she does.'

'You could go there first. It's on the way.'

'Uh-huh.'

'But, remember, they don't get along, not since, you know...'

'Yep, yep.' Bloody kids.

Back at home, I limped around the place, going through my normal routine of closing up for the night, checking and rechecking all the burners were turned off, wiping down my stainless steel counters and the flystrips, mopping the chequered floor.

Shop closed, we got on with tea. Fish and salad, minus the fish, since Brad (while I was at Perry Lake, busy being bitten) had decided I would become a vegetarian, to reduce my carbon footprint and the misery we humans have imposed on all creatures, including fish. So he'd gone through the fridge and binned the salmon.

'Fish may not be cute and cuddly and have eyelashes, Mum, but they can feel pain. More than probably. If you watched more TV, you'd know all this. You'd know, for instance, that an octopus can plan, can figure out how to defend itself with a coconut shell it's found. They're capable of making all kinds of decisions. Don't tell me that an animal that can plan like that can't feel pain.'

'Jesus, Brad. I can't believe you've thrown out good food. What a terrible waste.' I put down my fork and stared out the window. The sun was setting. It looked as though someone had taken a blood orange and smeared it across the sky.

'Now, listen,' I said. 'We'd better pool resources. Tell me what you know about this Alexandra.'

'It was in the *Muddy Soak Express*. Big story, didn't you see it? Their father, James L. Hocking, left his estate, including Hocking Hall, to Mona when he died eight years ago. He left next to nothing to her sister. Just an allowance. Alexandra was married at the time to Grantley Pittering.'

'As in Pittering and Son?'

He nodded.

I ate a lettuce leaf.

'So tell me, Mum, what information do you have to pool?'

I glared. 'I'd have time to look things up too, Bradley, if my days weren't filled right up with running everything.'

Galvanising Brad. And Ernie. The shop. Galvanising every damn thing for everybody else.

I started early. Soon I was into red sand hills and abandoned farms. I passed a derelict homestead, a mass of
broken timber, red-brick chimney standing all alone.
Maybe I should start up one of those schemes like they
have in Wycheproof. Rent out a house for a dollar a week
to some nice family and boost the population. Ernie's
shack. Brad could do it up. Although we'd need to choose
a family that likes takeaway.

I unstuck my thighs from the car seat, massaged my
dog-bitten leg. I sailed on through Hustle, past their public
toilets. I refuse to use those toilets, no matter how badly I
need to go. Those bastards nicked the design from Rusty
Bore, back from when we had a public toilet.

Grey wheat stubble thickened to shimmering green as
I got closer to Muddy Soak. I passed a fancy farm stay,
excessively surrounded with lacy ironwork verandahs. The
rounded Dooboobetic Hills were hazy in the distance.

I crossed the river, more a string of muddy waterholes than a raging torrent, as I entered town. Red banners hanging from every street pole proclaimed the Christmas Fringe Festival. I parked outside Déjà Vu Antiques Boutique, in the tree-lined main street. Everywhere you looked in Muddy Soak, there was green. It was a place well-endowed with shady trees, football teams, fringe festivals, drama groups. And antiques boutiques.

There was a closing-down-sale sign in the window.

I snapped off my seat belt, stepped out of the car.

I opened the shop door and three anorexic dogs leaped towards me with a surprising abundance of licking and enthusiasm for such bone-bag animals. I staggered back, guarding my bitten leg. Italian greyhounds, I found out later. They wore diamante collars and fleecy blankets.

A woman stood at the cash register, on the phone. 'Well, you'll just have to. Sort. It. Out. Grantley.' She wore more silk scarves than I would have considered possible, all different colours. Latin music strummed in the background.

The dogs took turns to sniff my nether regions. I pushed them away and looked around. Antiques boutique? A dump for junk, more like. Inside a glass case by the door, a stuffed parrot in moth-eaten red stood on a dusty branch. A sign below: *Our dearest Rufus. We'll never forget you.* The place was chock-a-block with chipped plates, bent saucepans and a sea of books. I screwed up my nose at the smell of incense. A multitude of Chinese lanterns, red and white, hung from the ceiling.

'No. You will pay me *now*. I'm not taking any more of your excuses.' She slammed down the phone.

One of the dogs barked, a deeper sound than I'd expected.

The woman strode over, grabbing the dogs by their collars. 'Get here. Traitors.' The last word was just a hiss. She was a woman who jangled as she moved. 'Can I help you?' No welcome-smile.

I collected myself. 'Alexandra Hocking?'

'Depends who's asking, darling.'

'Mona left this behind in my shop.' I held up the briefcase.

'What kind of shop?'

'The Rusty Bore Takeaway. We're known for our quality fish and chips...'

'Friend of Pauline Hanson's are you?' She laughed, a hard tinkle like a detonating chandelier.

For years the female fish and chip shop monopolist has been saddled with the flak created by that woman, her destruction of our good name. 'There are hundreds, probably thousands of towns in Victoria,' I said. 'And almost every one of them has a takeaway shop. Not a single one is run by Pauline Hanson. So, no, I don't know her.'

'Hit a nerve, my sweet?' A nasty smile. 'Anyway, Mona wouldn't go anywhere near oil. My precious sister doesn't do grime.' She blinked her long black eyelashes.

'Well, she came in,' I said, 'and I think the case belongs to Clarence.'

'What's Mona doing with Clarence's case? And why's it all torn?' Her irises were purple. Contacts maybe.

'I don't know.' I held it out for her to take.

She didn't take it. 'Take it back to Mona, sweet pea.'

'Um...I don't know where she is. Do you?'

'I wouldn't have the vaguest idea where Mona is at any given moment.'

'You don't see her often?'

'Just who *are* you?' Her eyes were post-box slits. 'The police?'

I cleared my throat. 'Look, I'm just trying to do the right thing here. Are you going to take this briefcase or not?'

She tilted her head to one side. 'That's a not, my honeydew. I don't go near Mona or her toxic grandson, not anymore. Take it to Mona's lovely little PA.' She waved a hand towards the door. 'Ravi'll look after it.'

I tried another tack. 'I see you're closing down,' pointing at the sign.

'Yes. Time to move on, I'm starting a B&B not far from the Soak. You could send along your customers.' She laughed, more shattered glass.

'At Hocking Hall? It would make a terrific B&B,' I said.

She stared at me a long moment. 'Yes, wouldn't it. Not Mona's thing though. Too busy with all her charities.' She paused. 'But Mona won't be around forever, will she?'

Back in the car, I passed the derestricted sign south of town. There was uninterrupted green hedging to the left, paddocks of greying grass to the right. Black cattle nosed around the grass, winding long strands around their tongues. Then, on the left, there was an opening in the hedge. Tall pink gates, a sign, 'Hocking Hall'. I pulled in, stepped out and pressed the intercom.

'Cass Tuplin to see Mona Hocking-Lee,' I said.

'Mrs Hocking-Lee is away. Do you have an appointment?'

'No, but...'

'I'm afraid we don't admit visitors without an appointment.'

'I need to return a briefcase.'

Some rustling, as though someone was looking through papers. A murmured conversation.

I leaned in, resting my arm against the wall. 'Actually,

the briefcase looks quite expensive.'

More rustling. The gates opened with a hum.

I steered along the driveway, a gravel ribbon lined with trees, leading to wide green lawns, and the spouting lion fountains I'd seen on the internet. Finally I saw the house, large, turreted and surrounded by verandahs.

I parked by the sign that said 'Visitor parking.' Another gate, another intercom. No rustling this time, the gate hummed open.

A young man met me at the door. He had dark brown eyes, straight black hair, a sculpted face, the kind of body one of those Bollywood movie moguls would snap right up. His shirt was more unbuttoned than was warranted, in my opinion. Presumably this was Ravi. He held a mobile against his ear and waved me towards a room without interrupting his phone call.

I tip-tapped across the marble floor into a large, dim room. Brown leather armchairs were arranged around a fireplace. Bookcases lined three walls. I took a squiz, running a hand along the shelves: all kinds of books; cracked leather covers, creased paperbacks, rows of slim journals with wearying names—*Ecological Economics, Corporate Social Responsibility, Business and Sustainability*. Near the floor, two shelves of mystery books. Old ones, with lurid covers.

'Look, Grantley, Mona isn't here at the moment.' Ravi spoke from the doorway into his phone. 'I'll let her know you called.' An English accent. He saw me looking, closed the door.

I stood near the door, listening carefully.

'Clarence? I have no idea where he is. Isn't he at work with you?' Ravi's voice was muffled.

I pressed my ear against the door.

'What?' Ravi's voice rose a few notes. 'Mona will be very concerned about this. She's terribly keen for this intern thing to work out. That's the only reason she agreed to your excessive fee.'

I looked around. There was nothing homey about the room, no family photos, footy trophies or kids' basketball awards. A wall full of photos of Mona at business dinners, collecting awards. She was a woman who knew how to look good in her clothes.

'What do you mean he's stolen your property? What kind of property?' said Ravi.

I held my breath.

'Personal? Look, Mona will need full details.' He paused. 'Absolutely not. No. Anyway, I don't have the authority to make that kind of payment.'

I peered at her awards.

Fairleigh Special Programmes Award presented to Balance Neutral for outstanding practical work in the field of sustainability.

LiveWell Best Practice Not-for-Profit Award. For Balance Neutral.

Good Giving Guide Award. Balance Neutral again.

'I have someone here,' said Ravi. 'I really must go. Yes, yes, of course I'll let Mona know.' The snapping sound of a phone closing.

The door opened and Ravi walked in, swinging his hand onto his hip.

'So what's all this about a briefcase?' He looked me up and down, taking in my bandaged leg.

'Cass Tuplin,' I said, holding out my hand. 'And you are...?'

'Ravi Gounder.' He shook my hand for only the briefest moment.

'Yes,' I said, 'Mrs Hocking-Lee left this case with me. I thought I should return it.' I held it out.

He took the case from my hands, turning it over, studying it. 'This isn't Mona's.' He gave me a sharp look. 'Where did you get this?'

'Oh,' I waved a hand, 'she asked me to hold onto it for a day or two. I understand it belongs to her grandson, Clarence. He's renting Mr Jefferson's charming lakeside cottage. The one near Rusty Bore. I am his agent.' I used my most dignified tone.

'Clarence is in Rusty Bore?'

'Yes, in the environs,' I said. It didn't seem the moment to mention Clarence and his handcuffs. 'You know Mr Jefferson, of course? I believe he and Mrs Hocking-Lee go back a very long way.' Ernie would understand the imperative for a little fiction.

'Never heard of him.'

'Oh? I must say I'm surprised she hasn't mentioned him. Perhaps,' I paused. 'Well, their relationship is quite personal.'

Ravi's face darkened.

'Not *that* personal,' I said quickly, and added a light and tinkly laugh. Maybe Mona and Ravi were an item. Maybe she'd been a woman with a lot of pent-up energy. Although my guess was Ravi wasn't primarily focused on the energy of women.

'He's always been a father figure for her, I understand. Mr Jefferson is quite elderly. He doesn't have quite...the vigour he once had. Anyway,' I paused, thinking quickly. 'The point is, I have some disappointing news. I'm afraid there's been some damage to the cottage.'

Ravi looked like he was having trouble taking all this in. I'll admit I was having a bit of trouble keeping up with it myself. 'What kind of damage?' he said, running a hand across his forehead.

'Well, a lot of broken crockery. All of Mr Jefferson's lovely willow pattern plates, smashed into tiny pieces. He was terribly fond of those, they were his mother's. I always told him it was a mistake to leave items of sentimental value in a rental cottage.' I clicked my tongue. 'There's some structural damage too, I'm afraid. A door has been torn off its hinges. And,' I paused, 'there was a lot of ripped-up women's clothing in the bedrooms. Mr Jefferson was rather shocked about that, to tell you the truth.'

Ravi swallowed.

'You're sure you don't know Mr Jefferson?' I said. 'Ernest Jefferson. You must have heard of him, surely. He has a whole suite of agricultural machinery businesses throughout the north-west. Terribly successful.' Well, Ernie did have a rusting pump by Perry Lake he'd once tried to flog off to Vern.

Ravi, looking bewildered, shook his head. 'I don't understand any of this. What's Clarence doing in Rusty Bore?'

'Something about writing a book.' I gave another little laugh.

'Book? Clarence? He can't even spell.'

'Really? And after all those bedtime stories Mr Jefferson read to him when he was small. Oh, he will be disappointed. He's been so looking forward to the book. Although I'm not sure what it's about...?'

'That makes two of us.'

'Anyway,' I said, 'as you can imagine, Mr Jefferson is keen to resolve all this with as little fuss as possible. The trouble is...well, I've had no success at all contacting Clarence. He's not at the property. Perhaps if you could try to phone him? I'm happy to wait,' I said with an officious smirk.

He snorted. 'No point in calling Clarence.'

'Oh?'

Ravi gave me a dishwater smile. 'Family business. There's no need to go into...'

'I see. Well, if you could perhaps call Mrs Hocking-Lee?'

'The trouble is,' he ran a hand through his hair, 'I've just tried her mobile, it's switched off. It's been off for days, actually.' He paused. 'Oh dear, this is all rather inconvenient.'

'Isn't it.' Another light click of my tongue. 'And she's due back when...?'

'Well, yesterday. I don't know what could have delayed her. It's unlike her not to let me know,' he said.

'Ah. Now that *is* a little worrying.' I leaned in closer and adopted a confidential tone. 'I'm actually a bit concerned for Mrs Hocking-Lee, Ravi. I do hope everything's all right, but...'

'But what?' Poor Ravi. His eyes were restless pools of black-gloss ink.

'You know I really don't have a good feeling about this. Mrs Hocking-Lee seemed terribly...anxious when I saw her on Saturday. And with all that torn-up clothing, well...I hope Clarence isn't a violent person?'

'Violent?' Ravi's eyes widened. 'But he would never harm her. Surely?'

A pause.

'Mona works so damned hard.' Ravi seemed to be talking to himself. 'It's simply unjust she's been inflicted with that appalling grandson. She gives him everything, money, that car, his own flat here in the hall, but no, he has to steal and cheat. She's tried everything. Threats, bribes, motivational therapists. He's just...'

Yep, I understood. A dropkick.

'Any recent disagreements?' I said. 'In particular...?'

'Well, there are so many...' he paused.

I waited. The key to effective grilling is knowing when to wait.

'He said she'd held him back from his dream.'

'And that was...?' I said.

'He wanted to be a professional gambler.'

'Oh? Is that an actual occupation?'

Ravi snorted. 'She thought the internship with Grantley...'

'Grantley's a professional gambler?' I said.

'He was. Unsuccessful. Now he's an accountant.'

An accountant with a past as an unsuccessful gambler. Not the best of looks.

'Well, Mr Jefferson is quite worried,' I said. 'In fact, he said to me this morning, as he wrung his work-worn hands, "Cass my dear, the only responsible course of action for us now is to phone the police." You know, Ravi, it was truly heart-wrenching to see the pain in that poor man's honest face.'

'Police.' Ravi's eyes bulged.

'So,' I said, 'shall we do that? I mean, really Mrs Hocking-Lee is sort of missing, isn't she?'

'Missing,' said Ravi, a panicked expression on his face.

'Oh my God. Here, use my phone.' He held it out.

'Actually, it's probably better coming from you,' I said.

'Right.' Ravi opened his phone. 'Yes. Sod Clarence.'

'Exactly,' I said, in a brisk tone. 'Now, I don't mean to worry you further, but there were several bullet holes in the kitchen wall at the cottage.' I paused. 'I think you'll probably need a taskforce. As it happens, I have the number of a terrific police officer in Hustle. He'd be the ideal lead for that taskforce. I'd suggest you ring him direct.'

He gave me a look like I was offering him week-old snapper. 'No, thank you.' He sniffed. 'I'll call our local police, here in Muddy Soak. They'll work out the best approach.'

At last. Mona was missing. Officially. Once Ravi made that phone call. Now the police would have to get involved. I started the car, a smile on my face. A wedge-tailed eagle soared across the sky. I snapped shut my seatbelt, then drove on through the pink gates, turning onto the highway. I'll admit I was pretty proud of myself, the way I'd handled Ravi. I was starting to think I could be good at this. It was like playing tractor chicken. Like that scene from *Footloose,* where Kevin Bacon wins. Against that fella in those tight jeans.

I grabbed a ham and cheese sandwich from one of Muddy Soak's multitude of up-market cafes, then set off in search of Pittering and Son. It turned out to be a dingy accounting establishment, with a small window looking out over a dusty yard. A rat-faced man met me at the door. Silver hair, navy suit. He moved stiffly, like he carried an old injury or had bad joints.

'Grantley Pittering,' he shook my hand. 'The son. And you are?'

'Cass Tuplin. Major retailer in Rusty Bore. Looking at expansion down the track, but before that...' I glanced at the leaflets on the counter.

'You're in the market for a top-notch accountant?' He smiled, rubbing his hands, dark pouches below his eyes. A faint waft of old alcohol rose from his skin. 'You've come to the right place. But I warn you, we're about far more than mere number-crunching here. Business has to be transparent, truly porous, these days. Don't you agree?'

'Wipe your feet,' screamed a voice behind him. A grey parrot in a cage.

Grantley waved me to a seat in front of his desk, settling himself on the other side. I gathered up some of the leaflets. 'Well...' I started.

'Yes, many of our customers are unsure at first which package floats their boat.' He held out a coffee-stained brochure. 'We specialise in bookkeeping and can furnish a full suite of BAS-related services. And we offer a multi-faceted approach to your taxation situation. Perhaps you're planning for retirement, looking at an intergenerational property transfer?'

Retirement? Thanks, Grantley. I flicked through the leaflets. North-West Parrot Trust. Balance Neutral. Pictures of smiling people, colourful birds.

'Our gold package is popular,' Grantley said. 'It's favoured by many of our self-fundeds, those with appropriate liquidity, of course.'

'Actually, Mona Hocking-Lee sent me,' I said.

Grantley's flushed face turned grey. 'Mona?' He didn't seem to know where to put his hands. He tried running them through his hair. He put them in his pockets, took them out again. 'And your connection with her is...?'

'She's invited me onto one of her boards,' I said, suddenly inspired.

'I don't recall her mentioning that.' Grantley flicked through a notepad.

'No, I haven't accepted yet. She suggested I come and see you. To help me decide.'

'I see. Which board?'

Good question. 'Mona said she was looking for someone independent, unconnected...'

'Unconnected with what? Which board?' said Grantley.

The thing is, Kevin Bacon only won at tractor chicken because his foot got stuck. I looked down, sweating. 'The North-West Parrot Trust.' I held up the leaflet.

Grantley licked his lips. 'First-rate little trust, that one. Does terrific conservation work in the region. You're a bird enthusiast, Mrs Tuplin?'

'Fanatic,' I lied.

'Don't you touch me, Kev,' the parrot screamed. Some clicking while it ate some seeds.

'Tuplin,' said Grantley. 'A familiar name. I had a Tuplin in here this morning, I'm sure of it.'

Dean, on the case at last.

'I'll pull together some documents for you,' he said. 'Mona's portfolio is tremendously successful. She's my biggest client.'

I glanced around. Three overfull filing cabinets, their drawers not quite closed. A row of grubby-looking files on the floor. A lamp hanging crookedly on its stand.

Was Grantley still gambling and if so, still unsuccessfully? What signs should I be looking for? Mounds of old Tattslotto tickets? Torn-up form guides? RSI of the pokies wrist?

'Actually, I've been trying to contact Mona all week.' Grantley loosened his tie.

I clicked my tongue. 'Such a busy woman. All those charities. And her family takes up a lot of her time.'

I leaned an arm on Grantley's desk. 'In fact, there's another matter I'd like to discuss. I'm looking for a trainee and I immediately thought of Clarence. But Mona said he has an internship here?'

'Ah. He started four weeks ago. But, ah...'

'Good little worker?'

'Early days, of course. But, ah...Clarence has enormous potential, just enormous.' He sounded like he had something stuck in his throat. 'One or two minor training issues we're working on. Attendance, that type of thing.'

I leaned in close, like we were conspirators from way back. 'I'm more familiar than I care to admit with problems of this nature. I've seen too many employees who are all yack and no yakka. Take my son, Bradley, who's...'

'Actually, Clarence might enjoy a change,' said Grantley. 'You have a son working with you in your business? Clarence would flourish with company his own age. Have you spoken to him to assess his interest?'

'Not in detail,' I said. 'It would be terribly useful to have an informed perspective on his performance. An honest view. So many employers won't tell you what they really think. And Mona,' I was on a roll, 'did mention there'd been...a little crisis...'

'Oh, no, no. Not what you'd call a crisis.' Grantley's hands shook.

'If I took Clarence on, I'd need to understand him.

Fully. Comprehend all his strengths and weaknesses.'

'I tried explaining it to Mona in my phone messages.'

I nodded.

'I hope she's not...?'

'Oh no, no.' I used my most soothing tone.

'Well, Clarence came to me with an odd story. Rather unpleasant, in fact. Still, I don't need to go into details.'

'Grantley, I'm sure Mona would prefer that you and I were completely honest with each other.' I gave him the threatening smile. The one I used on the boys back when they were kids.

Grantley reached into his drawer and took out a bottle of Bakery Hill Classic Single Malt. He poured three generous glassfuls.

I held mine carefully so it didn't spill.

Grantley threw back a glassful, rapidly followed by the second. 'I need you to understand we have very high standards in this organisation.' His hands were less shaky now.

'Of course.' I raised my glass and wet my lips.

'And just because Mona is my biggest client doesn't mean I'd do *anything* for her. I do have my...err.'

'I certainly understand integrity.' I sipped again.

He poured another drink and knocked it back.

'Clarence crossed a line, you know.' Grantley was slurring a little now. 'I had no option but to have him leave my office. I wouldn'a had him here in the first place, but my brother...'

'Your brother works with you?'

'Not any more. He's dead.'

A dead Pittering. Taylah's voice in my head.

'Ah. Was he involved in a drama group?'

'Yes, poor Kev would have loved this ridiculous Christmas Fringe Festival.' Grantley swayed a little in his chair. 'In my day, entertainment was entertaining. None of this heads on sticks insanity.'

Heads on sticks? Maybe it was a bit early for whisky. 'And Clarence...?' Did what? Killed Grantley's brother? Put his head on a stick?

'Clarence said he'd found the truth in my brother's old briefcase. At first I thought he was talking about some demented religious experience. Then he said someone would be sorry.'

'Sorry for what?'

'Didn't say.'

'What happened to your brother?'

He paused. 'He died in a train accident. Six months ago.' His voice was flat.

'Organised, I need things bloody organised, Kev,' screamed the parrot.

Grantley stood up, a little unsteady, and put a black cover over the cage.

'Sorry to hear it, Mr Pittering. Never easy losing someone. I lost my husband almost two years ago.' I put down my glass. 'Was there...any suggestion your brother's death was suspicious?'

He squinted at me. 'You're asking a lot of very odd questions, Mrs Tuplin.'

'Oh, just ensuring I understand all the people I'll be working with.' I waved my hand.

'Well, I'll have you know Muddy Soak has a record. It's been crime free since 1988.'

'Records can break, though, surely.'

'Perhaps.' Grantley put the bottle back into his drawer.

'Still, none of this is relevant to your decision. I suggest you talk to Clarence and assess his interest. I haven't seen him all week, so he obviously isn't interested in working here any longer. Perhaps when you see him you could ask him to return my brother's briefcase. It would mean a great deal to my mother.'

I was glad I'd left the case in the car.

'And now,' he glanced at his watch, 'I'm afraid I have a meeting.'

I stood up, shook his hand.

Outside the door, I paused. I figured I'd pop back in, Columbo-style, and ask one last, naive-seeming question, the one that finally dredges out the truth.

I opened the door.

Grantley was on the phone. 'Sergeant Monaghan?' His voice was low.

Thing is, I didn't know the question. And Grantley wasn't supposed to be phoning the police. I closed the door quietly and left.

I got into the car, drummed my fingers on the steering wheel. Maybe I shouldn't have pretended Mona sent me. Maybe Grantley knew I was lying, that's why he phoned Monaghan. Maybe Grantley killed his brother. He wouldn't want anyone snooping in that case. And it wouldn't have been easy for him to get out of gambling; Ravi said he'd owed a lot of money. Maybe Grantley had powerful friends. Not very friendly friends.

I phoned Brad.

'You have to take that briefcase to Sergeant Monaghan. Today.' Brad's voice was grim.

'No way. That lot's for Dean, it's obviously important. Clarence found something in that briefcase, something I haven't located yet.'

'Jesus, Mum. Can't you leave this Clarence bloke alone?'

'Brad. Mona is dead, shot through the head. Clarence is missing. And Aurora. And there are bullet holes in the wall at Ernie's shack. Of course I'm not going to leave this alone.' I paused. 'You do believe me, don't you?'

'Well...'

'Come on, son. Don't get all Dean on me here.'

'OK, let's say, just hypothetically, just for a moment, that what you're saying is true.'

Hypothetically was a start, at least.

'In that case, tell Dean. Or Monaghan,' he said.

I sighed. 'Keep up, son, I've tried all that. Look, think of it this way. It's like when you go off to do your fighting for the river. Sometimes you just can't rely on those in charge. You have to sort things out yourself.'

A pause.

'Well, what about those charities of Mona's?' he said. 'They might have something to do with it. What's the bird one? The North-West Parrot Trust?'

Good on Brad. Any opportunity to weave parrots into his day. 'I need a list of Mona's exes,' I said. 'Exes kill all the time. Everybody knows that.'

Some keyboard clicking noises. 'On their website the North-West Parrot Trust say they're a group of bird breeders and collectors.'

'Brad.' I put the leaflet on my lap and smoothed it out while I chose my words. 'I know you're interested in birds and rivers and trees and everything, love. That's terrific. Nothing wrong with an interest, but we need to focus here. Not get too distracted by things that are beside the point.'

'Mum, listen to me. Some bird clubs are a front for wildlife smuggling. It's worth billions. The trust could be a cover for poachers, stealing eggs from bird nests in the wild, smuggling them overseas.'

I unfolded the leaflet. A familiar face stared up at me. 'Jesus, Noel's in this brochure!'

A pause while Brad digested that.

'Did Noel mention any specific birds when you saw him?' he said. 'Major Mitchell cockatoos maybe? They nest at Perry Lake and they're worth big money overseas. Not to mention they're a threatened species in Victoria. Bastards.'

What birds had Noel mentioned? All I could remember was his lack of binoculars. And the esky. I looked out at the street. Watched a thin, grey-haired man hurry past holding a child by one hand.

Maybe Mona saw Noel. And he killed her to shut her up. I pondered, staring at Muddy Soak's stately honey-coloured post office, the huge green park with its open-air fernery and tumbling waterfall.

'Hey, I'm looking at the website for Balance Neutral,' said Brad. 'They do carbon offsetting. Voluntary. When you get on a plane Balance Neutral plants trees on your behalf. For a fee.'

'What an atrocious waste of money. Who'd pay for that?'

Brad sighed. Like I'd confirmed something he'd long suspected and not a good kind of something. 'You don't listen to anything, do you? You watch the news? Read anything? Heard of carbon dioxide, Mum? Air; maybe you've heard of that?'

'There's no need to be condescending. Not all of us have the entire day to do as we please, demonstrating all over the place against every little thing. Some of us have lives, Brad. Real lives we're busy getting on with.'

A silence.

'Thanks for reminding me,' he said.

'You're welcome.' My voice sounded more prim than I'd intended.

'Yep, that'd be me.' He paused. 'No real life.'

A gust of wind whipped some leaves against the car.

'Brad, I didn't...'

'I was going to leave this hopeless bloody place once you know, leave my hopeless bloody mother and go to uni. But...'

Hopeless bloody mother? What uni?

'I couldn't leave you on your own. Not after Dad... And I knew Dean wouldn't be any use. I'll go next year, I thought. Or the next; I'd go later. But the question is, when is that? When is later?' He spoke in a whisper, like he was talking to himself, not me.

There was a nasty silence and he hung up.

Gripping the phone, I focused on the road ahead, blinking fast.

Brad would hate the city, course he would. Busy freeways, surly people, murders everywhere. And there are a lot of people's feelings he needs to consider here. Ernie. Dean. Madison, the ferrets. And now there's Claire and, soon, the baby, they'd all miss him. They're used to him. A lot of people are used to Brad. A lot.

A white Commodore pulled up across the road. It looked familiar and…shit. Monaghan.

I grabbed my seatbelt and flung it on, started up the car.

Monaghan got out of the Commodore, leather coat flapping in the wind, and headed into Pittering and Son.

I drove out of Muddy Soak quick smart, past the red Christmas Fringe Festival posters, the shady trees, the waterfall, all the fancy cafes and patisseries.

My phone rang: Dean. I pulled over.

'Mum? Where are you?'

'In the car.'

'What are you up to now?'

None of your bloody business. 'Needed a few supplies from Muddy Soak,' I said. 'Had a bit of a dim sim emergency.'

'I was in Muddy Soak. I didn't see you there.'

'Big place, son. Anyway, why were you there?'

'Police business. Following up on your dog bite. Noel's van is registered to an address in Muddy Soak. Care of Pittering and Son.'

So Dean *was* there. 'Why's it registered with Grantley?'

There was a pause. 'How do you know about Grantley?'

Ah. 'You mentioned him, didn't you?'

'No.' Dean's voice was rock-hard cement.

'I must have heard the name somewhere, probably Ernie. You know what he's like—a walking map of the Mallee. Anyway, how did you get on?'

'Van's registered to a Donald Streatham. Grantley Pittering said Donald is an old family friend. Grantley hasn't seen him for months.'

My phone hand went cold.

'You still there, Mum?'

'Did Noel kill Donald and steal his van?'

'Whoa, Mum, hold on. We're dealing with a dangerous dog, not your cast of imaginary murderers. In imaginary handcuffs.'

'What do you mean, imaginary handcuffs?'

He sighed. 'Mum, admit it. There was no one hand-cuffed to a bloody tree.'

'Yes, there was!'

'For God's sake. Look, I just wanted to reassure you that I'm working to find Noel and remove his dangerous dog.'

'Noel could be responsible for Mona's murder.'

'Christ, you're not still on about your fantasy dead woman, are you?'

'She's missing, Dean, as you'll find out very soon. And Brad reckons Noel's a bird smuggler.'

'You need rest, Mum. A break from worry. I want you

home with that leg up. And Brad needs to get himself a job. Did he follow up on that contract at the Hustle abattoirs? Robbo still needs someone to skin the carcasses. Brad'd be good at that, he likes animals.'

'I'll remind him. Anyway, my leg hardly hurts. Do it good to get out. I can head up to your station. Brad's minding the shop. You want me to man the radio? I'd be good with a radio.'

'Mum. Go home. Stay away from Noel and his dog. And leave the police work to me.' Dean hung up.

En-route home, I stopped in Hustle. I got out of the car and headed into Whitey's before they closed, in need of Panadol. Sophia was coming out the door.

'*Ciao* Cassie.' She kissed me on the cheeks.

Claire stepped out from behind her. 'Hello, Mrs Tuplin.'

'Just call me Cass. So, how's it all going with the rellies?'

'Good.'

'You know Claire's rellies, Sophia?'

'Ah *si, si*,' she said, avoiding my eye. 'Come on Claire, we running late.' Sophia bustled off, Claire following along behind her.

Back in my shop, I spent the next hour cutting up onions and making burger patties, wondering if Ravi had made that phone call yet. I was elbow-deep in mince when Monaghan strode in, his leather coat draped over an arm.

'Mrs Tuplin.' He didn't sound too friendly. Not an *I'm-pleased-to-say-we've-discovered-you-were-right-all-along-about-that-dead-woman* tone of voice.

I washed my hands and dried them on my towel. I

remembered how Monaghan had marched into Grantley's place after I left. He wasn't going to arrest me for
impersonating a board director, was he? I mean, I only
said I was a *potential* board director. And Mona wasn't
around to dispute whether she'd sent me in to see Grantley.
Breathe, just breathe, I told myself.

'There's no need to look so frightened, Mrs Tuplin.
I've come here for a meal, not a discussion regarding all
your eccentricities, your non-existent corpses and so on.
Fascinating though such topics always are, of course.'

Well, thanks. So Ravi hadn't made that phone call, then.

He looked up at my blackboard. 'Oh, I see you do
home-made sausage rolls.' A wistful expression on his
face. 'My mother used to make sausage rolls. Yes, I'd
come home from school to the smell of them cooking, just
wonderful...' He stared off into a happy-pastry-childhood
distance.

That eye was looking extra weepy. Maybe I should
duck out to Whitey's in the morning and get Monaghan
some drops. If the eye felt better, he might be able to
concentrate properly. He'd be in need of plenty of top-
notch clear thinking, once he caught up with the Mona
situation.

'Are they low fat?' he said.

Low fat? The comfort food specialist knows the whole
point of a sausage roll is its fat content. That's what makes
them taste so good. 'Not exactly,' I said.

'And what kind of oil do you use in here?'

'The cooking kind.'

He stood there, looking uncertain for a tick. 'The thing
is, I'm trying to transition to the raw food diet.'

'Oh?'

'A whole range of health benefits, Mrs Tuplin. Schizandra berries, for instance. Terrific for the liver. You don't happen to stock them, by any chance?'

I shook my head. 'Right out of them at the minute,' I said. 'I can make you a salad sandwich though? Without butter?'

'Yes, I suppose that would be best.' He flopped down into one of my plastic chairs, looking weary suddenly.

I rounded up a couple of slices of wholemeal bread and started making his sandwich. He wasn't a fat bloke, plenty of space in that almost seven foot for one tiny sausage roll, I'd have thought. Maybe Monaghan had cholesterol. Keeping Muddy Soak crime free must be pretty stressful. 'I hear you were in Muddy Soak today, Mrs Tuplin.'

Oh shit. Here it comes. He *was* going to arrest me, then. Or give me a warning at the very least. I flicked him an anxious look. 'Yep, had a slight dim sim crisis. Needed urgent supplies.'

'Really.' It didn't sound like a question. 'So why were you asking questions of Mr Pittering? A lot of rather odd questions.'

I cleared my throat. 'Ah, yes. Well, I'm quite keen to find Clarence Hocking-Lee. Mr Jefferson asked me to... sort of look into things. He's pretty anxious about his tenant, as you might imagine.'

I wrapped up his sandwich and put it on the counter.

He fished out his wallet. 'I suspect you're a woman who...likes to solve things? For herself?'

I looked at him. Maybe he hadn't swallowed the Mr Jefferson line. Maybe Monaghan was smarter than I thought.

'Mrs Tuplin, this is serious police business, completely

unsuitable for some kind of deep-fried Miss Marple.' He handed me the money. 'Clarence Hocking-Lee could be extremely dangerous. I'm warning you in the strongest terms. Stay right away from him.'

Terry was late, then later, then obviously not coming. No phone message, no go-between popping by with secret notes. It was a busy evening in the shop, a drab type of busy. My head hurt, my leg ached under the bandage. I needed chocolate biscuits.

At eight-thirty I closed the shop, a pile of invoices waiting. But first I flicked through the North-West Parrot Trust brochure. Balance sheets, accumulated deficits, endless columns of numbers. Paragraphs of glowing guff about increasing membership, aviary design, events for kids. I turned to the other brochure. Balance Neutral had more pictures. Orderly tree plantations, koalas, happy kids holding seedlings in eager hands.

Then I saw his photo.

Was it really him? I held it closer. Terry. In a red cap, standing beside a mob of smiling kids. Underneath the photo, *Local contractors do our tree planting. This means we reduce travel emissions while utilising local expertise.*

'Mum?' Brad slouched in the doorway. 'Dean's been on the phone.'

'Oh?' Maybe Ravi had called Dean about Mona after all.

'He's on about a contract at the Hustle abattoirs. Skinning carcasses. He said you'd said I should do it.'

'Ah...'

'You both bloody know I'm a vegetarian.' He punched the door frame.

'Apart from the bacon, son.'

'Yeah, well, I'm in the process of giving up bacon. And I'm telling you, I'm not skinning any carcasses.'

The thing is, Brad could do with a decent opportunity. One with a bit of clear direction. I had an idea. I filled him in on the owner of Noel's van, poor Donald Streatham, quite possibly Noel's latest murder victim. 'And, actually, Dean's asked for our help on this.' I crossed my toes.

He paused. 'Seriously?'

'Yep. He wants you to arrange a birdwatching outing with Noel.'

'No way. That dog could have killed you.'

'You'll be fine. You're just arranging a perfectly safe birdwatching trip. I'll be hiding in the scrub, keeping the binoculars trained on you.' Brad would be all right, of course he would.

'And Dean?' His voice was suspicious. 'Where will he be?'

'He'll be with me, deep undercover. You'll be perfectly safe.'

'Why didn't Dean mention this to me on the phone just now?'

'He's a busy bloke, son. Anyway, this'd be better than skinning carcasses, don't you think?'

He sighed.

'You'd have a contact for Noel; didn't you say he emailed your blog? I bet he's got the internet in that van.'

'Mum, this is probably the most stupid idea you've ever had. Up there with what you did to Showbag.'

'No need to bring Showbag into this. That was just an accident. Anyway, it's Dean's idea. It'll be simple, just email Noel and say you've seen the most amazing rare parrots, he'll be there like a shot, to smuggle them. Probably best if you use a false name.'

'And as this false, as yet unnamed, person, how exactly did I get his email address?'

'Through the parrot trust, of course. You're a new member. An eager-beaver member, recent retiree, moved up from the city.'

'How am I going to look like a bloody retiree, Mum? I'm twenty-two. Noel will suss it out and set his dog on me. Or you. And you'll be killed this time.' Calamity and catastrophe; you can always count on Brad to hunt for woe, just like his father always did.

'An appropriate wig and costume will be provided from the Victoria Police wardrobe. Dean mentioned that, specifically.'

'What? I can't believe Dean's suggested this. What's the objective of this stupid meeting?'

'Find out what Noel's done to Donald Streatham, of course. Find out where Clarence is, and Aurora. Find out what happened to Mona. See if Noel's doing something evil to your parrot eggs.' I counted the flush of find-outs on my hand.

A pause.

'I can always just do it all myself, Bradley. Although there is the injured leg to consider, of course.' I gave it a rub, and winced a bit for effect.

'You can't go hurting yourself again, Mum.' He paused. 'Christ, OK.'

It was a pretty good plan. At least it seemed that way for a day or two.

I started working through my pile of invoices. Pretty soon, the desk was in disarray and my neck was sore.

'Just heading over to Madison's.' Brad paused at the door. 'Will you be OK on your own? You won't go doing anything stupid?'

I let that one slide by. Seemed like Brad was getting kind of close to Madison. How close? I didn't fancy being mother-in-law to a load of hissing ferrets. And what about Claire? She'd phoned earlier and talked to Brad. He'd acted all strange and hush-hush on the phone.

Anyway, Madison's animals were probably just child substitutes, a cheering thought. If things got serious enough for mother-in-lawing, the ferrets would be on their way out. Life is full of change. Although sometimes not as much change as you might hope for.

Brad tried looking casual. 'Madison needs a hand with Janette. She's got dermatitis. You have to hold her by the tail and dip her in a bag of powder. It's not easy, powder-dipping an unwilling ferret.'

'You done that email yet to Noel?'

'I'll do it later.'

'You need to send it, son. Dean's counting on it.'

'I'll do it when I get home. That'll be bloody soon

enough.' He turned and left, slamming the door.

I wandered into the kitchen, took out the briefcase from the cupboard. I ripped out the lining, in case something was stuffed inside a secret pocket. No secret pockets.

The books. Maybe there was a cipher? A heap of circled letters spelling a significant someone's name or a vital rendezvous. I flicked through, checking every page. Nup, zero circling. The books looked new, hardly read. I flung them and the shreds of lining back into the brief-case, snapped it shut.

I lay on the couch with a packet of Mint Slices and had a longish worry about suspects and their motives. I wrote myself a list.

1. Clarence. Motive: Mona's money (and she didn't like his book).
2. Noel. Bird smuggler. Mona objected. Donald collateral damage. Or objected too.
3. Grantley. Killed his brother. Mona knew. How?
4. Stu McKenzie. Revenge for Adrian's suicide.
5. Alexandra. Needs Mona's money for the B&B.
6. Aurora. Motive: money.
7. Ravi. Seemed worried about Mona, no obvious motive.

A knock on the door. I jumped, whacking my bitten leg against the table, then limped over to the door and opened it.

Terry looked at me. I looked back.

'Sorry I'm so late. Had a problem I had to...' he trailed off.

I brushed the biscuit crumbs from my dress. 'No problem. I expect you've been busy with the investigation. You're too late for potato cakes, but I can make you a cuppa. Maybe a Mint Slice? I suppose you'd like to chat about Mona. I've had an instructive day.' I was talking too much. I've never been able to wait quietly around the strong, silent type.

'Let's sort out your car door, Cass.'

We headed outside. The sky was dark blue, a lemony smudge on the horizon. He got into the driver's seat via the handbrake manoeuvre.

I sat beside him. 'Yep, had a useful day in Muddy Soak. Saw all the key suspects.'

'Key suspects in what?' he fiddled with the door.

'Mona's murder, of course.'

He looked at me. 'Why did you really phone me that night?' His voice was low, like he didn't want us overheard. Who'd he think could overhear?

'Because her body was there, Terry. I wouldn't make up a thing like that.'

He took off the door panel and handed it to me. 'Could have been a trick of the light. Maybe you saw something else. A sheep, perhaps.' He sounded like he was trying to convince himself. He turned back to the door innards.

'A sheep?' I balanced the panel on my knees. 'What sort of twit would confuse a dead woman with a sheep?'

He stiffened. 'People can make mistakes.'

Bugger. I'd offended him.

Something clunked and he pushed the door open. I got out and held the door, watched him roll up his sleeves. I liked the set of his wide shoulders.

'You're obviously a woman who notices things,' he jiggled the door handle. 'A smart sort of woman. But you'd have been on edge. You're probably worried with Clarence on the loose.'

A woman who notices things. I wondered if Terry

was partial to a rumball. He was a fella who deserved a rumball, a hard-working decent bloke like him.

'You...ever considered acquiring someone to look out for you?' He looked up at me, a long steady look from those blue eyes.

I smiled. I might be used to running my own show, but I'm quite adaptable to change.

He smiled back.

'What's Clarence done that I should be so worried about?'

But Terry just shook his head.

Door fixed, he stood, brushing his hands on his trousers. Strong-looking legs, despite the limp. I tested the door, enjoying watching it close.

'Right then...I'd best be off,' he said.

'Oh no, I'll put the kettle on. Fancy a rumball? I made them fresh today.'

He followed me into the kitchen. I filled the kettle. 'What happened to your cheek?' I touched his bruise lightly.

'Boring story. Involves a door.' Another steady look from those eyes. 'And Dale.'

'Sergeant Dale Monaghan?'

He nodded.

Who did this Monaghan think he was? No wonder Terry dreamed about his wood-carving life by the sea, miles from here. He deserved some quiet; long peaceful evenings eating rumballs with a decent woman. A mature woman who noticed things.

'Maybe you should request a transfer. I'm not sure Monaghan's the right boss for you.'

He laughed sadly. 'There's some bosses you can't ever leave.' He looked down at his hands.

He had nice hands, square, solid hands. They'd known exactly how to fix that door, would probably be good at other things as well. Knocking up a coffee table, working on your broken bed-head. Hands that were lingering and warm and would know how to hold your shoulders later on, much later on, after he'd finished with the fixing and the rumballs.

Get a grip, Cass.

'Nice place you've got.' His lips were parted.

Close enough to feel his breath, warm on my face, I swayed slightly. I glanced around for distraction; saw the Balance Neutral brochure. 'You're a busy fella, all your tree planting plus being a cop. Your work must never end.'

He stared. 'Me? A cop? Ha, that's good. Nah, I'm self-employed. Do a bit of this and that.'

Huh? Didn't he say Monaghan was his boss? 'But Monaghan relies on you?'

'Yeah, course. He's my brother.'

I got out the rumball container, started struggling with the lid.

'Need a hand?' His warm fingers touched mine. Fingers that would be warm on your face, moving along your arms, your neck. Deft fingers that would know how to unbutton a woman out of silk.

The kettle boiled.

Moving away, holding onto the table for balance, I carefully filled the mugs, arranged the rumballs on a plate.

'Terrific rumballs, Cass. I'm very partial to a rumball.'

I made my decision. 'Got something to show you, Terry.' I grabbed the briefcase. 'Reckon it's Clarence's.'

He stood so close beside me, I could feel the heat of his body.

'Jesus, Cass. I knew you knew something. You better take this in to Dale.' Those blue eyes gazed at me. I'd never realised something blue could burn like that. My thoughts drifted, a rapid type of drifting over which I had no control, way beyond briefcases, onto shoulders, buttons, skin, his skin on mine.

Terry reached out and gently took my hand. He kissed the back of my hand, my wrist, my arm. Drawing me towards him, he kissed me then, a proper drawn-out kiss.

It wasn't any trouble kissing him back.

Something turned to liquid in the region of my knees. He held me tight against him, his mouth moving to my ears, my neck. It's possible I let out a little sigh. Looking at me, a hot molten look that didn't help the knee condition, he slowly untied my apron, hung it on a chair.

'I can't resist you,' he breathed into my ear.

'Actually, don't feel you need to,' I whispered back.

He sat me on the kitchen table and kissed me a whole lot more. When I started unbuttoning his shirt he didn't try to stop me. I opened it to his belt, ran my hands down along his chest, felt the line of hairs leading into his jeans. He shivered, pulled my hands away and put them by my sides. More kissing, then he unbuttoned me, an urgent unbuttoning, rough-sliding my dress off my shoulders. His hands were hot on my breasts, his mouth firm against my neck. He pressed his body, long and hot, against me, kissed me, touched me more, more. My back cracked a bit. I didn't care.

His pocket pulsed. I may have moaned a bit. It kept pulsing.

Terry sprang away and took out the phone. I leaned on the table, trying to catch my breath.

'Yep, yep. On my way.' He hung up. 'Sorry, Cass. I'm not meant to…I've gotta go.' He stumbled towards the doorway, doing up his buttons, tucking in his shirt.

What, now? What type of emergency required him this very minute?

A marital bloody emergency.

'Course,' I stood, buttoned my shirt, tied on my apron, as if nothing had nearly happened. I breathed deeply in and out.

'Thanks for the rumballs,' he paused by the door. 'Best I've ever had.'

I knew it. No wedding band, but there's a wife. Or an STD. Or bloody both.

A disturbed night with dreams of blood and multi-killing. Grantley shot Brad, then Terry. Dean chased Grantley; Mona, eyeless, managed to stab them both. She ran off hand-in-hand with Aurora, throwing the briefcase through Ernie's window. Glass shattered everywhere.

I woke with a start, lay awake, listening. Nothing. I switched on the light, started reading *Death of a Lake*. My attention wandered. Arthur Upfield never had female characters I liked. Misogynistic times, perhaps.

My thoughts drifted to Terry. Was he just pretending he was interested? He'd been amazingly convincing.

I woke just before dawn, as Brad was getting home. Groaning, I decided to get up. I found him hunched over the kitchen table.

'Might call in on Dean before we open,' I said. 'You want to come?'

'No.' He played with his toast.

'Pleasant evening at Madison's? How'd the flea dipping go?'

His shoulders slumped.

'Ferrets OK? Not depressed? They didn't bite you, did they?' I searched his hands for signs of bites. 'Dangerous little animals.'

He sighed. 'I'm not really a ferret person, but I try. You know that, don't you, Mum? That I try?' His eyes were a bit too shiny.

I patted his arm. 'Course.'

'Madison said she needs someone the ferrets can look up to. She's decided to go to the Christmas Fringe Festival with Logan.'

'I thought she'd split up with him.'

Brad shook his head. 'Not exactly. He's out of jail.'

'And into Christmas fringe festivals now?'

Brad shrugged. 'Apparently he's interested in all the heads on sticks.'

'Oh.' What Madison thinks she's doing with Logan 'Skull' Mathieson is beyond me. Drugs, theft, jail time, Logan's done it all. He was a nice little kid, way back. A maths whiz. Helped out after school in his auntie's clothes boutique in Hustle. Until she discovered he was a bit too good with the credit card machine. He's muscular though, maybe that's what appeals to Madison. And it's possible they share an interest in animals. After all, he's got that giant squid tattoo covering the whole of his right arm.

'Well, never mind,' I said. 'Plenty more girls out there for you. That Claire, she seems nice. And Aurora. If she didn't kill her nanna. You sent that email to Noel yet?'

Brad shook his head.

'Want me to send it? I'll need his address.'

He stood up, hurled his toast into the bin. 'Leave off about the bloody email, Mum. I can't concentrate. My life's in crisis.'

Crisis? 'Listen. I'll call in on Logan, point out some facts.'

'You stay away from Logan.'

'I'm just trying to help get your life on track.' I poured some cornflakes into a bowl.

'You lied to me. Dean didn't ask us to meet Noel.'

'Course he did.'

'He did not. I texted him last night.'

I scowled. 'Checking up on me, are you?'

'I asked him when I should pick up the disguise. Thanks to you, Dean now has new evidence that I'm not only a waster, but a gullible one as well. Listen, Mum. Just leave this alone. If not for your own sake, for Dean's. Monaghan's got the power to close Dean's station.'

'He's hardly going to close Dean down for solving a big murder case.'

'He could if he knows Dean's family is interfering in the investigation.'

'There isn't any investigation to interfere in. That's the bloody point.'

'If Monaghan wants Dean's station closed, he'll make it happen. Loads of one-man stations have been closed.'

I pushed away the bowl. 'Well, let him! It could be Dean's chance to be promoted. The change he needs, so he can move up into Homicide.'

'Mum.' He sighed. 'Dean doesn't want to go to Homicide, even if they'd take him. He'll be made redundant. And you know how hard it is to find work around here.'

'There's always the shop to tide you boys over.'

Although Dean has his fish allergy, unfortunately. 'Well, I'll have a chat with the people up at headquarters. Don't you worry, I'll sort this out.'

Brad sank into a chair. 'Jesus, Mum. That's just it, isn't it? You're so sure you can sort everything out. All you do is make things worse.' His voice was low. 'Will you ever let Dean grow up?' He whacked the table, dishes clattering. 'Or me?'

'A mother knows what's good for her child.' I took a dignified sip of tea.

Brad stood. 'Good for us? You don't know the first bloody thing about either of us. You ever listen to Dean? His incessant rants about the technicolour Mallee sunsets, terrific neighbours, mates you can count on, blah blah? He'd hate living in the city. But you wouldn't know that, would you? You never listen.' Stamping out, he slammed the door.

Oh, for God's sake. Twenty-two and still slamming doors like a teenager.

'Vern. Come to pick up my drycleaning.'

Vern rolled himself out of his hammock and walked inside, clutching his notebook. 'Where'd you go yesterday? Gone all day. Bloody outrageous.'

'Had to go to Muddy Soak. Dim sim emergency.'

He brought in my dress from the back room. 'Someone came by your place while you were out. That scraggy-haired fella with the white van.'

Noel? Out in broad daylight, while Dean was looking for him?

'He was peering in your windows, tried your door. Thought he might intend breaking in, so I strolled over.'

Brad hadn't mentioned any of this. 'Where was Brad while this was happening?'

Vern shrugged. 'Musta had to duck out. Probably helping out with those ferrets. Hell of a lot of work, those animals.'

Great. Thanks for your reliability, Brad.

'Noel say what he wanted?'

'Nah. Asked me where you were. Gave me a shifty look. You been up to something not quite right with him?' Vern's eyes narrowed.

'What do you mean?'

'Well, I don't know what you get up to in your private life, Cass Tuplin. Widow like you could be up to anything.'

'I'm not up to anything. His dog bit me.' I pointed at my leg.

He glanced at the bandages. 'Probably had its reasons. Anyway. He had a young girl with him.' Vern laughed, a sound like a tractor firing up. 'Reckon you mighta missed your chance there.'

I didn't laugh. 'What kind of young girl?'

'Blonde hair, scruffy-looking.'

'Orange dress?'

'Maybe.'

'She say anything? Her name?'

'Thing is, she did. Weird type of name. Fella jumped quick-smart into the van, started her up. The girl sidled up to me and said, hush-hush voice, she needed to see you. Urgent, she said. Course, if I'd known where you were, I could have pointed her in the right direction. Shame when people decide to act all secretive.' He made a minor adjustment to the crotch of his shorts.

'What she want to see me for?'

He shrugged.

'What did you tell her?'

'Told her to wait, you'd be back eventually. "Can't wait," she said, "got to get it now."'

'Got to get what now?'

He smoothed out a non-existent crease in my drycleaned dress. 'Didn't say. She pushed a bit of paper into my hand. Then the fella yanked her into the van. Sped off.'

'Jesus, Vern. Why didn't you call last night and tell me?'

He scowled. 'I could see you had a visitor. I'm not a person that pries into other people's business.'

'What was on the paper?'

'Got it filed somewhere.' He bent down. Paper rustled as he searched through the shelves below his counter. He pulled out a heap of invoices, scrappy handwritten notes, a pile of dog-eared Tattslotto tickets, three postcards of bronzed topless women lying on beaches.

Vern might not be intact but he's fully functional.

He put all the bits of paper on the floor while he searched.

His phone rang from out the back. He stood up. 'Gotta get that. Waiting on a call.'

'What was on the paper, Vern?'

But he'd lumbered out to his back room. The curtain of blue and white fly strips swished behind him.

I stood and waited. What was Aurora doing with Noel? Why did she want to talk to me? To murder me? My hands went cold.

Or was Aurora some kind of hostage?

Vern took ages, his voice murmuring from the other side of his flystrips. It'd be quicker to search for the note myself. I knelt and rummaged through the pile of papers.

Nothing. I stood up. Waited some more. How long can a man talk on the phone, anyway? He'd left his notebook on the counter. Maybe Aurora's note was in there. I opened it, had a quick little rootle through.

'What you think you're doing?'

I jumped.

Vern can truly slither when he wants. He doesn't make a single sound.

'That's bloody personal property.'

'Just looking for that girl's...'

He snatched the notebook from me. A photo of a naked woman fell out.

'Get out.' Vern's face was hot red.

'Vern, I don't care about your photos. That girl could be in mortal...'

'Bloody industrial espionage.' He flung his arm towards his front door. 'Get out!'

Yeah, right. As if there'd be anything in Vern's shop any self-respecting espionage person would care to expose. I picked up my drycleaning and sailed out.

I tried the official approach first, calling Dean, filling him in on Noel and Aurora's unexpected visit.

'Right,' his voice was grim. 'I'll cruise around again today. I've told everyone to watch out for the dog. Vern should have called me.'

'Aurora could be Noel's hostage.'

'Mum. I know you're worried about that dog. But try to keep your imagination in control. Put your leg up. Brad can run the shop today.'

Terrific. I hung up.

I checked my watch. There was time to call in on Logan before opening the shop, if I made it quick. I'd set Logan straight on a few facts, and possibly a few small unimportant fictions. A brief update on Madison's sexual health status, since Logan had been away in jail, and Brad's path to bliss would be swept clear.

A blissful Brad would be calmer, more pleasant and

more accepting of our need to email Noel.

I rapped on Brad's door. 'Mind the shop, Bradley.' He poked his head out. 'And really mind it this time.'

'What's that mean?'

'It means stay here, unlike yesterday.'

He turned red, mumbled something.

'What?' I said.

'I said, yes. After all, I don't have anywhere else to bloody go, do I?' He slammed his bedroom door.

Logan lives in the old shearer's hut at the Ryan place, sixteen k's out of Rusty Bore. Passing the row of silos, I found my thoughts drifting back to Terry. The way he'd rushed off. Taylah would be able to update me on any wife-de-facto-infection situation, she knows everything about everyone.

Or was he somehow embarrassed? Why? The state of his assets? He had his own business. His ute. And there he was, helping out his brother, Sergeant Monaghan. A decent family man.

Discarded plastic bottles on the roadside rolled in the breeze. My phone rang. Terry! I pulled over, tyres skidding on the gravel.

'Cass. Where are you? I want to apologise. Any chance we can start again?'

'Look, are you married?' I might as well come straight out and ask.

'What? Ah...I can see how it might have seemed. Nah, it's just...work. It's complicated. Can I tell you about it over dinner? Tomorrow night?'

I hesitated.

'They do a decent roast at the Hustle RSL.'

It's never easy to resist a good roast. 'Terry?'

'Yes?' His voice was soft, eager.

'You know anything about the Hocking-Lees?'

'Not really,' he said.

'Aurora? She in trouble with the law?'

'Nah, Aurora's a good kid. Helped me with some tree planting.'

I pulled in outside Logan's place, behind a white car. An array of gas cylinders lay strewn across the yard, broken glassware in a glittering pile. I stepped out of my car. This place smelled seriously of cat pee.

I limped up the front steps of the house, pausing outside the door. A lot of shouting and banging was going on inside. I suddenly went off the idea of calling in on Logan. Brad could find his own solution to his love life. I started quick smart back down the steps.

The door behind me opened. A voice: 'I suggest you give it some careful thought, Logan. You don't really have a choice. Since no one will believe you.' A voice I recognised.

I turned around. A tall man stood in the doorway staring at me. A very tall man in a long leather coat. Monaghan.

He strode over and grabbed me by the arm. 'What are you doing here?'

He marched me to my car and stood, coat flapping in the wind. Smiled, a strained type of smile like he was working hard to be polite. Ravi must have reported Mona missing, surely. Was Logan involved? And maybe Monaghan was going to be a whole lot more polite to me, now he knew. 'Let's get you home. It isn't safe here.'

He practically pushed me into my car.

I wound down my window. 'What's the problem?'

'Get out of here, for God's sake,' he shouted.

I looked in my mirror as I drove off. He stood at the roadside watching me.

When I got home, I realised what the 'it' must be that Aurora had said she needed. I charged into my lounge.

The briefcase wasn't where I'd left it on the couch. 'Brad?'

He shambled up the hall.

'Did you move the case?' I said.

'No.'

The curtain flapped at the window. I looked at Brad, at the window, back at Brad. My windows are the ancient kind, not entirely lockable. 'You hear anyone open the window?'

He shook his head.

'You been here the whole time?'

'Bloody *yes*, Mum.'

Who? When? I could have kicked myself. Why didn't I just lock the damn thing away?

Well, I wasn't going to let a stolen briefcase get to me. Investigative setbacks are a given for any criminologist. Dean would find that out when he transferred to Homicide. Maybe I could help him prepare for it emotionally.

'It confirms the briefcase is important, Brad.'

'You'd better open the shop, Mum. It's already eleven.'

'In a minute. Good thing I kept the key. Maybe they'll come back for it once they see it's missing. We could set a trap.'

Brad sighed. 'You want me to open the shop?'

'Could you, love? Now I think of it, the leg is hurting. I suppose I should rest it a bit.' I gave him a valiant little smile. 'I'll join you in a tick.'

He scuffed off into the shop, the connecting door closing with a click. I leapt off the couch, crept down the hall, popped my head around the doorway of Brad's room.

There was the laptop on his desk, up and running. I thought about my wording for a moment.

Noel. If you're interested in nesting Major Mitchells, meet me 8 a.m. Monday at Perry Lake. And I've got something else you're looking for.

I hit send, then headed into the shop.

After the lunchtime rush, three customers, my phone rang. Dean.

'Mum, Sergeant Dale Monaghan is here. Mrs Mona Hocking-Lee has been reported missing. We need you and Brad to come in and answer some questions.'

Finally.

Dean's station is on the southern edge of Hustle, a weatherboard place with a metal fence framing the dusty yard. His house is out the back.

I opened Dean's gate. 'Now, don't mention the briefcase. It won't help Dean that you lost it.'

Brad scowled. 'Who lost it?'

'We haven't got time to go into all that now.'

Dean met us at the counter. 'Brad, you wait in the cell while we interview Mum.'

'The cell?' said Brad.

'Don't argue with me.' Dean grabbed his arm and marched him down the corridor. I heard a key grate in a lock, then Dean was back.

'The cell?' I said.

'No arguments from you either, Mum. I've had it up to here with you.' He jostled me into the interview room.

Not quite the way I'd expected to be treated, given that I'd been right all along and he'd been plain old wrong. Still, maybe it was procedure, locking up Brad, jostling me.

I sat down, gave Dean a deluxe star-witness beam. He didn't smile, just sat next to Monaghan, facing me across the white table. White walls, white ceiling, fluorescent lights. Dean seriously needed to redecorate.

I got myself ready for Monaghan's apology. That eye was still oozy. Nothing too transmissible, I hoped. He was sitting close by Dean and Dean needs both eyes operational.

'We're recording this interview,' said Monaghan. 'State your name and address please.'

I did.

Dean fiddled with a pen.

'Interview conducted by Senior Sergeant Monaghan and Senior Constable Tuplin.'

'Leading,' I said.

'Sorry?'

'*Leading* Senior Constable Tuplin.'

'Of course. Now, Mrs Tuplin, please describe your relationship with Mrs Mona Hocking-Lee.'

'Relationship? I hardly knew her.'

'Knew? Past tense?'

'Like I said, I found her on Monday, dead, in Ernie's shed. Then she disappeared.' No need to mention I'd found her the day before as well, no need to embarrass Dean.

'Senior Constable Tuplin...Leading,' Monaghan corrected himself, 'advised that you told him something similar on Sunday morning,' he looked at a notepad, 'at Perry Lake. Although there is no police report of that matter.' His lips tightened.

I looked at Dean, staring at his pen. I knew he should

have believed me and written up that report.

'He's probably got it all typed up.' I smiled. 'Dean has terrific typing skills. One of his best subjects at school. He's just in the process of remembering exactly where he put the report, aren't you, son?' I gave Dean a significant nod.

Dean gazed out the window, like he was hoping he'd be abducted out of here.

Monaghan made one of those steeple thingies with his index fingers. 'I searched Mr Jefferson's shed, after your call on Monday night. I found no dead body anywhere in the vicinity.' His voice was slow, like he was talking to a child. 'And no sign of one ever having been there.'

'Well, the murderer moved her. Obviously. Probably while I was chasing Aurora.'

'Senior Constable. Did you find a body when you were called to Perry Lake? Was a body mentioned in the report you can't locate?'

Dean shot a look at Monaghan, shook his head.

'You'll need to speak for the recording.'

'No. I didn't find a body.'

'How would you explain that, Mrs Tuplin?'

'Like I said, she must have been moved.'

'Twice?'

'She was definitely there.'

A pause. 'According to the senior constable, you phoned on a previous occasion, six months ago, to report a suspicious death. You phoned and said,' he read from his notepad, '"Come quick, Dean, Ernie's been strangled." For the recording, Mr Ernie Jefferson resides at the Garden of the Gods Extended Care Nursing Home.'

'A misunderstanding,' I said. Bloody Dean didn't need to have winched that one out and slung it on the shore.

'And was Mr Jefferson dead?'

'Not exactly.'

'Yes or no.'

'No.'

'No. Happily, Mr Jefferson wasn't dead or in the least bit strangled. And I'm pleased to say we've located the relevant police report. It states quite clearly he was asleep.'

Well, I knew all that.

'Did you check Mr Jefferson's breathing? Feel for a pulse?'

'Look, there's no need to hash over this old history...'

'Yes or no?'

'No.'

'Did you alert the staff at the nursing home?'

'No. I was bit upset.' I squirmed in my chair.

'And Brad? Was he with you?'

'Brad was parking the car. When I saw Ernie, I rushed out, grabbed Brad's phone and called Dean.'

Monaghan moved the steepled fingers to his chin. 'Whose idea was it to phone?'

'Mine.'

'You're sure? It wasn't Brad's suggestion?'

'No.' I paused. 'Look, this was all a long time ago.'

'Did Brad try to stop you from phoning?'

'It was over so quickly. Anyway, we need to focus. On Mona...'

'We're getting to that. So, at Perry Lake, whose idea was it to phone the police?'

'Mine.'

'You're sure? Take your time answering.'

'Mine,' I said firmly.

'Brad didn't try to stop you?'

'Of course not. He wasn't even there. Look, I'll admit that business with Ernie was a mistake. But Mona's really dead.'

'There's a big difference between someone sleeping and someone dead, Mrs Tuplin. You're aware of the difference?' He'd slowed his voice again.

'Of course I am.' Bloody man.

'Did you try waking Mr Jefferson that day, six months ago?'

Oh for God's sake. 'I don't remember.'

Monaghan read from the report. '"I didn't try to wake him. I was a bit worked up."' He looked at me. 'Could you have been worked up at Perry Lake?'

'It was completely different. There was a bullet hole in her head. And her eyes were missing.'

Monaghan unsteepled his fingers, then flicked through some files on the table, took one out. 'I have another police report featuring you, Mrs Tuplin. A rather worrying one. It states you shot someone, twelve months ago. Samuel Jenkins of Rusty Bore. A shooting that could have easily been fatal.'

'Showbag? But that's got nothing to do with anything. Just an accident. I was learning how to use a gun.' I glared at Dean, who maintained his stare out the window. Dean had done a whole lot of deep-sea bloody dredging for Monaghan this afternoon.

'Whose gun?'

'Ernie's. He said I should learn how to protect myself.' Ernie and his good ideas. Look where they got him. After all the fuss, Dean insisted on putting Ernie in the home.

'You pointed a loaded gun?'

'No one told me it was loaded. But, look, Dean knows all this.'

'The gun was discharged accidentally. My mother isn't an expert with firearms. The matter was investigated in detail.'

'I understand it was you who investigated, Senior Constable?'

'Yes,' said Dean.

'Alone? No other police officers involved? I don't recall you reporting a potential conflict of interest. Or has that been mislaid as well?' Monaghan smiled, a stretched-plastic type of smile.

'No.' Dean's voice was low.

'A lot of your police work seems to involve your family. I hope you're not in the habit of misusing your position for family favours, Senior Constable.'

Dean rubbed his forehead. 'Of course not. It was only Mum, I knew it was an accident. It didn't seem worth bothering you in Muddy Soak.'

'It's *always* worth following proper police procedure, Senior Constable. Now, Mrs Tuplin,' Monaghan stared through me. 'Victoria Police is undertaking some strategic realignments.'

A pause.

'Your son will be redeployed. He's been offered a role in Transit Safety. In Melbourne.'

I glanced at Dean, saw the shadows underneath his eyes.

'So you'll be dealing with me in future. And you'll find me much less tolerant of your mistakes.' Monaghan looked at his watch. 'Interview ended at 15:05.'

*

Dean saw me out. He wasn't chatty. 'Wait in the lounge.'

I fidgeted in the prickly armchair. A key scraped. Dean's and Brad's voices. Brad would straighten all this out. He and Dean together. I could see it might be hard for someone who didn't know me. The Showbag incident didn't make me look too good.

Poor old Showbag. I did apologise. And of all the things to hit. Not exactly the largest item in the room, not that I'm intimately familiar with his anatomy, and possibly not the nicest way to be emasculated. Assuming there is a nice way. Anyway, he was only fifty per cent emasculated. Before all that, Showbag used to pop by my shop, quite regular. We don't see a lot of each other nowadays. I think he's gone off takeaway.

I tiptoed down the hallway. Voices murmured inside the interview room. I bent down to listen at the keyhole.

Brad's voice. 'Yeah, Mum can get...a bit carried away.'

'Your mother's mental health is a consideration, of course. Now, I suggest you tell us what you've done with Mrs Hocking-Lee. Where are you holding her?'

'Holding her? Why would I hold her?'

'Mr Tuplin, there's a seven-year jail sentence for hindering a police investigation.' Monaghan's voice was deep. Trapped-in-a-lightless-cave deep, rather than the reassuring, broad-shouldered kind.

'Brad's no kidnapper.' Dean's voice.

'You're not exactly an independent authority, Senior Constable.' Monaghan paused. 'Mr Tuplin, I understand you're an active member of DirectAction, the extreme environmental group.'

'Not really. I...'

'You're aware DirectAction is responsible for a number

of criminal activities here and overseas?'

'Criminal? They're just concerned for the earth's welfare. It's called positive direct action.'

'Setting fire to the homes of people who own four-wheel-drives is hardly a positive action. I suppose you know Mrs Hocking-Lee is the president of the Wimmera Four-Wheel-Drive Club?' said Monaghan.

A nasty silence.

'We're working to identify the people involved in these fires. And we will find them, we will find exactly who has orchestrated these acts of eco-terrorism. He or she will serve a prison term, I can reassure you.' Monaghan's voice didn't sound reassuring.

'Um. Do I need a lawyer?'

'I'm just saying I'm worried about your associations, Mr Tuplin. Your behaviour could be regarded as suspicious.'

'Suspicious?'

'Especially for someone with your past.' Monaghan paused. 'Four arrests for burglary.'

'I wasn't stealing anything. I was working on behalf of the environment.' Brad's voice rose.

'Where were you the day Mr Jenkins was shot, Mr Tuplin?'

'Away. Probably.'

'Probably? You don't remember?'

'It was ages ago.'

'I think you know exactly where you were. You weren't "away" at all.'

Through the keyhole, I saw Brad shrug.

'It wasn't your mother who shot Mr Jenkins, was it? It was you.'

'No way!'

'I understand you and Mr Jenkins had an argument the day before his shooting.'

A pause.

'Mr Tuplin?'

'Six of his budgies died that day. It was forty-four degrees and they had no water.'

'And has Mrs Hocking-Lee offended your environmental sensibilities as well? Is that why you've kidnapped her?'

'Of course not. What a ridiculous question.'

'Mr Tuplin. I am watching you carefully. Don't leave the district. Interview ended at 15:45.'

'What's this Action Direct outfit?' I got into the car.

'DirectAction, Mum. You weren't listening at the door? In a police station?'

The heat mirrored above the road ahead.

'What exactly is DirectAction?'

'It's an activist group. Based on the idea of deep ecology. Humans aren't the only species on the planet, Mum. There are some who consider humans to be a...a kind of disease. A plague.'

'Plague? Jesus, Brad, this kind of attitude can't do you any good. You need to get out and mingle with normal, happy people. There's a perfectly decent pub in Hustle. You'd meet some terrific people in there.'

There were dark smudges beneath his eyes. 'Everyone I used to know has gone now. You know that. They went to uni or moved interstate, they're miles away from their bloody mothers. There's nothing for me in Hustle and, anyway, who'd drink with a loser like me? No wonder Madison's back with Logan.'

'Madison will realise your full appeal eventually. And if not you'll have escaped a lifetime of ferret-dipping. Anyway, there's always Claire. You could ask her out somewhere. She seems a nice girl.'

He glanced at me. 'You really have no idea, do you?'

'About what? Christ, Brad, it's your baby, isn't it? I bloody knew it.'

'No.' He paused. 'Look, Claire will tell you herself soon enough.'

'Tell me what?'

'It's for her to tell you, when she's ready.'

We passed a dead snake hanging from a fence.

'Anyway, the thing about DirectAction is, they're saying the time for peaceful protest is over. It's time to attack on behalf of the environment.'

Is that why Monaghan had been on about eco-terrorism? But Brad wouldn't set someone's Pajero on fire. Would he?

A blast of dust buffeted the car.

I rolled my eyes. A good thing Piero wasn't alive to hear all this.

Back at home, I put the burners on. Two regulars came by. Then a French bloke on his way up north, keen to chat about the history of fish and chips.

'Flake? But is he sustainable? There are large declines in shark populations around the world,' he said.

Brad scuffed around, cutting up the chips, his movements lethargic. He didn't discuss the state of sharks, not once, with the French fella, who left eventually, staring at his dim sims like they'd been shipped in express-post from Mars.

I wasn't going to let Monaghan get to me. I knew exactly who shot Showbag. It was me. And I had a whole array of witnesses. Vern. Ernie. Showbag himself.

Brad wouldn't have done anything to Mona, no way.

I thumped the freezer closed. We were getting low on calamari. I phoned Rae with my list for next week's order. 'And bloody Brad's joined a gang of crooks, Rae. DirectAction. Turn your back for one second, and your kids turn into eco-terrorists.'

'Nah, you've got good kids Cass, no worries there. Brad's solid. I reckon it wasn't DirectAction set fire to those houses anyway. Wouldn't be surprised if it was that bastard Clarence Hocking-Lee. Saw his sister recently. With Donald Streatham. Buzzed past in that old van of his.'

I stood still. 'When was this?'

'Yesterday.'

So Donald had got his van back. And he was alive? Where was Noel, then?

'Rae, what's Donald look like?'

'Scruffy fella. Long white hair and beard. Got an awful black dog.'

'Dean?' I said into the phone.

'Yes, Mum.' His voice sounded weary.

'Donald and Noel are the same person. Noel's just a false name.'

'Good.' He didn't seem that enthused by my break-through.

'Listen, you can't let that Monaghan get to you. I'm

sure he can't close you down.'

'It's happening. I was told officially this morning. Thanks to you, Hustle will be a non-twenty-four-hour station. Permanent station at Muddy Soak.'

I let the 'thanks to you' slide by. Dean sometimes outsources the blame when he's stressed.

'Transit Safety. Great. I'll be trapped indoors, wandering up and down suburban trains. I won't know a soul.'

'But that's terrific! Places you right on the doorstep of Homicide, for when they need some extra help.'

'Mum. It doesn't work like that.' He sighed. 'Anyway, Melissa's said categorically she won't go. She'll never live in the city. Ever. I've requested a transfer to Muddy Soak. That's my best option now.'

'Reporting to Monaghan?'

'Uh-huh.'

'But Muddy Soak's been crime free since whatever-whatever. They don't need another cop. We need you here. This place is turning into Australia's murder capital. I'll have a word with headquarters for you.'

'Mum!'

'Come on, Dean. Everybody knows how persuasive I can be.'

He snorted. 'You're off your head. Everybody knows that.'

Another stinging bullet I let whip past. 'Sounds to me like you're in urgent need of a plate of home-made lamingtons.'

A strangled sound. 'Stay away from me, Mum! You've done enough damage already.'

'Not even with some lamingtons? Chocolate, of course, I know they're your favourite.'

'What bit of "no" don't you understand? I don't want to bloody see you.'

'You know the Great Pacific Garbage Patch? All the tiny bits of plastic floating in the sea?' said Brad.

I suspected I would shortly. I carried on wiping out the freezer.

'It now covers an area three times the size of Victoria. Can you believe it?'

'Excellent. How are we going for dim sims? Got enough for Madison? I assume she'll be in later. You two sorted things out?'

'Kind of. Logan's been arrested. She's a bit down.'

'What's he done?'

'Meth lab.'

'She'll soon forget Logan once he's in jail. You need to get a move on though. Take her out for dinner, quick. And pass me that box of prawns.'

'I'm telling you, you have to stop selling prawns. Those nets do horrific damage to the sea floor. Most of what's pulled up is hurled back into the sea, dead. Sea horses, sea snakes—all dead, dead, the whole lot. Anyway, no girl's interested in me, Mum, not with you around.'

I sighed. The thankless work of motherhood was feeling a bit too bloody thankless. 'I'm worried about Dean, son. We need to help him.'

'If you want to do something helpful, drop all this Miss Marple crap and focus on the shop. Turn it into a vegetarian fish and chip shop.'

I straightened up, leaned against the freezer. My back hurt and my neck was cricked. 'Tell me, what exactly constitutes vegetarian fish?'

'You make burgers from wheat gluten, then flavour them with seaweed and spices.'

'Jesus. I have had it with this claptrap.' I flung down my cloth. 'No one would pay good money for something so ludicrous.' I stamped out.

Almost six and Terry was due any minute. Thing is, when a person hasn't been out with a fella (even if he's only a platonic type of fella, someone she's meeting for an informal briefing on police matters) in roughly a million years, she doesn't always have the full range of up-to-the-minute outfits at her disposal.

She'd probably seek a simple black dress, not too tight across the hips, something a bit Helen-Mirren-edging-on-Debbie-Harry-with-a-hint-of-Catherine-Deneuve. She might search her wardrobe: no black dress. Slinging the contents of her wardrobe onto her bed, she'd avoid the fluoro pink leggings, the lime high heels, the jeans that haven't fitted since 1989.

Pretty soon, the room was a despairing mound of outdated clothes. I looked at the time and sucked in a frantic breath.

'For the mature woman, it's all about décolletage.' Madison

stood in the doorway, a ferret squirming in her arms.

'And decorum, Mum,' said Brad, marching through to the shop. Brad, the expert on decorum. He'd come home last night encrusted with ferret powder.

'Madison?' I said. 'Did Taylah mention anything about wives, de factos, that type of thing?' I held up a short red skirt.

'Terry's divorced. His wife left him three years ago.'

I tugged on the skirt. The zip snapped.

Madison put her head on one side. 'You maybe don't want to risk looking trashy. I'd steer away from anything skin-tight.'

I pulled off the skirt. Finally, I found my red silk top, good lowish neckline, sleeves covering an adequate portion of the upper arms. Black pants, not too tight, covering up the bitten leg.

Madison nodded her approval. 'And have you decided on your signature sex move?'

'It's just a discussion about Dean's career,' I said. 'Terry's brother is a cop. It's not like it's a date or anything.'

The ferret squealed in her arms. 'Well, don't forget, your underwear should make you feel sexy. I always find a G-string works well.' She headed towards my kitchen. 'Come on Hazel, time for your bath,' she said to the ferret.

I directed my mind firmly away from images of Madison, ferrets and G-strings. The RSL was hardly G-string central. I fought my way into my best hold-me-even-tighter underwear, leaning against the wall while I struggled for breath. I got dressed, lipsticked, then popped my head out into the hallway, looking left and right.

Brad's room was surprisingly tidy, no clothing on the floor. No mouldering socks in the corner. No half-made banners covering the floor. His computer was on. I scrolled through the inbox. No emails from Noel/Donald. Lots of emails from DA. As in DirectAction? I opened one.

> Everyone. We're on for Mission Capture & Storage. DA rocks.

Then:

> Tyre biters have got our list of members. Don't worry, we'll find the leak, whoever you are.

The message had been sent to a long list of people. I scrolled through the names, most meant nothing. Then ahlee93. A. H. Lee. Aurora Hocking-Lee?

'Mum?'

I wheeled around.

'You look nice.' Brad sounded surprised. 'What are you doing in my room?'

'Look at all your washing, Brad. I could smell your bedroom from the hall.' I pointed at the empty floor.

He looked puzzled. 'Listen, I'm going out after I close the shop. Decided to take your advice and invited Madison out for dinner. She said yes.' He beamed.

'Terrific. Must go; mascara.' I fled.

Looking around the RSL, I realised I'd never eaten in the presence of so many guns. Guns in paintings and photos, twelve actual guns hanging from the wall.

Sitting as quickly as my constrictor-pants allowed, I gave Terry a nervous smile.

We busied ourselves with the menu while the banks of pokies chirped in the background.

'What'll it be?' he said.

I glanced at my watch. A fast decision was in order.

The RSL special ends at seven. I went for the roast. You don't choose fish and chips when you're out, not when you're a professional.

'So.' He seemed nervous too.

We both reached for the wine list, our hands touching. A little sizzle travelled to my knees.

'Can I apologise? For rushing away like that.' His voice had more husk than a woman in death-grip underwear can generally withstand. 'It was rude. And pretty, ah, inconvenient.' He smiled. 'It's...work. I'm doing some tree-planting near Hustle.'

'You plant at night?'

'Yeah. We're up against a deadline. Things are a bit dicey at the moment.'

I fiddled with the wine list.

'Balance Neutral hasn't planted all the trees it should. We're way behind. The punters have to get what they've paid for. Their carbon offsets and that.'

I hoped Terry wasn't about to get all Brad on me. 'How about some of the local pinot grigio?' I said to change the subject.

'Sounds good.'

Before he could start up on trees again I said, 'I might forgive you, if you answer a question. When was the last time you were on a date? One without a blindfold, I mean.'

The Moisy-Taylah-Madison grapevine had said Terry lived next door to his brother, no post-divorce de factos, not gay.

He shrugged, thickly buttering his bread. 'A while. And you?'

'Same.'

The wine arrived, he poured us both a glass.

I drank mine more quickly than I'd intended. I needed to soften a few of the things on my mind. Son-related worries, closing police stations, un-fathered babies, murdered women. The wine helped. And it was nice to be out with someone friendly. Someone with warm hands and a deep voice.

Terry refilled my glass.

'I don't normally drink this much. It's been a bit of a week,' I said.

He gazed at me.

And there'd been that awful meeting with Monaghan, no doubt he'd have told Terry. Probably had a big laugh. I imagined them up there at Muddy Soak, somewhere swanky, trading hilarious yarns about that stupid rustic from the Bore. My eyes stung.

'You OK, Cass?'

'Had a meeting with your brother yesterday.' I stared out through the windows, at the kangaroo paws, their regimental rows blurring fast. I blinked the moisture back. 'He was a bit, um...'

'Pushy? Bossy? Completely up himself?'

'Oh, I wouldn't put it quite like that,' I said, cheering up. 'He's...into authority, though, isn't he?'

'He's a bully.' Terry tore his bread, a vicious type of tearing.

'Anyway.' Maybe his brother wasn't the best of topics. I drank some more, feeling a little dizzy.

'What'd he see you for?'

'He probably told you all about it. I bet you had a good laugh.' My voice was wobbly. I've never been much of a drinker.

'I would never laugh at you.' His voice was low.

'Anyway, Dale wouldn't tell me, he thinks I'm an imbecile.'

'I just wish one single person would believe me.' To my horror, my eyes filled with tears.

He put his hand on mine. 'I believe you.'

'You'd be the first.' I looked at him, at his anxious eyes. 'Anyway, no point in moaning.' I did my best to use a brighter tone. 'Terrific little place, this. Terrific decor.'

We looked around at the guns, the display case of figurines dressed as soldiers in Afghanistan, complete with a tiny toy mine-detecting dog.

He held out a hanky. 'Reckon you need a moan. Get it out.'

I pretended to dab my eyes with his hanky. It had a lot of oily stains.

My roast arrived. Huge piles of meat on a giant plate.

'Your brother's blaming Brad for Mona's disappearance. And closing down Dean's station. That stupid briefcase was nicked as well.'

He stroked my hand, an absent expression on his face.

'Your parmigiana's getting cold, Terry.'

He smiled. 'You're more important than a parma.'

I drank another glass of wine. I was starting to feel better. Terry's hand was warm and kind, the underwear was clamping less, in fact, I was probably getting thinner from all the worry.

'You need to eat something, Cass.'

Suddenly hungry, I cleared the plate.

'You ever fancied travelling?' he said.

I nodded.

'I wouldn't mind getting away from the family for a while.' He wiped his mouth.

'Yeah. You can have too much of family.'

'Happiness is having a loving, close-knit family at the opposite end of the bloody state,' he said.

I laughed.

'I nicked that from George Burns.' He leaned over the table. 'How about we get out of here?'

'Without dessert?'

'I know a place does a terrific line in rumballs.'

'Oh no, I'm right out of them.'

He whispered in my ear, 'I've always wanted to learn how to make a quality rumball. Any chance of a...lesson?'

It was probably the wine that made me swoon.

We took precautions this time. Terry removed his phone from his pocket and put it on the mantelpiece. Then we got started on the rumballs, and towards the coconut finale we started on some sticky kissing, followed by urgent-style unzipping. My skin tingled beneath his hands. He liked my underwear, liked it more as it came off. He held me, tight and hot, against the fridge.

Later, a sticky condensed milk, chocolate and rum kind of later, Terry was ready for another lesson.

'I didn't follow it all. Can we go over the recipe again, slowly?' He stood behind me, arms around my waist, hands moving across my skin. My breathing quickened.

I've always had a lot of sympathy for a slow learner.

There was a noise at the front door. I grabbed Terry's hand and we scooped up our clothes and scampered to my room. We lay there, breathing hard, trying not to giggle at Brad clumping around the house. Finally, I heard his door click as he headed off to bed.

Later—much later—Terry and I sat against the pillows and got our breath back.

He stared out the window, at the moon rising across the railway line, then glanced down at his watch. Leaning towards me, he whispered, 'Let me help you with this briefcase thing. It's a big job, all alone. Tell me about it.'

'It belonged to Grantley Pittering's brother.'

He sat still.

'You know anything about him, Terry?'

'Yeah, Grantley's my cousin.'

And people say Rusty Bore's inbred.

'We were never apart. Dale, me, Kev and Grantley.'

'What happened to Kev?'

'He died.'

'How?'

He stared at me.

'Sorry, Terry. Sorry for your loss. I don't mean to be insensitive. I'm just worried...about Aurora.'

'Aurora?' He stiffened.

'Vern saw her outside my place with Noel. He's really Donald Streatham. They were poking around here. I bet it was Donald who nicked the briefcase.'

Terry expelled a breath. 'What's Aurora doing with him?'

'Maybe she's a hostage. Vern knows, but isn't telling me. He spoke to her.'

'What about?'

'She wanted to see me. Left a message with Vern. Who wouldn't hand it over.'

A silence while Terry took that in. 'Be careful, Cass.

Dale's a stickler for doing things by the book. He won't tolerate any kind of interference. Seriously.'

'I thought you wanted to help.'

'I do. I want to help you. I have an enormous need to help you.' He worked a slow line of kisses across my shoulder.

That sizzling feeling in my legs again. I had to get a grip. 'Focus, Terry.'

He snapped upright. 'OK.'

'How did Kev die?'

'He was hit by a grain train. At the Tallabung Road crossing.' Terry stared out the window.

'What, did his car break down on the line?'

'Nah, Kev was handcuffed to the line. Wearing a bridal dress.'

I hit him. 'I'm not stupid, Terry. Tell me the truth.'

He looked at me, dead serious. 'It is the truth.'

'Well, who handcuffed him?'

'Did it himself.'

'What, he killed himself?'

'No. It was an accident. Auto-erotic, the coroner said.'

'What does that mean?'

'Look, I don't really want to go into it, OK?'

A pause.

'It was awful, Cass. There was a fire. There wasn't much left of...'

I watched the moon come out from behind a cloud.

'What sort of fella was Kev?' I said.

'I dunno if our relationship is sufficiently advanced for me to update you on my family. You might not like them. I mean, I'm on probation here.' He looked at me with worried eyes.

'Very brief probation period around here, Terry. It ended around the desiccated coconut point in that batch of rumballs.'

'The coconut. Mmm.' He nibbled my ear. 'What do you do with it again?'

Later, the moon higher in the sky, I lay in the crook of Terry's arm. 'Tell me about Kev,' I whispered.

'Well, he was a sad sort of bloke. Never did what he really wanted to. He went into the family business...'

'Pittering and son, the accountants?'

'Yeah. His dad insisted. Uncle Tony wasn't an easy bloke. Kev did as he was told. He became an accountant, worked like blazes at that place. But what he really wanted was to be an actor.'

'Was he good at acting?'

'Yeah, pretty good. But he didn't look right. He could play minor parts, weedy henchman types. Character parts, I suppose they'd call them.'

'He was weedy?'

'Yep, weedier than anyone I've ever known except Grandad. Luckily, that aspect didn't pass down my side of the family.' He waited.

'You're not *very* weedy.'

'I knew he didn't like accounting, but I never knew it was that bad. I feel a bit...regretful. Like I should have done something.'

'Like what?'

'Dunno. Given him a cousin-to-cousin chat, maybe. Although he might have been just as miserable as a two-bit henchman actor.'

'People don't have to make it to the top to be happy.'

'Yeah. It's probably better to fail at something you love than be successful at something you hate.'

There was a pause.

'That's somebody's bloody quote, isn't it?'

'Yeah, another one I nicked from George Burns.'

'Have you memorised everything he said?'

'Not everything. He said a lot.' Terry smiled. 'Anyway, truth is I would have been sadder if Kev'd been, you know, someone I really liked.'

'What a terrible thing to say about your cousin. I hope that's not what people say after I die. "I'd be sadder if I'd liked her."' I paused. 'Someone must have missed him.'

'His mum.'

'Is that why he did it? Because no one liked him?'

He shrugged. 'Cass, this is more detail than I can give. When I said I wanted to help, I was thinking more along the lines of something physical.' He nuzzled my neck. 'Protection,' he whispered. 'You can outsource the non-thinking, beefy stuff to me. Leave you to focus on the brainy bits.'

The brainy bits. That sounded all right. Someone, at last, who appreciated my intellect.

'How can you be sure it was an accident?' I said. 'Clarence said someone would be sorry. Maybe Kev was murdered.'

'No, Dale investigated it himself.'

'Did Kev have any enemies?'

'Well, probably. Who doesn't?'

The moonlight lit up Terry's profile. He had a decent-sized, old-fashioned nose, not one of those little snub noses so many fellas go in for nowadays. Terry didn't have any enemies, surely.

'What was in his briefcase, Cass? Was there something in there makes you think it wasn't an accident?'

'Not really. Just those books. So, was there anyone who wanted Kev dead?'

'It was an accident.'

'I just mean…hypothetically. Did Grantley have his eye on the business?'

'Grantley? God knows what he's doing to that place. I want you to know I'm the decent one in the family.'

'What about Kev's clients?'

'What about them?' He started kissing my neck again.

I struggled free. 'Who were they? Was Donald Streatham one?'

'Donald was an old friend of Uncle Tony.'

'What type of old friend?'

'Well, he gave him that parrot, Baldy. Uncle Tony loved that bird.'

'What about Mona Hocking-Lee. She's a client, isn't she?'

'Yeah. Their biggest. And my boss.' He looked at his watch again.

'Have you got somewhere else you need to be? More trees to plant?'

'No, no. I don't want to be anywhere but here with you.'

'Take the watch off, then.'

He put it on the bedside table, Piero's old bedside table. Terry looked at me, took my face in his hands. His eyes were serious. 'I'm really not like my family. You do believe that? Tell me you'll always believe that. No matter what?'

What was he expecting would happen to change my mind?

'Course. I can see you're not like Dale. And you don't really seem the handcuffing-to-the-railway-line-wearing-a-bridal-dress type.'

'Thing is, I'd like to spend more time with you, Cass. A long, long time. I wouldn't want to lose you.'

Men. I'll never understand them. Why'd he have to get all negative and broody just when things are going well?

'Thing is, you haven't got the hang of the rumball procedure yet. I'll have to enrol you in an adult education course, some one-on-one tuition. Night classes, mostly.'

He kissed me, a slow style of kiss I felt I could possibly get used to.

Later, Terry's arms around me, I fell asleep.

The sound of a cat wailing woke me. I rolled over, remembered Terry, reached over for him. The sheet was cool, the bed empty. In the dark, I groped around for my clock, found it. Four-thirty. Where was Terry? Switching on the light, I scanned the room. No Terry's clothing on the floor, no Terry's watch beside the bed, no chewed-off arm lying on the pillow.

No note on the bedside table either. Huh. A fella could leave a fleeting note at least, wake up a woman to say goodbye. How much work is it to say goodbye? I had a heavy feeling in my chest. Was he off to see some other woman? Maybe he had a horde of them, different skin complexions and shades of underwear, in different towns.

Maybe that's what the 'will you believe me in the morning' routine had been about.

I stood up, took Piero's photo down from the chest of

drawers, dusted it. Piero was never one to nick off in the dark. He took up the whole bed and snored all night. I sat down, photo in my lap and cried a bit. Was I ever going to get over bloody Piero?

'I don't want to forget you,' I whispered to his moistened pic. 'But I'm still alive. Although I'll admit sometimes it's hard to tell.'

I headed to the kitchen to make myself a cold drink of Milo, crunchy across the top. Clicking on the kitchen light, the first thing I saw was Terry's phone, still there on the mantelpiece. I stirred my Milo and stared at the phone. I took a sip. Well, it wouldn't harm anyone to just take a little look at it. Everyone knows integrity has inbuilt flaws.

Picking up the phone, I scrolled though his contacts. No names that seemed especially female. Three messages from Dale. I took another sip of Milo. Maybe Monaghan had texted something relevant, something important that could help Dean keep his station. I clicked on the first message:

Mate. How'd it go?

Then:

Call me.

Third message:

Where are you? That stupid bloody woman sorted out?

And who exactly would she be? Gritting my teeth, I went into Terry's sent messages. One to Dale:

Got the old bag. Now what am I supposed to do?

I blinked twice. Old? I flung the phone across the kitchen, it smacked against the wall, I got up and stamped on it. Swore out loud.

Slumped at the table, I was holding the cool glass of Milo against my hot cheeks when Brad ambled in, yawning, his hair sticking up in tufts.

'What's going on, Mum? And why's there coconut all over the kitchen floor?'

'Long story.' I didn't move. I was considering staying slumped there for a longish period.

Brad pulled out a chair, sat down. 'I saw Terry's car out the front when I got home. Did you have a nice night?'

'Terrific.'

'Is everything OK?' He paused. 'Is that your phone smashed up on the floor?'

'Not exactly.'

He put his hand on my arm. 'You know, I was never too sure about Terry. There was something not quite right. Something about him didn't add up.'

'Thanks for that compelling data.' I sniffed.

'Come on, Mum. There's plenty more fish in the sea.' He passed me a tissue. 'Well, strictly speaking there aren't... But you know what I mean.'

He patted my arm. 'Lots of nice blokes out there. Looking for someone kind-hearted and loyal and conscientious, someone like you.'

'Thanks.' I blew my nose. 'Look, I'm fine. Having a quiet Milo. You go back to bed.'

Brad mooched back along the hall.

I crunched through my Milo. Terry probably left that phone there for a reason. One of those subconscious things, like how a person will be talking to another person, knowing there's one thing she mustn't say.

'Is that a wooden leg?' or 'How'd you lose that arm?' or 'Noel bought some moist-wipes,' that type of instance.

A person can freeze right up, in that position, can't think of anything except the one thing she mustn't say. Until she blurts it out.

I sat still. Yes, I still hadn't found out why Noel-slash-Donald bought those moist-wipes. Or why Aurora wanted to talk to me.

I limped along the street, torch in one hand, precautionary plate of lamingtons in the other. It was just after ten p.m. I'd had a slow day in the shop; plenty of time to hone my master plan.

Vern would probably be out, playing the pokies down at Hustle, Boofa tied up out the front of the pub. Going to make his fortune someday, Vern often tells me. See the world, pay off his debts. 'And what'll you say then to my little merger proposal?' he asks.

Vern would have information in that notebook, information he wouldn't even recognise as significant.

I scurried on past Showbag's gate. Arriving at Vern's out of breath, I paused. His hammock was swinging white and ghostly in the wind. A car's headlights approached and I froze against the wall, Cat Burglar Barbie. The car went by. I slipped around the side of the shop, to the house behind.

At the back door I heard a noise, darted a look over my shoulder. The Hill's hoist creaked, turning slowly in the wind. Vern's chooks clucked from inside their shed as they settled for the night.

No problem getting in. The shop's a different matter, but Vern never locks his house. By the door, I had a twinge of scruples. But it's not exactly breaking in, not when you've brought a plate of lamingtons for the fella. Freshly made. Vern's quite partial to a lamington, he's often told me so, with a hopeful look.

'Vern? You in?' My voice sounded edgy. Of course he wasn't in. The lights were off, his car was gone.

The only sound was something scratching in the roof. A small and scuttly something, possibly a rat type of something. I opened the door. I listened, plate balanced in one sweaty hand. No telly noises, no stomping around the house sounds, no bathroom sloshing. I slithered in, as noiseless as a scrap of whispered scandal.

In Vern's dim kitchen, my breaths came quick, in nervous pants. It was a kitchen full of dark corners. The air had the musky tang of bloke-on-his-own. Was that breathing I could hear? I clicked on my torch, flicked it round. The air moved behind me. I whirled around. Nothing. Just the back door swinging. Calm down, Cass. Just rats or mice.

How hard can it be to find a stupid notebook anyway? I searched all through Vern's bedroom, rootling through his drawers, rustling through the pile of newspapers beside his bed, flipping up his mattress. There was a pile of vivid magazines underneath that mattress. I flipped it down again real quick. For a fella his age, Vern has a shocker of a libido. Finally I found the notebook under the kitchen table and I limped home as fast as I could with the book tucked underneath my arm. I remembered to take the lamingtons as well, no point in wasting them.

Back home, I shoved Brad's magazines aside and sat down on the couch to leaf through the pages of Vern's book. I found notes on a bewildering array of cars coming and going from Rusty Bore, a list of Vern's customers each day, what they bought and what they said. All in his terrible spider-handwriting. It wasn't easy relearning how to write using his wrong hand, he told me once. Exactly how Vern lost that arm is a mystery. It was gone when he arrived in Rusty Bore twenty years ago, and he's never mentioned it. I asked him about it once, but he just frowned; puzzled, like he couldn't remember where he'd put it.

He'd noted down the details of that grisly day when Showbag had his accident. I didn't linger there, flicking forward to study these past few days, see who'd been in town. There was a lot about myself. *That Tuplin woman's holding back on something. I just know it.*

Another entry: *Why's that orange ute pulled up outside her place again?*

She came in today in that blue number she wears to show off her figure. She had suspicious drycleaning.

And another: *Is she up to something with that fella in the white van? She's a mantrap, that woman. She watched his every move around my shop with a hungry kind of expression. Was that what she was doing at Perry Lake? Has she been up to something filthy in the back of his van?*

This was followed by some densely written Vern-fantasy involving a swarm of energetic women who held him down inside a van and wouldn't let him out.

Finally, I got to the list of items Donald had bought. *Fella bought a pack of moist-wipes. What's a bloke like that doing with a moist-wipe? Can't be good.* Good old Vern, maybe he could recognise significant after all. Vern's a natural note-taker. He could have been a court reporter if he'd had the arms.

Come on Vern, I whispered, tell me about Aurora. What's her mobile number? I ate a lamington, then turned the page, looking for his notes on the last two days. Nothing. I held the book up to the light. Rough edges, where...What? Three pages had been ripped out.

I searched, no other torn-out sections. I remembered those sounds I'd heard in Vern's kitchen, the swinging back door. Had someone been in there? The hairs on my arms stood up like an Antarctic breeze just gusted in.

A mopoke let out a hooting call. My leg throbbed. I rubbed it and ate another lamington to ease the pain.

Torch in hand, I headed for my front door. I was turning the handle when I heard a car pull up outside. Opening the door a crack, I peered out.

'Mum?' Dean walked across the gravel, heavy crunching footsteps. 'You should have that leg up.'

Quick smart, I stuffed the notebook down my dress and opened the door wide. 'Dean, how nice! But I'm just heading off to bed.' The notebook was riding up my chest.

'Have you put on weight?' He peered at me. 'I don't know why you won't use that tongue patch Melissa found for you at Whitey's.'

Holding my arm, he walked me slowly towards my bedroom, like I was some kind of prehistoric invalid. 'Melissa could stick it on for you. You'd definitely lose weight. Apparently you get agonising pain on your tongue every time you eat.'

He paused outside my bedroom door. 'Look, I know it's late but I wanted to warn you about Donald Streatham. He's got history. Been in jail for smuggling native bird eggs to overseas collectors. He might be up here after local cockatoos. Worth millions to collectors, Mum, bloody millions.'

'Like Brad said.'

'Yeah.' Dean's mouth turned down like it always has when something doesn't suit him. 'Look, promise me you'll stay away from Streatham?' He gave me a pleading look, the kind he used to give me as a kid when he was after a third serve of ice cream. 'A bloke like that could be very nasty.'

I nodded, crossing my fingers behind my back. I wouldn't normally lie to a police officer. Dean'd understand, later on.

Waiting until his car started, I scurried out my back door. But as I limped along the road towards Vern's place, past Showbag's gate, I heard a car behind me. Dean again? I whirled around. A ute slowed beside me, the sound of country music surging out.

Vern wound down the window and leaned out. 'What you doing wandering the streets at bloody midnight?' He turned down his radio.

Quick as I could, I flipped up the back of my dress and shoved the notebook down my undies.

'You hiding something? And why have you got a torch? You're not thinking of snooping in my private regions again, are you?'

'A person has a right to walk around when she feels

like it.' I gave him my dignified expression. 'And I didn't mean to snoop the other day. I'm just terribly worried about that girl, Aurora. I think Donald's taken her as a hostage.'

'Donald Streatham?'

'Yeah. He's an international bird smuggler.'

'I know he's a bird smuggler, I'm not stupid. That's why he's in for questioning at Muddy Soak. Been in there all night, the pub was full of it. News travels like wildfire in that town. At least here people know how to respect a bit of privacy.' He paused. 'Some of us, anyway.'

'I was onto Donald, ages ago. I've been helping Dean. He doesn't mind me helping out, from time to time.'

'Can't see why he'd want your help. He's got that brother he could turn to; young, resourceful bloke. You'd prob'ly just end up shooting the wrong person.'

'There's no need to be insulting, Vern. A person does her best. And don't forget you were implicated in the Showbag incident, so I wouldn't get too cocky if I were you. Dean's still got his eye on you.' I always held it was unfair of Showbag to hold Vern partly responsible since Vern wasn't anywhere near the gun. But no need to let him know that.

'Ah.' Vern shot me an anxious look. 'Maybe I should nick off home and get my notebook. Do my bit to help. Could be something crucial in my book. I seen a few cars lately, heap of visitors too.'

'Oh? Anyone in particular?'

He paused. 'Well, a woman came in the other day after a big sack.'

'And her name was...?' I said.

'Didn't say.'

'What kind of sack?'

'Huge sack. Showed me how big with her hands. Yeah,' he licked his lips. 'Good big hands.'

A pause while Vern was lost in a reverie.

'What was she like, Vern?'

'Persistent type of woman,' he said. 'Not something I carry love, I told her, suggest you head up to Hustle, bigger range. But she wouldn't leave. Friend had an urgent need for a sack, she said, very particular about the dimensions. Anyway, wrote it all down in the book.'

I nodded. It wasn't in the notebook I'd just read. Was it on the ripped-out pages? 'This could be important, Vern. Reckon Dean'll want to know this. Do smugglers stuff birds in big sacks, you think?'

'Nah. Tuck 'em down their undies, don't they?' He tapped his fingers on the dashboard. 'Well, in the end, I went and rummaged out the back, found an old jute wool sack for her. No one's used them for years, mostly nylon now. Got a good price for it, too. See, just one of the many reasons you should give my merger proposal due consideration.'

I stood there a tick, pondering.

'You better get in,' he said, 'don't want to do too much on that buggered leg.' He leaned over and popped his passenger door open. 'In you hop. I know exactly where it is, that book. There's bits I reckon will be deeply relevant. Wrote it all up before I went out tonight, while the memories were fresh.'

I reached for his door.

'And you know,' he looked thoughtful, 'I've got a bit of a thigh problem at the minute. Could do with a touch of womanly massage in the vicinity.' He looked at me. 'Reckon you'd have not-bad hands for massaging.'

'Is that the time?' I said, looking at my watch. 'I'm feeling terribly tired, suddenly. I might head home to bed. Maybe we can chat about your notebook in the morning.'

I shuffled off as quick as any creeped-out person can with a large notepad stuffed deep inside her knickers.

Back at home, I worried. Maybe I should have gone back with Vern and slipped the notebook back while I had the chance. Had a quick rootle through his bins. I'd missed the moment now. Thing is, I wasn't wild about proximity to Vern's vicinity.

What if he found the notebook gone and got worked up? What would he do? Report it to Dean?

I parked myself on my couch, too tired to think clearly and feeling slightly nauseous. Maybe eating that plate of lamingtons hadn't helped. I wouldn't have minded heading to bed but I knew I'd have to wait up a bit and then take the notebook back. Give Vern time to go to sleep, then return it on the quiet. I'd be as soundless as a tiny sigh, he wouldn't hear a thing.

Yawning, I put my feet up, like Dean said I should. I leaned back, closed my eyes a moment. I tried to relax but I could feel the wind was building. The lounge window rattled. A loose piece of corrugated iron scraped across the roof and the wind whipped the flystrips against the shop door.

The last time I'd waited up like this was the night Piero didn't make it home. The CFA siren went off around midnight, all the town's dogs howling along with it. Piero leapt out of bed and into the truck with Ernie. I waited right here for him, on the couch. And waited. The news report said the flames broke over the truck like a wave. Ernie didn't say much at all.

The dream started, the one where I'm running, the red wave a roar behind me, spitting tiny burning sticks into my back and legs. My hair catches alight. I scream, keep running, holding Brad—a much younger Brad—by his wrist in death-grip.

His hand wrenches free. I turn and he's fallen into the flames. I scream again; my dress is on fire. His small dog, Blacky, whines near Brad. I grab Brad's arm, heave him up. Blacky snarls, and in one twist, turns into Bubbles. She spits a blast of white-hot embers, setting Brad on fire. Smoke everywhere, I can't breathe. Choking, dragging Brad, I crawl low to the ground. The wave surges, hot wind roaring in my ears. There's a ripping, a crack, a boom. The fire wave breaks over me and everything goes black.

I woke in a white room, feeling like a piece of mutton scrag. There was something hammering behind my eyes. I looked around, trying to figure out where I was and how to turn the hammer off. Brad sat in a chair beside my bed, hunched over a *New Scientist*, his left arm in a sling, his face red and blistered. I read the headline upside down, 'Mammoth clue to climate change'. A picture of a frozen baby woolly mammoth lying stiff and desiccated, white-coated people peering at it. I could identify with that baby mammoth. I felt pretty stiff and desiccated myself.

'Where am I?' My throat felt like it had been done over with a set of skewers. It didn't feel good to move my head.

'Don't you move,' said Brad. 'The doctor said you have to take it easy.' He resumed his reading.

'What happened?' I lay still a moment, then lifted the bed cover an inch. Legs, two; one still showing dog bites.

Arms and hands accounted for. It didn't look like I'd had any surprise liposuction either.

He sighed. 'Be quiet and rest, Mum. Just do as you're told for once.'

Someone was lying in the bed opposite, a mop of grey hair. I hoped she wasn't dead.

'Well, I'd find it a lot easier to rest if you told me why I'm here.'

I was on my couch, last time I looked. When was that? My memory was fuzzy, like I was peering through a film of oily steam.

Brad gave me a frightened look like people get when they're about to tell you something nasty, like they're sorry and really didn't mean it, but they've run over your dog.

'What?' I snapped, then coughed.

'Did you leave a burner on, Mum?'

He wasn't making sense. 'I never leave the burners on.'

'I woke up to find the house on fire. You were unconscious on the couch, breathing in the smoke.'

'And the shop?'

'The shop's a big pile of ash.'

I caught my breath.

'We'll talk about it later,' he patted my arm with his un-slung hand. 'When you're better. There'll have to be some changes.'

'Changes? What kind? Is my house OK?'

'All gone,' he said in the falsely bright voice used on those who've lost the greater part of their brain. 'Although I saved your handbag. Anyway, I'll go and find the doctor.'

He loped off down the hall.

Gone? I tried to comprehend the enormity of that, while the hammer kept on hammering. My box of photos of the boys. My framed photo of Piero. Brad's whole series of sea monster drawings from when he was eight. Gone? I slumped back on my pillow. And my insurance, was it up to date? Thinking about paperwork didn't help the nausea. I closed my eyes and went over shutting up the shop, my endless cleaning routine. I'll admit I do it all on autopilot.

Had I checked the burners? I must have, surely. I remembered the wind, all those banging sounds. The back door, I never lock it. An icy feeling crept up my arms.

In bustled a plump, bright-eyed figure in a white coat, looking more than ready to assist any baby woolly mammoths that came his way. A badge on his coat said Doctor Rangarajan. Brad followed in his slipstream.

'Mrs Tuplin. Marvellous!' The doctor beamed. He had a face jam-packed with enthusiasm. Picking up a chart hanging from the bed, he did some rapid ticking.

'You've done extremely well. We'll just need to keep you in a little longer. Smoke inhalation can be a serious business.' He hung the chart back on its hook.

'How much longer?' I tried sitting up, feeling sick, 'Thing is, I'm not sure I'm safe in here.' I've seen enough midday movies to know how easily your average murderer gets into a hospital when he's motivated. It only takes one discarded white coat and he's in. Then he creeps up to your bed, gives you the nasty final look and *bam* he pulls out all your plugs.

Doctor Rangarajan stared. 'Of course you're safe. Our care here at the Hustle Public Hospital is absolutely first-rate. And you have your son here,' he beamed at Brad. 'What a son, you must be proud.'

Brad looked at the floor.

'If only I could be fortunate enough to assist my own mother in such a way, but sadly, she's passed away.' His smile faded. 'At least we believe she has. She disappeared, climbing Mount Kilimanjaro. It broke my father's heart.' He stared off into the distance. 'And my heart too, of course.' Hauling himself away from his African-mountain middle distance, the doctor gave himself a little shake.

'Yes, your heroic Brad. Saving your life like that.'

Brad? Saved my life?

'A little bump on the head as he dragged you from your burning house.' He waved a hand. 'Thus the bandages. But you'll be fine. Astonishingly fine. All thanks to Brad's quick thinking.'

Brad turned red.

'And did he tell you he sat here by your side these last two nights? He maintained a constant vigil. Beyond compare, this young man.' He thumped Brad on the back.

Brad staggered and coughed.

'But you know this, of course. You're his mother.' The doctor gave me a radiant we're-all-happy-families smile. He swept out of the room in search of other baby woolly mammoths in need of cheer.

Brad dumped himself into the chair, reaching for his magazine.

'Brad. I didn't leave the burners on.'

'It's OK, Mum, accidents happen. The important thing is you're alive.'

'Did you turn them back on?'

He flung down his magazine. 'Bloody typical. I should have known this would all be my fault.'

I was too nauseous for an argument. 'I'm not blaming

you. I'm just trying to work out what happened. You didn't turn anything on after we closed, you're sure?'

He nodded.

'Nor me. And the shop smoke alarm. It wasn't going, was it? It would have woken us. And Showbag would have heard it. You know he hears everything.' Showbag doesn't sleep too well, not since the accident. He can't get comfortable, or so he claims.

Brad spoke slowly. 'There was a car...'

'What car?'

'It drove off while I was getting you out of there...'

'The arsonist!'

'Calm down. Maybe the alarm was faulty, we hadn't tested it in a while. Anyway, the CFA will look at all that.' He sounded like he was trying to convince himself.

'I bet someone took out the battery. That someone snuck in the back and set the place on fire. To kill us. Me.'

'Jesus, Mum! I told you not to get involved. How many times?'

Dean walked in, heavy boots clomping on the hospital floor.

Good old Dean, six foot one of reassurance, dressed in blue, his gun close at hand, hanging in its holster. He held a bunch of deep pink roses. General MacArthurs, my favourite. Trust him to know that.

Dean'd sort this out, especially now he knew about Donald, and with Mona reported missing, he'd believe me now. Dean wouldn't leave me on my own to grapple with a faux-doctor-murderer.

'Thank God you're all right.'

His voice was gruff. He bent down and kissed my cheek, looking deep into my eyes like he was searching for something he'd lost down there. 'You remember me, don't you? It's Dean.'

I struggled up against the pillows.

'Perfect timing, son.' I lowered my voice. 'Can I borrow your gun?'

Dean stared.

I suppose there'd be regulations about lending out his weapon, even to his relatives.

He cleared his throat, looked at the roses in his hand. 'Anyway, let me put these in some water. I see Brad didn't think to get you flowers.'

Brad humphed, got up to fetch another chair. He plonked it down like he was planning on using it to stab a hole right through the floor.

Dean gave Brad a little nod. 'Colours are good for them, Brad, smells, sounds, anything that stimulates the brain.' He spoke in a low voice, as if he thought I couldn't hear.

Brad looked at Dean from under lowered eyelids.

Moving his chair closer to me, Dean said, 'Now, Mum. You can't go on like this. I'm really worried.'

He wasn't the only one. 'I don't mind if you lend me some old spare. As long as it shoots OK.'

Dean patted my wrist. 'Poor old Mum. When you're better, we'll have a little family talk.'

'I could be dead by the time I'm better, Dean. I'm telling you I need a bloody gun.'

'We'll have a proper family conference.' Dean sailed on. 'There'll have to be some changes. It's sad you lost the place, but it's time you made a change. It's a young person's game, takeaway. Time to put your feet up.' He smiled a Gladwrapped smile.

What did he think I'd be doing with my feet up? Sounded boring as all hell. 'Anyway,' I said, in a louder voice, 'Can you spare a few minutes today to show me how to use it? So I'm ready for tonight? Although I don't mind if you stay here and fight him off yourself. Actually, I can see how you might prefer that.'

I glanced at Brad. I could have done with a little help but Brad was busy glaring at his magazine.

Dean had the sort of look he gets when he's about to announce something worrying, like the day he told me Melissa was pregnant.

'Mum.' He rubbed his chin. 'It can happen to anyone. Early onset dementia doesn't mean you're old, or anything. It can come on really, amazingly early. It's better if we just accept it. You know I only want the best for you.'

Brad gave Dean an eye-flick glare.

'Dementia?' I struggled onto my pillows, who cared about the nausea. 'Who says I have dementia?'

'Yeah,' said Brad. 'Who?'

'Well, no one,' Dean took his hand away. 'Not yet. But that's just because Brad hasn't had anyone look. I'll have a little chat with the doctor. It's the obvious explanation. For your...muddled behaviour.'

'Muddled? Dealing single-handedly with a murderer because my cop son won't believe a word I say? There's nothing bloody wrong with me.' I looked at my hands. 'Apart from a few burns.'

'And a nasty dog bite,' added Brad.

A pause.

'Some smoke inhalation. And a unique range of irritating habits.' Brad scratched his arm. I don't know what he thought he was smirking at. Kids.

'Yes, apart from those, there's nothing wrong with me,' I snapped. 'I don't know how many times I have to tell you, Dean, there's a murderer out there. You need to focus on the facts. Instead of all this waffle about dementia.' I grabbed his arm. 'Listen, the fella's burned my house down. He's dangerous. And single-minded.' More than I could say for Dean.

Dean shook his head.

'You need to whip me away into a witness protection scheme. Do I get a say in where I'll be relocated? I wouldn't mind somewhere green. I can draw you up a shortlist.' They'd need to give me a new face, of course. I'd have to consider my choice of nose.

'I don't know how you could have let things go this far, Brad, without getting her to a doctor.'

At last Brad closed his magazine. 'Well, I reckon Mum could have a point. There's a lot here that you're ignoring.'

The last time Brad stood up to Dean was when Brad was twelve. Brad lost, as I recall. He always did.

'So, let me get this straight,' Dean's voice was low. 'You and Mum, in the absence of any evidence, have decided that someone set fire to the shop. To kill Mum.'

Brad nodded.

'And why?' said Dean.

'Because of the body,' I said.

'Ah, yes. Because of all this crap about a body.' Dean sighed, stared at the wall. 'Look, we're checking the place for cause of fire. OK? The CFA are looking for any signs of accelerants, signs of arson. All part of the routine. Probably, and it's early stages, but probably all post-fire indicators will show the fire started in the deep fat fryer. The most plausible scenario is that a burner was left on. By Mum,' Dean turned his gaze on his brother, 'or more likely by you, Brad.'

'What?' said Brad.

Dean held up a hand. 'I know you don't like it. I mean, who'd be OK with the idea that his negligence could have killed his mother? I'm afraid you'll just have to live with that. In the meantime, we're waiting on the evidence. The professional knows not to rush to conclusions before reviewing all the evidence.'

That's Dean all right. He'd be reviewing the evidence before deciding to clip his toenails.

'Consider this, Brad. There are many, many ways in which a fish and chip shop can burn down. Burners left on, faulty thermostats, cheap power boards, dodgy wiring, just to name a few. We professionals must consider everything. That's why we investigate the cause of the fire. *Properly.*'

'I know,' said Brad, 'but...'

'The professional works for a living, Brad.' Dean's voice rose. 'He doesn't fill his days demonstrating and protesting. He compromises. And he doesn't have his aged mother look after him all his life. He doesn't leave her to work forever. In a bloody. Death. Trap.'

So much for the early onset. I'd moved rapidly onto geriatric, it seemed.

Brad's face turned red.

'So, whatever paranoid little fantasies you need to clutch onto to tell yourself you're worthwhile, you just clutch away. But Mum will be staying with me and Melissa from now on. And I'll be watching all her comings and goings, let me assure you.'

'You'd lock me up?' I said.

The grey-headed body in the bed opposite perked right up. She wasn't dead, as it turned out. She fluffed up her pillows with her skinny hands, then sat upright, settling in to watch. Her head moved from side to side, like she was at the tennis.

'If that's what's needed, yes,' said Dean. 'Actually, that's a good idea. The cell's quite comfortable and Melissa's not keen to have you in the house. Nothing personal,' he said quickly, 'Melissa thinks you're terrific Mum, just terrific, but she's busy packing for the move. We're going to Bendigo. Traffic. Monaghan didn't want me at Muddy Soak, thanks to you.'

A nurse came in. 'Time for your injection, Mrs Flanders,' she said to the tennis-watcher in the other bed.

'Buzz off. Can't you see I'm busy?' Mrs Flanders batted her away.

'And to top it all off, Vern phoned this morning.' Dean gave me a glued-on stare.

Jesus, Vern's notebook. Had it burned?

'He said you broke into his house and stole important records. He mentioned industrial espionage. He wants me to investigate. He wants Monaghan involved. He wants all the bloody detectives in the state involved.' Dean rubbed his forehead. 'Tell me it's not true, Mum. Tell me you didn't break into his house.'

'Well, I only just...' I didn't get to finish.

'Mum! From here on, I have to know where you are. At. All. Times.' A vein bulged in his neck.

Dean needs to attend more carefully to the state of his blood pressure. The stress of the job's not doing him any good. Maybe he's not cut out for it. It takes a certain type of person to cope with this detecting trade.

'Look,' Dean used a softer tone, 'Dad would want me to look after you. And Brad, well, he's not the right carer for you. He's too busy wasting his life to notice what's happening to yours.'

Brad jumped up, his magazine sliding onto the floor. 'I carried Mum out of that bloody fire. And sat beside her for the last two nights. Where were you?'

Dean snorted. 'I don't have to answer to you. I was doing my job. More than I can say for you.'

'What's *wrong* with you, Dean? Why won't you give me credit for anything?'

'Because, Bradley, you're a parasite. If it was just one event, I could get over it. But a lifetime of disappointment, mate, that's harder to forget.'

'Lifetime of disappointment? What sort of bullshit parent-talk is this? You're not Dad, Dean. He's dead. Get over it.'

Dean sighed. 'You know, I tried so hard with you. Footy. Volleyball. All those jobs I put your way, the chicken factory, the abattoirs, that lamb emasculation contract. You could have done any one of them. But no. I've come to realise you're just a blood-sucker, mate. Someone has to say it.'

Brad's ears turned red.

'So don't go thinking this little heroic act of yours changes anything,' said Dean.

I flopped back on my pillows. 'So. You locking Brad up too?'

Dean stood up. 'No space.' His voice was a rim of ice on a dark pond. 'Brad needs a short sharp shock. It's time he found his own way in the world.'

A nasty silence.

Brad picked up his magazine, folded it carefully and put it on the chair. 'You always were a bastard, Dean, and a stupid one. If you had anything at all going on inside your head you'd be able to see just how stubborn you are.'

He swung around to me. 'And as for you, Mum. Yeah, you made up your mind about me a long time ago, didn't you? Well, you'll both be bloody sorry. I'll show you.' He stalked out, leaving behind his magazine.

Mrs Flanders stared after Brad, boggle-eyed. We were all pretty boggle-eyed. Her lips moved. I thought I heard her whisper, 'Good on you, son.'

'Good riddance to a waste of skin,' muttered Dean.

After Brad had gone, Mrs Flanders curled up beneath her covers. Dean stayed on, looking grim, watching me eat my dinner, a meal of mostly lettuce since it was Brad who'd filled in the meal slip. Finally, Dean stood up.

'I'll be back in the morning. And don't worry, you'll be comfortable in the cell.' He kissed my cheek. 'Most importantly, you'll be safe.' He walked out, heavy steps, a man with work, kids and now an insane mother to worry about.

I lay there, TV flickering, showing floods and earth-quakes and starving people crying out. I tried calling out a friendly hello to Mrs Flanders, still beneath her covers. No reply. Maybe she really was dead.

Time to review the situation. The situation wasn't going well, that much was clear. My shop had burned down, and my house. There was at least one dead body, two missing people, a murderer on the loose and no one that believed me.

Only Brad, and only possibly. And where was he?

I tried his mobile. No answer. Madison said she hadn't seen him, through the sound of ferrets squealing in the background. 'He said he'd come around tonight to help get Tim settled in. Poor Timmy, he was abandoned.' She spoke in an agonised whisper. 'An abandoned ferret is a sight to break your heart.'

I hoped Brad didn't feel abandoned. 'Ask him to give me a call, will you Madison?' Although it was possible I might be killed by then. I should give her some final words for him, just in case. I couldn't think of anything worth saying. Only that I was sorry.

A nurse came in. Her name badge said 'Wendy' and she wore the expression of a person who'd seen the world and found it wasn't to her liking. She turned off the TV. 'Time to sleep.'

'But...'

'No arguments.' She pulled up the bed covers, tucking them in more tightly than I needed.

The room grew darker. I waited, buzzer finger at the ready, tensing up as people passed the door. Mrs Flanders started snoring. It was reassuring to know she wasn't dead.

The hospital settled for the night, the night-shift staff came on duty, hushed tones in the corridors, soft-soled shoes squeaking past. What kind of shoes do faux-doctor-murderers wear? Do they squeak or are they completely soundless, leaving you no time to summon help?

I tried not thinking about Brad and whether he was safe, whether he was busy turning into a bedraggled homeless fella on some cold wet Melbourne street. I tried not thinking about him shivering in the rain, the lack of hope in his eyes. I tried not thinking about how much I'd miss him in the shop, at home. Everywhere.

I tried not thinking about how my life was shaping up, assuming I survived the night. Living in Dean's prison cell. Watched every minute, never going anywhere. I'd never get to travel around Australia. I'd have to be polite every morning to Melissa. Admire their girls' latest navel piercings, so they'd smuggle me in a slice of bread. I'll admit a tear slipped out and trickled down my cheek.

Was it true what Brad had said? Was it possible I didn't listen? *You made up your mind about me a long time ago.* I tried, most of all, not to think of that. Or the distance in his eyes.

I woke to the sound of footsteps in the corridor. Heavy-sounding, no squeaking, no soft soles. I held my breath. They came closer, paused. A shadow fell across the doorway.

I reached for the buzzer but it wasn't there. Gasping, I fell back on the pillow, woozy-headed.

'Mrs Flanders,' I croaked as loud as I could muster. 'Help. I'm being murdered.'

No response.

Surely the buzzer had fallen on the floor. I surged out from the covers, ignoring the woozy head. There it was, shining white on the floor. I reached down, down, down for it, feeling dizzy, my hand closing around the white plastic.

Something cracked against my skull.

'We can't tie her down, it's unethical.'

I struggled to open my eyes, to get up off my back. My head felt like a train smash. The murderer had got me—but he didn't want to tie me up? Seemed a strange, politically correct type of murdering. I managed to raise my eyelids. A figure in white floated nearby. I sucked in a breath. So I was dead? In a place where tying up was considered, but forbidden by a code. What type of place? I blinked and a name badge, 'Wendy', came into view.

'Mrs Tuplin?' A voice that was too loud. 'You fainted and hit your head. Can you hear me?'

'Loud and clear,' I croaked.

'I hope you'll understand now why you should stay in bed.' Some vicious tucking-in movements.

'The murderer was here.' My voice was raspy. 'Donald Streatham, it must have been. He came right up to the door. I saw his shadow.' I paused. 'Mrs Flanders, is she...alive?'

'Mrs Flanders is fine, apart from having her precious sleep disturbed by your antics. Now, you will NOT get out of bed again. Understood?' She turned away. 'She's not in a marvellous state, Sergeant, her blood pressure is very low. Do you have to see her right now? Surely this could wait until the morning.'

Monaghan? What was he doing here? I turned my head. He was sitting on a chair against the wall, that long black leather coat draping across the floor.

'It's vital I speak to Mrs Tuplin now.'

'Five minutes, that's all.'

He nodded. 'Understood.' He paused. 'You can leave us now, Wendy.'

But she sat down next to him, fiddled with her watch. 'I've set my stopwatch.' She smiled a plastic smile.

'This is a confidential police matter.'

She nodded. 'Four minutes and fifty-five seconds left.'

He stared at her, a stare full of longing hatred. 'Mrs Tuplin is a potential witness to a homicide.'

At bloody last.

Wendy nodded. 'Four minutes, forty seconds remaining.'

He stood up, a sudden, angry movement. 'I need to speak to Mrs Tuplin privately. You will leave right now.'

'Anything you discuss will be treated as completely confidential. You have four and a half minutes left. Or, of course,' Wendy smiled sweetly, 'you can do as I suggest, and speak to our patient in the morning.'

Monaghan turned his glare onto me. 'Mrs Tuplin. Donald Streatham is dead. A traffic accident. It appears he lost control of his vehicle and hit a tree.'

I stared.

'An empty bottle of Jim Beam was found on the

passenger seat next to the body of a black dog. And there was a jute wool sack in the back of his van. The sack contains human remains.'

'Mona?' I croaked.

'We don't have a definite ID yet, but it appears to be the body of a woman of mature years, wearing a gold-coloured dress.'

I kept quiet. I didn't want to waste the precious minutes Wendy was counting down.

'We also found a laptop in the van. Your son Bradley's laptop. What exactly is the nature of your son's relationship with Donald Streatham?'

'Relationship? They don't have a relationship.'

'We have examined your son's emails and it appears he does have a relationship with him. So there's no point in lying to protect him. It's possible...your son is involved in a bird-smuggling ring involving Clarence and Aurora Hocking-Lee. Where is he?'

Bird smuggling? Brad? 'He left. We had...an argument.'

'What about?'

'Just family business. Nothing important.'

'Everything is important in a murder investigation.'

'Brad just got into a tiny huff.'

'You must phone me immediately if you hear from him.'

'Is Brad...in danger?'

Wendy snapped me a look from her stopwatch.

Monaghan didn't answer.

'What about Clarence and Aurora, where are they?' I said.

'We will find them. We will find your son, as well.' Monaghan had the kind of face that didn't need his lips drawn into a thin white line like that. He'd look grim enough when he smiled.

'Mrs Tuplin,' Monaghan paused, 'This may come as a shock, I'm afraid. It's also possible your son...started the fire in your shop.'

'Bradley? No way.' Brad might hate the place but he would never torch it. Would he?

'Did you see or hear anything suspicious that night?'

I shook my head, not a good idea as it turned out. I felt sick.

'I understand you followed Donald Streatham on Tuesday.'

'His dog bit me.'

'You must stop meddling in a police investigation. It's unhelpful and dangerous, especially for someone with your...mental health issues.'

'Twenty-five seconds,' snapped out Wendy.

I was starting to warm to Wendy.

Monaghan gave her a look designed to wilt, but Wendy didn't seem the wilting type.

'Is there any reason Bradley may have tried to kill you?'

'Of course not. Donald's your man.' Clearly, Muddy Soak had been crime free so long Monaghan was out of practice. 'Donald must have killed Mona and knew I was onto him, wanted me out of the way. I don't get out of the way all that easily, though.'

'Yes, I can believe that,' he said.

'Time's up.' Wendy shepherded Monaghan out.

I lay there, staring at the ceiling. At least the police were finally involved. Properly. Now that Mona's body had turned up. But why was Brad's laptop in Donald's van?

No way Brad would involve himself in bird smuggling. And he would never leave that computer. Not unless he'd encountered an emergency. What type of emergency? Panic rose in my throat.

Breathe, breathe. You need to think.

It must have been Donald who'd killed Mona, as I'd long suspected. But the more I thought about it, the more loose ends appeared. Aurora, for instance. If she was that ahlee93 on Brad's email, one of that group of committed eco-warriors, surely she wouldn't be smuggling birds? Had Clarence forced her into it?

I rootled out my phone, tried Brad again. No answer. He'd turn up, of course he would. *I'll show you* he'd said. Had I driven him to do something stupid? Something bloody ghastly?

I transferred my stare from the ceiling to Mrs Flanders, snoring in her bed. Pretty soon, I'd be out of here, back to the disappointment of my life. Without my shop. Without even my dusty photo of Piero.

I'd have to think about what to do. Rebuild? I would have liked that trip around Australia with Terry. Bloody Terry. I hoped he was missing his stupid phone. I hoped he'd caught something deeply infectious from one of his other women, something truly painful.

And no doubt Vern would be on and on about his notebook, once I was allowed visitors. So that jute wool bag he'd sold, he'd said a woman came in and bought it, she must have wanted it to put Mona in. Have to be the same wool bag, surely. Couldn't be that many jute wool sacks floating around the Mallee. So who was the woman who'd bought it?

It's never pleasant for a person to be locked in a police cell by her son. There were no bars for me to hang from to rail about the injustice or even run my tin cup along. No filthy pail of excrement to pose dejectedly beside for a photo in the *Herald Sun*. A clinical type of room, white, it smelled of disinfectant. A screened window looked out on the dusty world outside. I had a door. A door Dean had locked.

He'd put some flowers in a vase. 'There, that cheers up the cell...the room. And I'll bring in the old TV for you, it'll keep you occupied. Essentially, you're free to come and go, Mum. Just give me a hoy if you need the loo.' He'd left, turning the key.

I don't know where Dean picked up such a warped idea of freedom. Through the internal window I could see him busy yapping down his phone. Had Dean always parted his hair like that and combed it down so neatly?

The sheer tidiness of him had started to get on my nerves. I sat, and the prison bench creaked.

Too early that morning, Doc Rangarajan had bounded to my bedside, pronouncing I was in outrageously good shape, all things considered.

'And her mind is just absurdly clear,' he smiled, giving Dean's hand a hearty shake. 'What Mrs Tuplin needs now is her family.'

Dean frowned. 'Well, we'll need a second opinion. Still, she doesn't need to worry now, I'll take good care of her.'

After everything, after all my investigations, after it turned out Mona was really dead, Dean didn't say one word of thanks. He just push-guided me into his van and snapped on my seatbelt. He got into the driver's seat.

'Look, it's attention-seeking behaviour on your part, I know.' He started up the divvy van. 'A cry for help. Melissa looked it all up on the internet. Well, Mum, we've heard your cry. You're going to be fine, living with us. We'd never put you in a home, Melissa will always take care of you.' He paused. 'And I will too, of course.'

'Melissa?'

He turned the van onto High Street. 'Yes, we've talked it all over and she's fine. Madison drops the ferrets off each morning on her way to work but Melissa will still have time for you.' He paused. 'I told her you don't need help with eating or anything, not yet anyway. Melissa thought you could help with the ferrets on the days she's at work. Madison doesn't like them being left alone for long. They have a lot of health-care needs.'

'But Madison won't be dropping them off to you in Bendigo. It's too far away.' I rubbed my face, I seemed to be developing some kind of nervous facial twitch.

We sailed past the shops on High Street, Whitey's chemist, the mural.

'Madison's moving too. She's got a remedial massage job lined up in Bendigo. She and Melissa couldn't bear to live that far apart.'

'No, no,' I said in a strangled voice. 'Look, I'll be fine living on my own. I'll rebuild. My customers demand it.'

'I don't think that's a good idea, Mum. Not while you're injured.'

Maybe he had a point. I was still having a bit of trouble breathing, especially when people upset me. I wasn't staying with him long term though, just a day or two, while I recovered. And I wasn't having anything to do with those ferrets.

'I'm worried about Bradley,' I said. 'He would never leave his laptop. What was it doing in Donald's van? Is Brad in danger?'

'Brad? Don't go worrying about him, Mum. He'll have found a new demonstration to hang his banners at. Or some chicken farm or abattoir to trespass in.'

'But he's not answering his phone. Even Madison hasn't seen him.'

'I have enough problems at the moment without running around after Brad. He'll be sulking somewhere. I'm not wasting police time on this stupid family. Not any more.'

He turned the van into his drive. 'And Vern's phoned Armed Robbery now. You know his niece's ex's wife's cousin is a superintendent there?' His hands were white-tight on the steering wheel. 'I really need this bloody family to stop embarrassing me.'

Embarrassing? I couldn't be held accountable for Vern

and his hysteria. There was no way I was armed when I nicked that notebook. Not unless you count a plate of lamingtons as weaponry. 'Listen, Dean. Family's everything. Your father knew that. It's a damn good thing he's not around to hear you talk like this.'

'Dad?' Dean stared out the windscreen. 'Ha!'

'What's that supposed to mean?'

Dean turned and looked at me. 'Oh, Mum.' His eyes softened, less the endless-night type of black, more like treacle. 'I have to tell you something about Dad. Something important. Before you lose any more of your mind.'

'I'm telling you, son, my mind is absolutely fine,' I snapped.

But Dean carried on as if he hadn't heard. 'The thing is, Dad wasn't, ah, exactly how you thought he was.'

I stared at him.

'You know how he went away a lot?'

'Yeah. He took all those photos. All over the place. Piero was an ace photographer.'

'Yep, but he had another reason for travelling.'

'What other reason?'

Dean took his hand off the steering wheel and gently stroked my arm. 'He had another family, Mum. And you know the saddest part? Everyone knows, except for you.'

Something caught in my throat for just a second; a lost fly perhaps. 'That's not funny, Dean. In fact, it's plain mean.'

'It's not a joke.'

I looked at his face. 'So who's this other family?'

Dean's phone started ringing. 'Sorry.' He grabbed the phone.

Something hot rose in my throat. I flung open the car door and threw up.

Now, on Dean's prison bench, I shifted uncomfortably. I held out my hands; they were still shaky. Dean was busy rushing around his station, dealing with phone calls from assistant commissioners, superintendents, Vern's relatives. He seemed pretty stressed. It did cross my mind that maybe he'd made up this whole Piero-other-family business. After all, stress can do strange things to a person. I tried using that line of thought to reassure myself. It didn't work. I needed Brad. He'd explain. I tried calling him again. No go. I tried Madison.

'I still haven't seen him,' she said. 'I was hoping he'd bring over something tasty to perk up Tim. Moving to Bendigo isn't what my new little boy needs right now.'

'Madison.' Jesus, how to ask? Still, no point in holding back. Dean had said everyone knew. 'Ah, do you recall Piero having any secrets?'

A pause. 'What kind of secrets?'

'Any kind. The secret kind.'

'Well, I'm not sure he would have told me his secrets, Cass. He'd of told you first, wouldn't he?'

'I mean the type of secret everyone knew, except for me.'

'Oh.' A long pause. 'That type.'

'So is there anything you're keeping from me, Madison?'

A strangled swallowing sound. 'Possibly.'

'Who is she?'

'Shit. Who told you?'

'Dean. So who is she?'

'Dean really is one heartless bastard,' she said. 'No offence intended.'

'Who is she? Who is this bloody other family?' My face was hot.

'Look Cass. It's not for me to say...'

'Well, who *is* going to tell me then?'

'Oh my God. Gotta go, Cass. Timmy needs me. Zara's got his throat in her jaws.'

I put down my phone and groaned. Melissa was out in the dusty yard, hanging out some washing. Maybe I should just focus on normality, do my best to stop thinking about philandering dead husbands. And stay away from murderers too. I could try to be a better mother. Especially to Brad. Maybe I should apologise. But for what? Holding him back from the world? He didn't need any help with that. I remembered what he'd said the day I went to Muddy Soak, the day I was all for forcing him into that undercover bird meeting with Donald. *I couldn't leave you on your own.* Is that really why he was hanging around, instead of going to uni, getting on with life?

Dean got off the phone, unlocked the door. 'That was Vern. I've asked him to come in. Now, I need you two to work this out. Be nice, apologise. Give him back his notebook.'

'It got burnt. Look, I'm a fire victim, Dean. And I'm in bloody shock, after your little announcement. Does anyone care about that? Does Vern care about that?' My voice grew higher. 'And who's to know Vern wasn't working with Donald, even helped him torch my place? Vern's always wanted to annex my shop. If Vern's going to go around making wild accusations, well, so can I.'

'Jesus, Mum. Calm down, will you? Offer to buy him a new notebook. Flirt with him. Anything. Just do whatever it takes to stop him phoning any more superintendents.

My career is hanging by a bloody thread.' He slammed the door and locked it.

I put my head in my hands. Why hadn't I taken that stupid notebook back? I should have known Vern would make a heap of trouble. I didn't even get anything useful from it. The important stuff was on those ripped-out pages. Ripped out while Vern was out. He'd said he'd written it all up before he left for the pub. So the pages must have been torn out sometime between Vern going out and my arrival with my undercover lamingtons. Donald must have got there before me.

I remembered the rustling sounds I'd heard in Vern's kitchen. Probably Donald in post-ripping mode, stuffing those sheets into his pocket. I stared out the window, searching for something green to rest my eyes on. Red dust, scrappy shrubs. Maybe we were in for another dust storm. Muddy Soak would probably get more undeserved rain.

Muddy Soak. I sat still. Donald was at the Muddy Soak police station that night, Vern had said. *Been in there all night, the pub was full of it.* So he couldn't have been at Vern's. My brain moved slow and careful. If Donald didn't do the ripping, then who did? And why?

Monaghan was missing vital details, that much was clear. And Rusty Bore was a town without protection from a murderer. Quite possibly a less-than-satisfied murderer in search of further victims.

Stay calm, Cass. All we need is for Dean to solve the crime, properly. Catch the killer. And then Monaghan and the hierarchy would see Dean's full worth. They'd reinstate him in an instant. I'd collect the facts, present them to Dean, that way he couldn't argue.

My phone rang. I grabbed it, hoping it was Brad.

'What's this about you picking up a nasty dose of dementia?' Ernie.

'Huh. Don't believe everything you hear. You seen Brad?'

'Brad who?'

Maybe today wasn't one of Ernie's good days. No point in asking him about Piero.

'Anyway, what the hell are you doing with my key?' he said.

'Key?'

'That key you had. Day you wanted me to open up that briefcase. What the blazes are you up to with the key to my gun cabinet?'

My hand froze. 'Why didn't you tell me?' When I showed him the key a million years ago.

'You expect me to remember every-bloody-thing? I'm eighty-seven. Christ, when does a man *hic* get a break?'

My mind whirled. Why was Ernie's gun cabinet key lying on the sand at Perry Lake? What was in the gun cabinet? I bet Monaghan didn't know anything about it. This must be it, the convincing evidence for Dean's reinstatement. Did I still have the key? I rootled through my handbag.

In my hand I held the key.

For your actual everyday criminal, Dean would surely guard the toilet door, listening for incriminating smashing sounds, ready to fly in with his handcuffs. No need for his demented mother though. He was busy on the phone again.

'If I can just explain, Superintendent Bartlett...' he said, as I closed the toilet door.

The window was surprisingly easy to open, just a little flick, but not so easy to wriggle through. I pushed and struggled in that window frame, kicking like a kangaroo. Wedged in tight around my middle, my arms outside the window, handbag dangling, my breath was squeezed into tiny gasps.

A dual-cab ute pulled up on the verge. It had a row of spotlights across the top, Australian flag fluttering above. Vern got out and shut the door.

I tried reversing back through the toilet window. But

the window frame just bit deeper into my stomach. I hung there, holding my breath, as silent as a heart murmur.

'Hah. What you bloody up to?' Vern let out a hooting laugh.

'Vern,' I gasped. 'Look, I'm real sorry about your notebook.' I had an idea. 'You couldn't help me out this window, could you?' I blinked in his direction, as best I could. It wasn't a top-notch flirting situation. 'I should mention though, I think my dress has all ripped away.' I tried what I hoped sounded like a seductive schoolgirl giggle.

Vern lunged forward and grabbed me. He yanked so hard on my arm that it felt possible I'd end up a one-armed person myself.

Finally I fell out onto the ground, slipping out into the world like a new-born calf, my dress reasonably intact.

Vern looked disappointed.

'Listen,' I brushed myself down. 'You're in terrible danger.' I gave him a few quick words re the notebook-ripping situation. 'There's clearly more to this than Monaghan realises. The murderer will be after you next, he'll know you notice things.'

Vern's face turned grey.

'We need to head to Ernie's shack. Take a look inside his gun cabinet. There's likely important evidence in there.' I held up the key.

Shaking his head, Vern jumped back in his ute. 'Nah. I'm not into getting killed. We're leaving. We'll head down south and change our names. Start up somewhere new. Hop in. Quick.' He started the ute and put it in gear with the special lever on his steering wheel.

I clambered in. 'But he could murder half of Rusty

Bore. You'd feel terrible deserting everyone.'

Vern gave me a look that suggested he could tolerate the guilt.

'And Brad's disappeared.' I rustled up some tears, it wasn't hard. 'He's got a burnt arm.' My burnt Bradley would represent easy pickings for your single-minded murderer. 'Please. I'd be terribly grateful.' I sniffed.

'Grateful.' He looked thoughtful. 'Well, we can't stay there long. Anyway, saw Brad driving towards Perry Lake last night.' He pulled the ute out from the kerb. 'Out on my hammock I was, taking the air. Watching this couple of flies. The male, he was going for it...'

I interrupted. 'Why was Brad going to Perry Lake?'

Vern shrugged. 'Had a fella with him.' He kept driving, watching the road.

'What fella? He's in trouble, I knew it.' My voice rose.

Vern glanced at me. 'Trouble? Nah. Brad's a sensible young bloke. Bright sort of fella. Held back by his family, poor kid. Birdwatching, be my bet. It's relaxing for the lad.'

Brad had said, *I'll show you*. That didn't sound like someone planning to wind down with a spot of bird watching. I picked my nails.

Locusts mashed against the windscreen, the bonnet and roof. A row of pulped green corpses on the wipers, spotted wings fluttering in the wind.

'Appreciate your help, Vern.'

'Any time.' A fine-tuning tweak to his groin. 'Thing is, you can't go round nicking people's personal property. There are bloody boundaries.'

'I said I was sorry.' I paused. 'What was in that note-book, anyway?'

'Huh. Don't pretend you didn't read it.'

I shook my head. 'I didn't get a chance. I fell asleep, next I knew I was in hospital. Everything got burnt.' A white lie wouldn't hurt, would help protect Vern's dignity.

He darted me a look. 'You telling me the truth?'

'Of course.' I folded my arms. 'And there was probably something vital in that notebook. You see everything.'

'Yep.'

'Anything stand out? Anything unusual lately?'

'Everything's unusual, when you observe things closely.'

'You see Donald?'

'Nope. Well, only that time he came poking around your place with the girl in tow, like I said.'

'Anyone else?'

'There was that Terry Monaghan. He's been around a bit. You seeing him or something?'

I flushed. 'Yeah. No. Not really. Bastard.'

'Why'd you give him that briefcase then?'

My nail-picking fingers stopped, snap-fossilised. 'What?'

'Saw him waltzing out of your place with a briefcase.' He paused significantly. 'A briefcase he didn't go in there with.'

Terry had nicked the briefcase? From under my nose? And Brad's. Why? For that Monaghan, I'd bet. Aiming to steal the credit from poor Dean. Good thing there was nothing in that case. Served them bloody right.

We arrived at Ernie's shack, the cars still parked outside, Mona's silver Mercedes, Clarence's black Lexus. And now there was another one at the back, a yellow-green Datsun 180B with a faded *Ten things you can do to save the planet* sticker on the back window.

My heart did a little skip. Brad was here! He wasn't

dying on some rain-slicked city street.

I flung the ute door open and hurtled across the sand to the shack.

'Brad,' I croaked, opening the front door, peering into the dim. I had a lot of things to say when he appeared, starting with the apologies. 'Brad?'

Silence.

Marching down the murky hallway, crunching over broken plaster, I peered into every room. Still a mess of torn-up clothes and cases in the bedrooms. No sign of Brad. Still a jumble of knocked-over chairs and smashed-up plates in the kitchen. And those bullet holes in the wall hadn't gone anywhere. 'Brad?'

I stepped outside. *'Bradleeeey.'*

Silence.

Steeling myself, I looked inside Ernie's shed. Empty. Nothing in the bath, no suspect mounds under suspect tarps. I rapped on the door of Ernie's outside loo, opened it. A wooden bracelet, sculpted into waves, lay on the floor. I picked it up and slipped it in my bag.

Brad's car was unlocked. I peered inside, keys in the ignition, binoculars on the seat. Closing the door, I saw big scuff marks in the sand beside the car.

'Brad?'

Just the wind sighing through the pepper trees. On the cracked earth beside the toilet, a wattlebird snapped down on a locust.

Vern and I marched all through the bush around Ernie's shack, searching, calling, searching. Nothing. We headed along the track to Perry Lake, crunching over the sand. I held up a hand to shield my eyes from the sun. Miles of pink–white sand, lapping mauve–brown water, scrappy trees. No sign of Brad. The wind was light, the sky a pale friendly blue, not the kind of day you expect to lose your son.

'Now don't go worrying yourself.' Vern laid his hand on my arm. 'He'll have just nicked out to do a bit of birdwatching and forgot to mention it. You know how engrossed he gets.'

'Without his binoculars?'

Vern paused. 'Yeah. Experts like young Brad don't need binoculars. They know a bird just by the way it hops, flicks its eyelash.' He was working hard to convince himself.

'Do birds even have eyelashes?' I said.

Vern shrugged.

I needed Brad here to clarify.

We headed back to Ernie's shack. Bradley would be all right, of course he would. I stared up at the sky. My legs started shaking, like they had nothing to do with me.

'Now, now,' said Vern. 'You need a little sit down.'

Back inside the shack, my phone rang.

'Jesus, Mum, I leave you for five bloody minutes and you nick off. Where are you?' Dean.

'I'm worried about Brad. His car's here at Ernie's place but there's no sign of him. He's missing. I need you to swing into action. Officially.'

'Do I have to tie you down? Vern'll be here any minute.'

'Vern's with me. Good suggestion of yours that we reconcile. We've sorted it all out. But we need to find Bradley. He's in trouble, I'm sure of it.'

'Uh-huh. Well, put Vern on. If he's really there.'

'Of course he's here. Listen, Dean, you need to hurtle into a missing person's whatsit. Right away.'

'Mum. Monaghan is on my back. Not to mention Superintendent Bartlett. They're all on about misuse of police resources. Brad's just sulking, I tell you. He'll turn up.'

'You'd rather I call Monaghan, register Brad as missing with him?'

Dean sighed. 'All right, if I look for Brad, will you promise to come back? Right away?'

'Of course.' We'd need to rootle in Ernie's gun cabinet first, whatever was in there could help locate Brad. No need to mention that.

'You'll phone me as soon as you find him?' I said. 'Call me in half an hour?'

'Mum, missing persons investigations aren't solved in thirty bloody minutes. It takes time. Bank records, for example...'

'What have bank records got to do with it? You need to get out there and look for Brad. Properly. Helicopters. Tracker dogs. No point wasting time down at the bank.'

'I'm not running around with helicopters, looking into all your stupid fantasies.'

'Brad isn't a fantasy, he's family. And Mona wasn't a fantasy either. She turned out to be dead, didn't she? Won't the Homicide taskforce be arriving any minute? They'll be very concerned about a missing person at a time like this.'

Silence.

'You get out there and find him.' My voice was shaking. 'He's your little brother, for God's sake.'

'You come back here right now.' Dean's voice was a hiss.

'You listen to me...' My face was hot.

Vern grabbed the phone. 'Dean. Vern.' He listened for a while.

I tried to breathe. Would Dean go out and look for Brad at all? Even open his stupid station door?

'Yep, well, I might withdraw the complaint about your mother,' said Vern. More listening. 'I could consider phoning Superintendent Bartlett.' A pause. 'You'll direct the taskforce to my shop? Currently the only shop in Rusty Bore. They'll need a bite to eat.' Vern glanced at me.

If I wasn't so worried, I'd have been gutted about the timing of that taskforce and their hearty bloody appetites.

'We could be a while, your mother and me. Everything's fine, no need to worry. She's in good form. Terrific. We've got a lot of important retail-efficiency arrangements to go

241

over. Probably be away a night or two. Madison'll run the shop for me. She can handle a taskforce. You will tell them to go to my place?'

He handed me the phone. Dean had hung up.

'All fine,' said Vern.

'I liked the bit about the retail arrangements, Vern. Very creative.'

He gave me a sideways look. 'Yep. We'll talk about those. In good time. Maybe tonight, when you're more relaxed. You're a bit too tense at the moment.' He put his hand on my leg, then inched the hand up my thigh, smiling.

My stomach moved uneasily. 'Just remember, I'm deeply vulnerable at the minute. I have a missing son.' I grabbed his hand and put it firmly on the table.

I tried Brad's phone. The call just went to his answerphone again. A tear slipped out.

'There, there.' Vern patted my arm.

I watched his hand carefully.

'Normal to be worried. But Dean'll find him. Now, you'd better tell me exactly what's been going on.'

I blew my nose. 'There's a whole heap that's unresolved.' I ticked the heap off my fingers. 'Why Clarence came here in the first place. Why Mona was killed. Who ripped out the pages of your notebook.'

Vern tensed. Oops. I moved on swiftly. 'Who burned my shop down. How Donald's bird smuggling fits in. What's in the gun cabinet.' I surged out of my chair before Vern had a chance to get started on his notebook. 'Come on. The gun cabinet. Could even be money in there, Vern.'

His eyes narrowed, a money type of narrow.

The gun cabinet was a grey steel affair attached to the

wall. I fiddled with the key, trying to open it. Finally, the door creaked open.

No wads of banknotes, no huge manuscript. No guns either, since Ernie had declared them all years ago under one of those early amnesties.

I reached into the back of the cabinet. There was a tiny something. I took it out and held it up. A computer memory stick.

'That all?' Vern bustled in, started rootling through. In case I'd missed something, I suppose. I didn't like being checked up on like that, but in a way, it was a relief to have someone else to do this with. I'd had enough of being alone, waiting in the dark to be murdered.

Of course, Vern found nothing. Any person knows how to check a gun cabinet.

Vern brought in green tea in tiny cups. I took a sip. Bloody disgusting. 'Very exotic,' I said.

'Yeah, got into green tea in Sarawak,' said Vern. 'I needed to get away from the authorities for a while. Terrific swamps in Sarawak. Nothing better than drinking green tea looking out over a decent bloody swamp. Nothing. Mostly buggered now, of course. Palm oil plantations.' He stared into the distance.

Maybe Sarawak was where he'd lost the arm. Maybe a motorbike mishap in a swamp. Possibly involving a young Malaysian beauty, a tragic story, that'd be why he never talked about it. Poor old Vern. I took another sip of green tea. If I turned off the normal-tea expectations, it wasn't too bad.

I'd never been inside Vern's house in the daylight. It was a whole lot cleaner than I'd expected, with an array of Chinese cabinets in deep red wood. Flinging one open, he

revealed a computer with an enormous screen. Vern probably needed that big screen for the full impact of all his
porn. I wondered if Vern knew about Piero's philandering.

'Vern? You knew Piero pretty well, didn't you?'

Vern glanced at me. He switched on the computer and
slipped in the memory stick, did some busy clicking.

'He tell you stuff?' I said.

'What type of stuff?'

'Personal stuff.' I sipped my tea.

'I'm not one to pry into people's personal lives, you
know that.'

'But you see things. You're observant.'

He hunched forward, peering at the computer screen.

'Piero had another woman, Vern.'

'Yep.'

'And a whole other family.'

'Yep.'

'You don't seem real surprised.'

'Like I said, people aren't always exactly what they
seem.'

'Where is she? This other woman.'

'I wouldn't go there, Cass Tuplin. There's no happiness for you down that path. Seriously. I know how this
story goes.'

I moved in my chair. 'Well, maybe not happiness. But
I've got a right to know.'

'Doesn't mean you need to.'

'Of course I bloody do. Jesus, Vern. My bastard
bloody husband bloody had another woman. And I've
been mourning the bastard every minute of every day
for almost two years. Christ. If my house hadn't burnt
down, I'd slice up his damn photo and fry it.'

'Yep.'

'And you all knew. How long?'

'A while.'

'And you said nothing?'

'Didn't want to hurt you, Cass.'

'Well, who the hell am I supposed to be angry with? A dead husband? The whole town? Myself?'

'Reckon you could take your pick. I tend to go for myself, personally.'

A pause.

'Did something like this happen to you? In those swamps?'

He shrugged. 'Had a few things happen. Now, look at this,' he pointed at the computer screen. 'There's an Excel file called Pocket Money. Clarence's book, you reckon? Strange bloody title. Strange sort of program to write it in as well.'

I peered at the screen. Lots of columns. Rows of numbers. It looked like something from my BAS return. 'Some type of accounting record.'

He leaned closer. 'Look at those names down the left hand side. Dodgy crowd. Logan Mathieson,' he stabbed a thick finger at the screen, 'Shane Yend, Gabbo Ford. All got drug connections, that little lot.'

'Why would this file be locked inside Ernie's cabinet? And the key left lying on the sand?' I said.

'Maybe a swaggie had it.'

'A swaggie with a memory stick wrapped in his swag? Which he put for some unknown reason into Ernie's cabinet? Then dropped the key near Mona's body?' I put down my cup. 'You reckon?'

Vern turned red.

'More likely Clarence nicked this file from Grantley and locked it in the cabinet.'

'Maybe Grantley's got some kind of racket,' said Vern, slowly. 'But Muddy Soak's been crime free since...'

'Yes, yes.' If I heard that one more time.

'It's an impressive record, Cass. That Sarge Monaghan's had a few awards.'

I wasn't interested in discussing Monaghan's awards. 'Reckon we need another visit to Grantley's place.'

He nodded; a rare event, someone agreeing with me.

'We'll take Ernie. He'll enjoy it.' Ernie would be essential, I was sure of it. Anyway, no more of the friendless routine. I'd take anyone I could get.

'Plus,' Vern's voice was low, 'Ernie's not bad behind a gun.'

I explained to Taylah that Ernie had to go to Muddy Soak for a while. 'A funeral,' I said into the phone. I used my Sunday-best doleful tone. 'Old friend of his.'

Taylah gasped. 'His friend wasn't murdered, was he?'

'No, no, nothing like that.'

'It's just terrible, that poor woman in the wool bag. I can't believe we're losing Dean, as well. We could all be murdered in our beds.'

'Don't worry, Taylah. They won't let Dean go, I'm sure of it.'

'You wanna collect your tickets? Moisy dropped them in,' she said. 'For the Muddy Soak Christmas Fringe Festival. Starts tomorrow.'

'Ah. Yep.'

'It's so exciting! All those *artistes* in Muddy Soak! I just hope none of them get murdered.'

247

'Now, now, no one will be murdered, Taylah.'

Wet sounds while Taylah worked her chewing gum. 'So who is it? This friend of Ernie's?'

'Awfully tragic,' I stalled. 'And sudden.'

'Uh huh?' A pause.

'Fella he knew from the war.' I had a moment of inspiration. 'No one local. Stanley Robbins. Lived down south. Nice bloke. Always wore a tie. Fell out the back of an Armaguard van, doing up his tie, would you believe. Hit his head and died.'

'Armaguard van?'

'Haven't got time to go into it all right now, Taylah. I've got flowers to organise. I'll be in to collect Ernie tomorrow morning. Don't be surprised if he doesn't seem to remember Stanley. You know what Ernie's like.'

I spent the night on Vern's couch, ignoring his offers to share his bed. After breakfast—muesli, starfruit and yet more green tea—we set off to pick up Ernie from the home.

Ernie was waiting in his room, dressed in a carefully ironed khaki shirt and matching shorts. He looked like one of those aged birdwatchers Brad is fond of bringing into my shop. The type that launches into earnest debates about sixth extinctions and carbon miles. Launched. Back when I had a shop.

'Managed to free up the diary,' Ernie brushed down his khaki. 'And a trip will do you good, Cassandra Ariadne. Might even find yourself someone. Don't know what you've been doing all these flamin' years. High time you found a fella, one that doesn't need too much improving and comes without a lot of debt.'

Ernie gathered up the tools he'd laid out on his bed: a hammer, some pliers, a crowbar, wire cutters, a hip flask, skeleton keys, a stethoscope. He crammed them all into a bag and hung it on his walker. I don't know how he got that stuff past Taylah.

We walked slowly down the corridor, and I reminded Ernie of Piero, since he seemed to have forgotten my marriage. I was starting to wonder if I'd be better off forgetting it myself.

He stopped a moment. 'Piero Tuplin? You want to marry him? Well, if you want my opinion, I'm dead against it. He'll be a faithless bastard. Stay right away from him, Cassandra Ariadne.' He stamped ahead.

He struggled into Vern's van, took off his hat, then stared out the windscreen, clicking his false teeth.

I felt a faint swell of pride as I looked around at our little group. We'd become our own version of the Fantastic Four, minus Brad unfortunately. Minus the superpowers bit too, of course. Vern took off at top speed, resting his arm stump on the window ledge.

As anyone will tell you, there's a lot an able, or reasonably able, group can achieve without any bloody superpowers.

I watched the world roll past while Vern drove. Salt haze trailed silver above a dry lake. A distant row of power lines, milky through the glaze. I wound down my window, ran my fingers through the curtain of hot air. I wasn't happy, not exactly, not with Brad missing and my house and shop burnt down and the humiliation thanks to Piero, but somehow, I felt free. On the loose.

Pocket money. Presumably Grantley wasn't paying money to those people. They'd be paying him. His pocket money.

'We'll need to interrogate Grantley,' I said. 'And maybe visit the people on the list.'

'We can't put you in danger, Cass,' said Ernie, leaning forward in his seat. 'You haven't even met a fella yet. No, I vote we bring Dean into the operation.'

Vern nodded.

So much for democracy. Terribly inefficient, democracy. No one ever mentions that. 'Here's the plan,' I said. 'Vern, your job is to distract Grantley while Ernie and I search his premises. You've always been good at extracting information without people knowing what you're up to.'

'Dunno how I'll distract him, though.'

'He's a reformed gambler. Tell him there's a terrific gambling loophole you've just found. A not-quite-right pokie you've found at the Muddy Soak RSL. It spills out all its money when you press a certain button.'

'Nah. No one would share that kind of knowledge. He'll be suspicious. And the RSL would fix that machine pronto, can't let a profit margin leak away.'

'Well, OK, how about you're an old mate of his brother, Kev. You don't know he's dead. Kev's got something of yours and you want it back. A book, a footy jumper, a DVD of something dodgy. You'll have to act all amazed and sad when he tells you Kev's dead. But you've always been a good actor.'

Vern grunted. I took that as assent, and dialled Dean's number.

'Yes Mum. I am, in fact, looking for Brad. Right now. I'm at Ernie's shack.'

'And the helicopters?'

'I don't need my mother to help me organise a missing persons search. Look, there's a lot of footprints around

Brad's car. I'm taking photos, measurements, all that. Or would be if you'd get off the phone.'

'Terrific, son.' I hung up.

I filled in Vern and Ernie.

'Good old Dean,' said Vern. 'Vital development, footprints.'

I stared out the window a tick, at the puffs of dry fairy grass on the fractured soil.

'As long as Brad turns up OK,' I said.

'Course he will,' said Ernie. 'And everyone knows how critical footprints are in your average criminal investigation. How many crooks don't leave a flamin' footprint? They can't help it, they all have feet.'

Grantley's mother, Mrs Pittering, must have been around ninety. She was bone-thin, her white hair worn in a wispy ponytail. She was in an emerald green silk outfit, her mouth a gash of red lipstick. 'Grantley isn't here. He has...an appointment at the RSL.' Her blue-veined hand was tensed on the door, ready to swing it closed.

Vern spoke. 'After Kev, actually. Friend of his. Vern Casey. Passing through the Soak with my colleague here, Dr Tuplin. She's an expert on historic homes, here to tour Hocking Hall. This is her uncle, Ernie. Anyway, thought I'd look up Kev while we're here.' Vern smiled a tooth-filled smile.

'Kevin passed away.' She moved to close the door.

Vern organised an ashen face. 'I didn't know. Been away.' He even managed some tears.

'There, there,' she patted his arm. 'Perhaps you'll come in?'

We trooped inside. I was worried about this Dr Tuplin

role, about Vern's too-inventive faculties. It wouldn't have hurt to have warned me. Just a few short words to assist a fellow-conspirator.

Mrs Pittering led us down the hallway, into a lounge room. Not the kind of lounge I was expecting, not what I'd call a normal old-lady lounge. No brown velvet armchairs or hypnotic ticking clock. The lime green carpet was covered with broken glass. One wall had been sprayed with graffiti. Tall red letters, spelling words some old ladies would profess they didn't know. Arranged across the room were three rows of plastic chairs, each containing a dead hand. The wall beside me was lined with decapitated heads on sticks, twisted faces full of pain.

We stood there in gob-smacked silence.

Mrs Pittering didn't seem to notice, just silk-rustled out to make some tea.

We found three chairs without dead hands and carefully sat.

'Milk and sugar?' Mrs Pittering put her head around the door. She saw us staring at the heads on sticks. 'Oh, don't worry, they're not real.'

I nodded.

'It's for the festival. We're envisioning and manifesting an immersion play.'

'I see,' I said, not seeing.

'The audience will be immersed in crime. Not real-time crime, unfortunately, but we've worked hard to do our best.'

'Very nice,' murmured Vern.

'Bloody creative.' Ernie leaned forward on his walker.

'It's a portal to the experiences of those in other towns, towns that aren't crime free.' Her voice had a hint of smug. She rustled back into the kitchen.

Ernie had been staring at the mantelpiece behind the heads, at a row of photos. He got up and shuffled closer. One young and lovely woman in a bathing suit, circa 1950, signed in the corner. A more recent photo of four young men in footy jumpers. Red and blue, Muddy Soak–Patchemilda colours. I picked out a young Dale Monaghan, then Terry, younger, thinner. There was a third bloke who looked like a shorter, dark-haired version of Grantley with a twisted nose. Kev? The fourth man looked familiar, but I couldn't place him. They stood in a row, muddy-kneed, all with their arms around each other.

Mrs Pittering came in with a tray. Vern surged forward to assist, earning him a red-gashed smile. She sat and poured tea into dainty, gold-rimmed cups.

Clearing his throat, Ernie said, 'Gladys Wilson!'

I'd never heard him so excited.

'I suspected when I first saw you, and that photo there confirms it.' He pointed at the mantelpiece. 'It was you who kept me going in 1944, love.'

She smiled. 'It's been quite a while since anyone called me Gladys Wilson.'

Ernie snickered. 'They didn't show all their bosoms…'

'Anyway,' I said. 'Thank you for the tea. Especially since you must be so busy at the moment.' I waved my hand at the sticks.

A pause.

'Where did you meet Kevin? In Bendigo?' she said to Vern.

'That's right,' he beamed. 'Through a mutual friend. Soon worked out we had a lot in common, me and Kev.'

'Acting? You'd get a lot of leading parts, good-looking man like you.'

Vern smiled. 'It was Kev who truly had the leading-man looks. Everyone told him so.'

'Really?' She looked puzzled, then sighed. 'He was a terribly gifted actor. He could have done anything.'

'He must have been a clever fellow,' I said, 'good at both acting and accounting.'

'Kevin never wanted to be an accountant, it was his father who insisted on it.' A tear slid down her cheek.

I reached out, patted her hand. 'You mustn't blame yourself, it's not your fault.'

She wiped her face angrily. 'Of course it's not my fault.' A pause. 'Kevin was murdered.'

'I thought the official verdict was...' I shut my mouth suddenly. I wasn't supposed to have heard about Kev's death. But Gladys wasn't listening.

'An accident, they said. But there is not the slightest chance that Kevin would have wanted to, would have done, would have...And ivory organza? How ridiculous. Kevin detested polyester.' She sniffed.

'Did you let the police know your concerns?' said Vern.

'Of course. And Dale investigated it personally. He was always terribly good to Kevin. He was such a support for him, after that little motoring misunderstanding. But Dale said he'd looked and he could find no evidence of murder.'

Vern nodded.

'My poor Kevin had just been offered a part he really wanted. A terrific play, in Sydney. He was finally going places.'

'His wife must have been pleased for him,' I said.

'Kevin wasn't married.'

'You'll have to forgive my colleague,' Vern said. 'Terribly nosy, writers. Part of the job description. She doesn't mean anything by it.'

She sniffed. 'What do you write, Dr Tuplin?'

My stomach did a little whirl. I gabbled, 'I'm writing a series of romances set in Australia's historic houses. And of course, Hocking Hall, being as it is, well, as you know...'

'I see.' She sipped her tea.

Cringing at my forlorn lie, I shot a look at Vern, but he just nodded as if everything was following his carefully plotted plan.

'Kev must've inherited his artistic streak from you,' said Vern, pointing at the heads on sticks. 'I'm sorry I missed the funeral. I'll bet it was a big crowd, he was such a popular fella.'

'Yes, he had many friends.'

'I should call in on some of them, pay my respects. Not sure if I remember many surnames, though. It's been a while. There was this one fella he used to mention...'

'Terry? Or perhaps Dale. He spent a lot of time with his cousins.' She waved a hand at the photo of the four footballers.

I peered at it. 'Is that Kev on the left? What a...handsome young man. Who's the other boy on the right?'

'Ford Hocking-Lee.' She looked at me with suspicious eyes. 'Don't you know him, Dr Tuplin? He was Mona Hocking-Lee's son.'

'Well, my focus has really been on the building,' I said, 'and the complexities of my storyline, not so much on the Hocking-Lees, not as such.' Now I thought about it, he did have Clarence's weaselly chin. 'The four boys are close?'

'Only two of those boys are alive today.' She sighed.

'Dale and Terry. Poor dear Mona. No mother wants to outlive her son. Not that Ford was...'

Ernie had been looking at Gladys in a dazed fashion. Now he leaned forward. 'That fella give you trouble? Attractive woman like you might have a bit of trouble.'

'Well...I never trusted him. I was worried he was a bad influence on Kevin. Little Kevin was easily led. I know how hard Mona tried with Ford. And then, of course, he died so tragically. With his young wife, in that traffic accident.'

'No,' I breathed.

She stiffened. 'You're not some kind of reporter? They're circling the town, since poor Mona was found.'

Vern reassured her, I reassured her, Ernie tut-tutted about the true evils of gutter journalism from across his walking frame. 'Gladys Wilson,' said Ernie. 'I don't suppose...' he paused.

'Yes?' she smiled.

'You probably get asked this all the time. But I'd love an autographed copy of one of your terrific photographs. Bloody patriot, you were.'

She beamed, got up and opened a drawer. Returning with a photo, she handed it to Ernie. In black and white, she sat against a striped beach ball, her fair hair streaming around her face. No heads on sticks anywhere near her back then.

Ernie and I sat on the bench outside the RSL, trying to look normal, trying to blend in. Red posters of the Christmas Fringe Festival were hanging from poles, glued to walls, displayed in every shop window. Endless drifts of shoppers inched along the street.

'That Pitterline bastard disappeared with my money, you know,' Ernie said to no one in particular. A CFA truck with Santa ho-ho-ing on the back sailed past.

'Yep.' I watched the door of the RSL, fretting over Brad, chewing a fingernail. The sky was a hard dark blue, black clouds on the horizon.

'Bloody oath. Owed me sixty dollars.' Ernie stabbed a bone-like finger in the air. 'Buggered off to the Northern Territory. 19-bloody-88. Shit year in a shitty decade.'

My phone rang. 'Brad! Where are you?' I said.

'Pittering.' His voice had a nasty, choking sound. The phone crackled.

'Where are you? Are you OK?'

'...locked me in...' More crackling.

'Where? Locked you in where?'

The wind wrapped an empty Twisties packet around my feet.

'I'm hanging...' something garbled.

'Hanging?' My voice rose.

'...middle...low...send help. Quick.' The phone cut out.

'Brad? Can you hear me?'

Silence.

'Brad?'

I dialled his number. My hands were shaking.

My call went to his answerphone. I tried three times, then waved my phone wildly at Ernie, as if that might make it work.

'Whole century was crap, you know. And Hugo flaming Pitterline...'

'Shut up, Ernie!'

I called Dean. 'He's locked inside somewhere,' I said. 'Hanging. In terrible danger. You have to *do* something.'

'Whoa, stop yelling, Mum. What are you talking about?'

'Brad, for God's sake.'

'Where is he?'

'I don't know. Why I am always expected to know every single thing? You're the bloody cop. Get out there and find him.'

'All right, calm down. Leave it with me. Where are you, anyway?'

'Be back soon.' I hung up.

I sat vice-tight on my hands. 'Brad's in danger and it's all my fault.'

'Can't believe you told me to shut up. And after everything I've done for you,' said Ernie.

'He told me not to get involved in this.' My voice was croaky.

'Help a person out, and that's the thanks I get.' Ernie shook his head. 'I spent years telling all those hanger-on women that Piero had something nasty.'

'Ernie. Please. I need to think.' I stood up, paced along the pavement. I should have let Brad waste his life with all those banners. It might have been a waste, but at least he'd be alive.

I stared up at the darkening sky, hoping I'd find some kind of answer. I set my shoulders. Pittering, Brad had said. Grantley, surely. 'We'll get that devious bastard Grantley to talk,' I said.

'Piero's got a weepy little infection, I told them, every one of them,' said Ernie. 'And now you just tell me to shut up. Brutal way to treat a fella in my time of life.'

When Grantley stepped out through the doors of the RSL, Vern was by his side. They wove a zig-zag line along the path towards us. Vern slipped his arm through Grantley's as they got closer.

I gave Ernie a nod. He stepped over to them, jabbing two fingers held together, into Grantley's back. Ernie's fingers are old-bone and icy, not a bad impression of cold steel.

'Hey?' said Grantley, staggering.

'Shut up and keep walking.' Ernie kept his voice dark and low.

Grantley's face turned grey. 'Look, I don't have any money, mate.'

'Keep quiet, and you'll live. We're walking to that nice park ahead. At a normal pace. Smiling.'

I marched on the other side of Grantley, hemming him in. Oblivious Christmas shoppers parted like the Red Sea around us. Grantley's face glistened.

The park was the huge, green kind that attracts the relaxed family visitor. I guided our little group towards an old Telecom shed, away from any happy families.

'Face the wall,' I growled. Not a tone of voice I'd used before. I sounded like Clint Eastwood. Vern held Grantley's arms up against the wall.

'Don't kill me.' Grantley's voice was shaky.

'Tell us what you've done with Bradley,' I said, 'and you won't get hurt.'

'Who's Bradley?'

'You bloody well know who Bradley is. Where is he?'

He swallowed. 'I know that voice. You're that woman who came to my office. Who *are* you?'

'You don't need to know. What have you done to my son?'

'Me?' His voice was a squeak. 'I haven't done anything to anyone.'

'Decent people stand up to hooligans, Grantley. Now, a woman has been murdered. That's not acceptable. And three people are missing. Including my son. And it all comes back to you. Where is he?'

'I don't know. Honestly.' Grantley started crying.

I wasn't going to let some blubbing get to me. Conniving, murderous bastard.

'I'll report you to the police. This is harassment.'

'Maybe he really doesn't know,' whispered Vern.

I shot Vern a warning look. 'You know something,

Grantley, even if you don't know—you know. So spill it.'

He stood there, head slumped against the wall.

Maybe I needed to be more specific. 'Brad's locked up somewhere. Hanging.' My voice choked up.

'God, you must be worried,' said Grantley.

A silence while I digested that. This was one crafty masterminding murderous type, offering sympathy like that.

'I am,' I said, snappy. 'Now, what's the Pocket Money bank account about?'

'The what?'

Vern twisted his arm.

'I don't know! Honest, I'd tell you if I did.'

Vern twisted harder.

Grantley cried out. 'All I know is...Kev wouldn't let me near it. Or anything.'

'Go on. You have my interest.'

'Junior partner, supposedly, but I knew nothing about the stupid business. It was a nightmare after he died. Took me ages to unravel things. Still haven't managed to.'

'Get to the point.' Ernie jabbed his fingers harder into Grantley's back.

Grantley cringed against the wall. 'Kev never took a holiday. Couldn't be out of the office, he had to control every little detail. Then last year he got the flu and couldn't get out of bed. I had to run the place on my own. Someone rang, asking about the Pocket Money account. I'd never heard of it. I went round, woke up Kev and asked him. "I'll deal with it," he said. Stared at me with big eyes. "You stay right out of it," he told me. Kev didn't trust me to do anything.'

'Get to the point,' I said.

'Christ, I'm telling you, OK? I was offended, naturally. I stamped off. Perhaps I should have asked him all about it. If I'd known I'd be held at gunpoint later on, obviously I would have.' He squealed as Vern twisted his arm another notch.

'Pitterlines never think, they're all the same,' muttered Ernie.

'What does Clarence have to do with the account?' I said.

'Clarence? Nothing.' He paused. 'Although he seemed to know all about it, that day he left. Strange. I'd never mentioned it.'

'So why did you kill Mona Hocking-Lee?' I said.

'What? I wouldn't...I couldn't...Look, you've got the wrong person. Honest.'

'Well, who is the right bloody person?' I snapped.

'I'm telling you, I don't know.' His shoulders shook.

'Reckon he might be telling the truth, Cass,' whispered Vern.

All of a sudden there was the sound of clapping. I whirled around. A huge crowd had gathered behind us. Christ, there must have been half of Muddy Soak out here on the street.

'Bravo,' a man shouted.

'Really professional,' called a woman. 'You must come back for next year's festival.'

Shaking off our adoring fans, we climbed into Vern's ute and charged back to Rusty Bore. I watched the telephone poles flash past, worrying. Stressing over Brad. The moon was a white disc rising over the Dooboobetic Hills.

Vern looked grim. Ernie was the only one in an upbeat mood, pleased with the newly discovered power of his fingers. We weren't any closer to locating Brad. Was Grantley, nerdy mastermind, just putting on a brilliant show to deceive us? He'd told us he'd need trauma counselling, as we left. 'And I'll be sending you the invoice,' he shouted, hoarse-voiced, crowd still clapping.

Maybe Kev had been blackmailing people around the Soak. And someone had got sick of it. 'We should talk to some of the people on the Pocket Money list,' I said.

'Dangerous lot there, Cass Tuplin. Reckon we'll need Dean along,' said Vern.

Ernie set off on another rant about Hugo Pitterline, so I didn't bother asking him.

I dialled Dean's station. 'You found Bradley yet?'

Silence at the other end.

'Dean?'

'Sergeant Monaghan speaking. How can I help you?'

'Where's Dean?'

'Who is this, please?'

'Dean's mother, Cass Tuplin.' That man knew my voice, he just wanted to annoy me. 'Shouldn't you be out helping look for Bradley?'

'Calm down, Mrs Tuplin. Senior Constable Tuplin is following up a lead near Bendigo. We're doing everything we can to locate your son.'

'Bendigo? What's he doing there? What about those footprints? I'll call him now and get him organised.'

'Mrs Tuplin!' His voice was tight and hard. 'This station is now under my jurisdiction, and I don't permit inter-ference.' He paused. 'Where are you? We don't want you in danger.'

None of his business. 'Visiting relatives.'

'Good. Stay indoors. Remain calm. And I must ask you not to bother the senior constable. I'm sure you don't want to have any further negative influence on his career. We'll call you once we have any information.'

I considered interrupting to tell him about the Pocket Money account, but somehow I wasn't in the mood. And he'd hung up.

'I bet he's sent Dean off on some wild bloody irrel-evancy,' I told Vern. 'Getting him out of the way, so Monaghan can hog all the admiration for those footprints. It was Dean who found them.'

'That Sarge Monaghan knows what he's doing,' said Vern. 'Got a whole swag of awards, that bloke. He'll find Brad.'

I stared out the window, hoping Vern was right, that Monaghan would find Brad.

I called Dean's mobile. No answer. Probably out of range. There's a lot of black spots en route to Bendigo.

Vern insisted we crash the night at his place. It was too late to take Ernie back to the home and I didn't fancy camping out in Dean's cell, especially with Monaghan around.

Vern rustled up a deeply vegetarian pasta dish, and more green tea. We sat and brooded around his kitchen table.

'So what was on those ripped-out pages in your notebook, Vern?'

He scratched his thigh. 'Main event that day was the woman who bought the bag.'

'You reckon she ran Donald off the road? Got him drunk? After tempting him with her charms?' I said.

'Not a woman with surplus charms. Definitely not a looker, poor bloody woman.'

'Donald must have known something. What could he have known?'

None of us had answers.

Once again I dodged Vern's offer to share his bed and set myself up on the couch. He ended up with Ernie in his bed. Vern didn't look too pleased about that but, as I pointed out, we couldn't expect Ernie to sleep on a couch at his time of life.

I lay there under Vern's spare blanket, worrying. Ernie and Vern snored in the room next door, out of sync. I closed my eyes but couldn't sleep. I just kept seeing footprints. Footprints in the orange sand around Brad's car, footprints in the pink sand at Perry Lake, around Mona's body.

There'd been heaps of footprints around her body. Those ravens had been hopping all around them, looking for grisly bits of her to peck. Footprints that broke through the surface crust of pale pink, to the deeper orange-pink, and then black mud, below. There was something about those footprints.

I closed my eyes, drifting in and out of sleep. Dreams of footprints, left and right. Rows and rows of footprints in the sand. Shallow, deep, shallow, deep.

I jerked awake. The footprints around Mona's body: they'd been like that. Alternating deep and shallow imprints.

No point phoning Dean, neck-deep in irrelevancies in Bendigo. I called Monaghan.

'You'd better sit down, Sergeant Monaghan. I've got surprising news for you.' I may have sounded a little satisfied, no one's perfect after all.

'Mrs Tuplin? You do realise it's two o'clock in the morning?'

'Listen, your brother's involved in Mona's murder. His footprints were around her body.'

Silence.

'His limping footprints. All over the place.'

'Look, Mrs Tuplin, I know how you, ah, imagine things.'

'I didn't imagine those footprints. I saw them. I'll bet you Terry's involved in the Pocket Money account. He's got some protection racket going.' I remembered Terry had told me he did a bit of this and that.

'The what account?'

I explained about the memory stick.

'Well, no one should ever underestimate your tenacity.'

Tenacity. I didn't mind that.

'This is a serious allegation, Mrs Tuplin. Listen, I know it's late, but can you meet me? We can't afford to delay, this may be why your son has disappeared. Bring the memory stick, we'll need that.' His voice was different. At last, a bit of respect.

'Where?'

He paused. 'Meet me at the silos. We'll go to Mr Jefferson's shack and re-examine the footprints around Bradley's car.'

I tiptoed out of Vern's, the back door creaking as I opened it. I froze, but the snoring symphony carried on.

I should have known all along it was Terry. I'd allowed myself to get distracted for too long by that Donald. Terry had been on the spot, at Ernie's shack, that morning we'd found Mona. And he'd nicked the briefcase from my house.

The roadside was grey in the moonlight, the silos tall black shadows against the sky. I marched along the road. And to think I'd slept with Terry! Allowed myself to imagine a little takeaway-wood-carving future by the sea together. What self-respecting person sleeps with a killer? Probably the same one who drifted through all those trusting, gullible years of marriage to an adulterous, cheating bloody bastard. My cheeks burned hot.

Definitely no need to involve Vern and Ernie. Or anyone from Rusty Bore.

I slogged along the road. A mopoke let out a hooting call. Really, Monaghan was the one to blame, if you thought about it. So obsessed with correct procedure and his stupid multiple awards. Muddy Soak: crime free since 1988. Yeah, right. He should have been misusing some police resources himself to investigate his family. You need to pay careful attention to your relatives.

I turned onto the track towards the silos. Car headlights flicked on. Monaghan was already here and waiting, then. He was efficient when he got motivated, I'd give him that. He wouldn't be real happy either with this turn of events. It wouldn't help his career when it came out he had a murderer for a brother. He'd need his own transfer, pronto. And how many towns would welcome a new cop with a serial killer in the family? Vic Police would have to boot him out, more than probably.

Poor bloody Monaghan. He'd be flicked off to some far-flung roadhouse. If he didn't shoot himself. I felt an annoying spark of sympathy. Maybe I'd have to offer some last-minute counselling to prevent his desperate suicide.

My feet crunched on the gravel. From here, the silos blotted out the sky. There'd be a policing gap in Muddy Soak, once Monaghan shot himself. Could be a Dean-sized gap. If they didn't promote him straight up into Homicide. I cheered up a bit.

The moon moved behind a cloud. I made my way through the bits of broken glass and discarded wrappers, towards the headlights. We'd have to find that woman, the one who bought the wool bag. No doubt some naive and unsuspecting female, one of Terry's assorted women from around the state. Maybe even poor old Mona was a love interest. Yep, if I'd been fooled (only momentarily, of course, I always knew there was something not quite right about Terry), there'd be plenty of other sharp-witted women taken in as well.

There'd be some poor old thing he'd convinced to buy the bag. The old bag. Hang on, that text. *Got the old bag. Now what am I supposed to do?* I stopped, dazzled in the headlights. Why had Terry asked Monaghan that?

The headlights clicked off.

A whack to my stomach. I staggered forward, winded. A push from behind and I pitched face first onto the gravel. Snatching a breath, I surged up from the ground. A torch blinded me. I kicked towards the light, hit something soft. A muffled shriek of pain. I started running, but then tripped. Hands grabbed my shoulders. Three cracks across my face with something hard. Warm liquid running down my cheek.

My arms were yanked, held tight as someone tied my hands behind my back. I tried screaming but all that came out was a winded gasp. He flipped me over like a chicken on a chopping board. Roughly taped my mouth.

Something pointy jabbed against my head. A cold, metallic kind of pointy. Definitely not a finger.

'I'll have the memory stick, thank you.' Monaghan's voice, short of breath. The light was above his face like a miner's torch. Searching my pockets with one hand, gun against my head, he took out the memory stick. 'Good.' He started dragging me across the gravel.

I stood, wobbling. Aimed another kick.

A deafening gunshot roar. He shoved me onto my knees, jabbed the gun against my forehead. 'You want me to shoot you?'

I shook my head. I felt dizzy.

He dragged me across the gravel.

'You're disappointed,' he said. 'Of course. But you won't be for long. And you'll be relieved to hear I know where Bradley is.'

My breath came in quick pants.

We were heading towards the silos, denser black ahead.

'Bradley was just as nosy as you. I don't like people nosing around in my financial dealings.'

Was? My knees liquefied.

'So many accidents in silos, aren't there? Young people looking for adventure...so many tragic deaths. And a woman your age should really know better than to climb inside a silo. Looking for your son, we'll all suppose. She always was mentally unstable.'

I gagged against the tape.

'Such a shame to have you silenced, Mrs Tuplin, I will miss all your witty conversation.'

Sarcastic bastard. The anger pumped the blood back into my legs.

'But you'd be a screamer, I can tell. Kev was a screamer. You know, I'm a modest man, with modest needs. I don't ask much. Just a small levy from those who break the law. No town is actually crime free, of course. But it's not that hard to keep things in order. All it takes is a little entrepreneurial spirit. And a decent accountant to keep track of things.'

The Pocket Money account was Monaghan's?

'I do prefer things organised.'

Grantley's parrot. *Organised, Kev, I need things bloody organised.*

'And I don't need some complete dickhead thinking he'll write a book about it. Well, he's been dealt with. Shame his nanna got in the way. There's only you left now, since you survived the fire.' He gave a short laugh. 'You won't survive this.'

We were at the middle silo. *Middle...lo,* Brad had said. *Hanging.*

'We're going to climb.'

A cold wave surged in my stomach.

Monaghan untied my hands with one hand, keeping the gun pressed against my head. Our feet clanked on the metal rungs, his breathing below, a step away.

In one swift movement, I tried stamping on his fingers. Another gunshot ripped the air.

'Next bullet is for you. No more warnings.'

I kept climbing, my ears buzzing.

At the top, the wind tugged my dress. The moon came out. We were high above the railway line. I clung to the metal bar while the world swirled below.

'Open it,' he waved his gun at the hatch.

I shook my head.

He pressed the gun against my head. 'Open it or I'll shoot you.'

I stayed put, clinging to the metal bar. A dull thudding in my head. Monaghan wouldn't shoot me. He needed my death to seem like an accident.

He gave an impatient little sigh.

'Plan A, Mrs Tuplin, is your tragic fall into the silo. But don't worry, I've got my Plan B organised.' He pushed the gun harder against my head. 'Plan B involves a bullet. And a burial. A private one. Just you and me.'

The hatch door was cold and heavy, my hands slippery with blood. I was too slow. When he whacked my face with the gun, my lip split but it didn't make me any faster. I wiped my hands on my dress and pulled at the door with a muffled grunt. Finally it opened with a metal-on-metal clang and a gust of too-warm air. I peered inside, holding onto the bar. Dark air filled with dust. A gut-wrenching stench of something dead. I gagged.

I ripped the tape from my mouth, screamed, turned towards him, kicked out. Monaghan smashed the gun underneath my chin, knocking me off-balance. I scrabbled to stay upright and grabbed at his long coat. He toppled towards me. I snatched at the rail, but with a twosome-wild-wail, we fell through the opening, into the dusty void of putrid air.

I fell for what seemed forever, scrabbling at the air. *Whack*, I landed hip-first on something squishy. Grain? No one ever mentions grain is squishy. I lay there a moment, winded, a dull thudding in my head. Black all around, just a square of moonlit sky above. It looked a long way up, that small square.

This would be my end, then. In a stinking, dusty silo. Monaghan would probably shoot me, then the grain would swallow my remains. A song popped into my head. 'Lost in Love' by Air Supply. I shook my head, feeling sick. But the lyric kept going round and round in my head. Jesus, I refuse to die with 'Lost in Love' my final bloody thought. Come on, move, Cass.

I felt around, then shrieked. A lifeless arm was sticking out from under me. On the other side, another one. Was that the something squishy? A body? I'd landed on a body? Agh. Holding my breath, I carefully rolled off.

I pant-gagged in the stench. Was it someone dead? I touched a wrist, felt for a pulse. How's a person supposed to know where to find a bloody pulse? I whimpered. Helen Keller could recognise people just by feeling their face. I ran my fingers over the eyes, nose and cheeks. No idea. Down over the collar. Leather. Lots of leather. A two-cow leather coat.

I snuffled, cowering back. I darted out a hand, looking for his gun. No go. I flapped my hand around on the grain. Bingo. I stuffed the gun deep inside my knickers. Grabbing his torch, I waved it at his face. His eyes were closed. Was that a flicker in his eyelid?

'Mum?' A whisper from above. 'Is that you snuffling and whimpering down there?'

'Brad!' I flicked the torch up. Brad was suspended from something by his belt. Not the most dignified of positions. But alive.

'You OK, Mum?' He spoke in an urgent whisper.

'Nothing broken.' I gagged again on the gut-wrenching stink. 'Monaghan's here with me though. I'm not sure if he's dead or just unconscious.'

'Jesus! We've got to get out of here. Stand on the grain. Reach up. I'll hang down and grab your hands. If you unhook my belt, maybe we can reach the hatch.'

'The wheat will swallow me if I stand,' I wailed.

'That's just a myth. It only does that if the auger's going, when they pump out the grain. Wheat's solid as the ground otherwise.'

'What about *McLeod's* bloody *Daughters,* son? That whatsername, blonde woman, nearly died. Lucky that good-looking fella swept her up into his arms at the last moment. What was his name...' I coughed.

'Focus, Mum! That was probably canola. Grab my hands.'

I stood, waved around, felt his warm hands.

'What's that awful smell, Brad?'

'You don't want to know.' He grunted, our hands slipping as he tried to lift my weight.

'Yes, I do.'

'I'll tell you when we get out of here.' More grunting.

My feet were still on the wheat. 'I don't think this plan's working.'

I let go, flopping back onto the grain.

'I'll phone Dean.' But Monaghan had my phone. I held my breath, felt around his pockets. A phone. Mine, mangled from the fall. I pressed buttons. Nothing. I grabbed his phone and stabbed at it. *Enter PIN.*

'Any idea of Monaghan's PIN?' I whispered.

Brad groaned.

'Your phone, Brad?'

'Out of battery.'

'Ah.' Blood trickled into my eyes. I wiped it away. 'Listen, we'll be fine. We'll just wait a bit. Sun'll be up any minute. Be heaps of people here when it gets light. We'll shout for help. And Monaghan *is* dead, I'm sure of it.' Fairly sure.

Brad slumped from his beam like a disheartened bat. In the torchlight, I could see his arm was still in the sling and his face was bruised. His trousers were hauled half-way up his back.

It was long past time for a little mother-reunited-with-her-bruised-son dialogue. If I could have reached him, I'd have wrapped him in a hug. 'I'm sorry, son.'

'What for?'

'For everything. For getting you into all this.' My voice was croaky.

'Oh, Mum. I got myself into it. I was angry with Dean.'

'Dean was plain wrong, Bradley. You could do anything if you put your mind to it.'

'Maybe.' He grunted, trying to ease his trousers.

'What happened, how did you get in here?' I said.

'I knew I'd seen a car outside the shop the night of the fire. Terry's ute.'

I sucked in another breath of putrid air. 'Is that smell a dead kangaroo?'

'No.' He paused. 'And I wasn't going to Monaghan, not after that dismal interview. Or Dean. I went to Terry.'

'Christ. Is the stink Terry?'

'Will you stop interrupting? I told him I had something that could help his brother's investigation.'

He cried out.

'Brad? You all right?'

'I think my trousers are ripping.'

'Well, we're all in a bit of discomfort here. No point moaning. Anyway. The smell?' I flicked the torch around.

'If you'll just bloody listen.'

Dead rats maybe. Have to be one big heap of rats to make a smell this gigantic.

'I guessed the key you found might fit something at Ernie's shack. So I told Terry we should go there and search. When we arrived, Monaghan was waiting. He slapped a pair of handcuffs on me and dragged me to his car. Terry seemed as shocked as I was.'

'He's a little Oscar-winner, that Terry.'

Brad grunted, fiddling with his trousers. 'So Monaghan drove and they started arguing. Terry's going, "How many will it take, Dale? How many more body bags do I have to buy?" He started saying he should never have got involved and from here on, Monaghan could count him out. Said he was reporting him to Dean.'

Wait. Terry was the woman?

'Then Monaghan pulled the car over, reached across and smashed Terry's face. He said, "Too late, mate." Terry went quiet after that. Monaghan dropped him off, then brought me here.' Brad sighed. 'I tried to run, Mum, but...And I lost half my trousers. Pathetic.'

'No way, son. You were brilliant.'

'Really?'

'Yep. Bloody courageous.'

'Must run in the family then.'

'Thanks.' I choked up. Probably something to do with the terrible smell.

'Yes, you might be misguided, reckless and naive, but you're definitely courageous, Mum.'

I lay on the grain soaking up our rosy moment. Apart from being trapped inside a silo with a dead-slash-unconscious murderer and a stomach-churning smell, this was quite possibly the best day of my life. The square of sky above softened to the pale grey of dawn.

'And the stink?' I said.

'Clarence. He was...' The rest of Brad's answer was drowned out by a metallic screeching. A train! A grain train was pulling up beside the silo. There'd be heaps of people. A driver, anyway.

'Help!' I shouted.

Brad joined in.

A hand grabbed my arm. Monaghan sat up, his face a nasty pasty colour.

I screamed, and just then a mechanical whirring started up below. Something shifted. Suddenly I was sinking, I was into the grain to my knees. Monaghan's hand bit deep into my arm.

'Brad. I'm sinking.' My voice was high. 'You said the grain's not a problem if the auger isn't on.'

'That *is* the bloody auger. Grab my hand.'

Jesus. I dropped to mid-thigh.

Monaghan plunged down to his neck, his grey face visible just above the grain. He grabbed me underneath the wheat, hands tight around my waist.

'Mum, quick.'

I sank again, to my knicker line. I let out another scream.

Brad swung back and forth from that beam like he'd worked the circus all his life. He grabbed my wrist. 'I won't let go, Mum. I'll never let you go.'

I believed him. My boy Brad, he'd never let me go. His trousers might though.

Brad pulled hard, my arm and shoulder burning with the impossible stretch. Monaghan gripped my waist, dragging me down. The grain kept sucking. I kept screaming.

'Shoot him, Mum.'

'Shoot him?' I whispered.

'I can't hold you both. He's too heavy.' Brad wheezed.

Still holding Brad one-handed, I scrabbled for the gun in my knickers. I pointed it at Monaghan. I looked at his bloodless face. Was that fear in the pinches around his eyes?

I shut my eyes. Squeezed the trigger. Deafening noise followed by a crazy pinging as the bullet ricocheted around.

I opened my eyes.

Monaghan stared at me.

Jesus. I should have aimed.

Monaghan's hand surged out in a burst of grain. He grabbed the gun. Held it against the centre of my chest.

'You stupid man,' I hissed. 'You gunna shoot me? I'm what's keeping you alive. Me and Brad. We're your human chain to out of here.' I sounded braver than I felt.

I looked at him, at his mad, dark eyes.

I grabbed his wrist, knocked the gun from his hand. It fell with a soft plop onto the wheat.

He grunted, let go of me and snatched the gun. Holding in it two hands, he pointed it up at my head. His finger pressed against the trigger.

I closed my eyes. The grain heaved again and I sank down to my boobs. I opened my eyes.

Monaghan was gone. Just the gun on the grain.

Brad started yelling, I started yelling, maintaining my death-grip on his hand.

The whirring auger slowed.

But no one came. Clutching the gun, I aimed towards the hatch and fired.

There was a sharp cry from above and the silhouette of a head appeared in the hatch.

'Down here,' I gasped.

'Jesus, Mum,' Dean groaned, 'I don't believe it. You've shot me in the bloody leg.'

Despite a nasty flesh wound, Dean managed to winch us out, one by one, from the silo, aided by the grain-train fellas. After he'd finished with the hoisting and a lot of shouting about safety, guns and the sheer stupidity of people who climb into silos, he finally let me explain.

Then, at last, Dean listened. Without interrupting, not even once.

He glared at me for a moment with those brown–black eyes, then got onto his radio to organise a police hunt for Aurora. He called up for tracker dogs, and helicopters and fifty cops from across two states.

'Let me call the ambos for you, son.'

He gritted his teeth, clutching firmly onto his radio. 'I'll do it myself, Mum.'

Nothing I could do, just do my best to bandage up his bleeding leg.

Afterwards we waited in Dean's divvy van for the

ambulance. A magpie warbled. The early morning air was cool. I rubbed my arms.

Dean grunted, said a quiet, 'Sorry, mate,' to Brad. Then, his eyes too shiny, he whispered, 'Why didn't you tell me, Mum? A good thing Vern called me. You could have been killed.'

The ambos arrived and whizzed Dean off to Hustle. He phoned me later that morning, to tell me he'd arrested Terry, who he'd spotted from the ambulance en route to the hospital. Presumably Terry hadn't been expecting to be arrested in a drive-by ambush by an ambo.

After three days of searching, a New South Wales cop and his dog, quite a nice dog, a friendly labrador called Trixie, found Aurora in the bush not too far from Ernie's shack.

She was in not-bad shape, in the circumstances. Dehydrated and somewhat hysterical, as any person would be after witnessing her nanna's and her brother's murders and fleeing into hot, ant-infested mallee country for the best part of a fortnight. She was whisked away pronto to Muddy Soak by Ravi and a swarm of trauma counsellors.

Aurora was carrying an important letter. A letter Kev Pittering had written and Clarence had found hidden deep inside Kev's briefcase. It was one of those *if you're reading this, I've been murdered* kind of letters, stating Kev was off to meet Monaghan to call an end to the Pocket Money arrangement.

Monaghan had roped Kev in as his bookkeeper, back when he'd started his little racket in the eighties. But Kev had decided he was finally leaving the accounting trade to pursue his acting career. He hadn't realised working with Monaghan was a job for life. Aurora also had Clarence's book, if you could call it that. Four versions of chapter one in barely readable scrawl.

'Terry's hairs were all over that wool bag,' Dean told me in a quiet voice, after he'd got out of hospital, leaning over his mound of vegetarian stir-fry. We were in Vern's dining room and Vern had ducked out to the kitchen to get another bowl of salad. Thanks to Brad, there's sixteen vegetarians now in Rusty Bore.

I nodded.

'Terry said he thought that bag contained a bloody sheep, can you believe it!' said Dean. 'Monaghan said he'd run over a sheep and didn't want the owner to know, in case they were upset. Incredible that Terry thinks we're so gullible as to believe that for a second. And with his footprints all around her body.'

'Yep, what sort of twit would confuse a dead woman with a sheep?' Number of legs for a start. I picked at my stir-fry.

'At least he's admitted he helped move her body. Twice. And he insists it was Monaghan who set fire to your place.'

'Well, I can half-believe that. Terry didn't seem the arsoning type. He fixed my car door, after all.'

'He was using you, Mum.'

I pushed my plate away. Stir-fry's never been my favourite.

'And if I have anything to do with it, he'll do the maximum sentence for accessory,' said Dean.

I don't know what Dean was so upset about. It wasn't him who'd slept with the man. Or who had lingering daydreams involving a fella with disappointed, faded blue eyes.

'How long would that be, exactly?' I kept my voice casual.

'Long enough for you to bloody well move on.'

'Why did Monaghan kill Mona?' I said, not only to change the subject. This fact was still unclear to me. Clarence I could understand, since he'd found Kev's letter and the Pocket Money file and been stupid enough to try to blackmail Monaghan. But what did Mona have to do with it?

'Wrong place at the wrong time. He was probably aiming at Clarence. Lucky for Aurora she was outside in the loo when Monaghan arrived at the shack. He didn't know she was there.'

Shame his nanna got in the way.

'The bullet in Mona was definitely from Monaghan's gun. And the ones in Ernie's walls,' said Dean.

Vern came back with the salad. 'What I don't understand is why he killed that Donald fella. Mind you, a lot of dodgy things probably went on in the back of that bloke's van.' He gave me a significant nod.

'Aurora asked Donald for help after she saw him in the bush near Ernie's. Monaghan had handcuffed Clarence to a tree.' Dean passed me the overflowing bowl of salad. 'Monaghan wanted the Pocket Money file. But Clarence couldn't give it to him, since he'd lost the key to the gun cabinet.'

'I told you Clarence was handcuffed to a tree. Didn't I?'

A pause. 'Maybe,' said Dean, the closest he could get to an apology.

'Why was the briefcase in the rubbish dump?' I said.

'Mona. According to Aurora, Mona thought Clarence was writing about her, about the Kota gas leak. So she dumped the case, thinking it contained his book, but he'd already emptied it.'

I took one lettuce leaf from the salad bowl. 'Aurora should have gone to the police. To you.'

'Come on, Mum. She saw a cop chase Mona and Clarence out of the shack while she hid in the outside toilet. And then found Mona dead and Clarence handcuffed to a tree. We weren't exactly looking like the citizen's friend.'

'And why did she steal my car?'

'She thought she and Clarence could get away, hide interstate. But your car ran out of petrol straight away. Don't you fill your car, Mum?'

So Aurora's failed getaway attempt was my fault now? 'And Donald?'

'He was stealing eggs, part of the bird-smuggling racket the North-West Parrot Trust was running,' said Dean. 'Aurora saw him and begged him to buy a hacksaw so they could open Clarence's handcuffs. And some food. Monaghan saw Donald and knew he had to get rid of him. So he got him drunk, crashed his van, pinning Mona's death on Donald.'

Yep, those moist-wipes must have been for Aurora. She would have needed to moistly wipe the dust off her skin, after all that.

If Dean had only listened, Clarence and Donald might have lived. And Monaghan, of course. Although I wasn't quite as sorry about him.

I zapped two Chiko Rolls in the microwave. It's not the same serving takeaway in Vern's old caravan. The impact on quality control is a worry. But good old Vern got that van cleaned up pronto, dredging it out from his shed once he got wind of the taskforce. He still sees many advantages in a merger, he tells me. I've told him I'm determined to rebuild.

'My customers demand it, Vern. Once the insurance comes through.' Me and my insurer are currently negotiating over the definition of a fire although personally I fail to see the area of ambiguity.

It had been a week since the silo and my split lip, bruised face and dog-bitten leg were almost healed. But it would take longer before I could sleep again. It wasn't just the lumpiness of Vern's couch. I kept waking at three a.m., heart jack-hammering, after dreams involving mad oozy eyes, guns and suffocation underneath a tonne of wheat. I'm probably too sensitive.

Between them, Clarence and Monaghan had turned the top-grade wheat in that silo into pig food. Still, their families gave them proper funerals. I didn't go, I was too busy serving takeaway to the taskforce. And all the TV crews.

Good little eaters, those TV crews. The ABC even found some money for a documentary. All about Monaghan and what drove him to do it. A sympathetic type of show. The producer, Quinn, told me about it as he waited for his burger.

'We're focusing on the strain country police officers are under. And the terrible isolation of the psychopath. It's an under-explored area.' Quinn put his elbows up on the window frame.

I nodded, as I wrapped up his order. It didn't sound to me like the show would have much of an audience.

'Shoot the flaming bastards, every one of them,' said Ernie, his yellowed moustache quivering.

Quinn raised his eyebrows.

Ernie was on day-release from the home.

'Fella's already dead, Ernie,' I said. 'Not to worry, I'll do you a nice piece of grilled whiting.' I grabbed Ernie's fish from the mini-freezer. 'See ya, Quinn.'

It's not been easy to settle Ernie down after recent events. Poor bugger still thinks Grantley Pittering is somehow related to Hugo Pitterline and therefore Grantley should be forced to hand over Ernie's unpaid sixty dollars plus inflation since 1988, however much that is.

But I had good news for Ernie. Aurora didn't want Clarence's five grand, she'd said she wanted to have nothing to do with Clarence's affairs. After I wrapped up Ernie's whiting, I presented him with his cash.

'Five bloody grand?' Ernie spat on the ground. 'Mafia money? Not on your life. Filthy people.' He threw the money back at me.

'Clarence wasn't...'

'Lack of bloody judgment, Cassandra Ariadne. It's always been your problem. That's the reason you're still flamin' well single after all this time.' Ernie snatched up his fish and shuffled off.

Brad paused from cutting up the chips. 'Don't worry, Mum. There's someone out there for you, I'm sure of it.' He must have seen my face.

'Yeah. Listen, give that microwave a little wipe-over for me, will you?'

'Look at male chimps. They're totally into older females—they don't let a bit of wrinkled skin or weird bald patches put them off.' He waved the dishcloth. 'And chimps are our closest relatives. Only two per cent of our DNA isn't in a chimpanzee. There'll be a nice bloke for you out there somewhere.'

'Thanks son. Although to tell the truth I'm not really in the market for a chimp.'

I went through the contents of the mini-freezer. I'd be needing more whiting before tomorrow. Bloody Ernie. Lack of judgment. Thing is, Dean had made that point as well. *A person has to be careful about the company she keeps.*

Turned out Victoria Police could reverse a decision, like I'd always said. Instead of transferring Dean to Traffic Management, they lined him up quick-smart to take over Muddy Soak. He'll be busy: that town is just teeming with crime. There's even talk of awarding Dean a medal.

Injured in the line of duty. There'll be no need for him to mention exactly who injured him.

I had a thought. 'Brad? Why was your laptop in Donald's van? Was that something to do with Direct-Action? Monaghan mentioned it.'

Brad looked up from his potatoes. 'He lied, Mum. Murderers do that.'

'And you and DirectAction? No orchestrating?'

'No.' He gave me a smile.

Working in the van hasn't exactly hit Brad's G-spot, but it's giving him a chance to save up for university. He'll soon be starting his course in eco-bio-whatsit. I'm getting ready to miss him.

While he cut up the chips, he started on a mini-lecture: how small, fast-moving birds experience an entire lifetime in what seems to us barely an instant.

'Their perception of time is quite different to ours, Mum. To them, we move as slowly as a sloth.'

'Yep. Speaking of which, you gunna clean that microwave?'

'There's no way I'm letting incredible animals like that just disappear, Mum.'

I've never seen Brad look so determined. His face is all aglow. It's possible he's in love, Madison's been around a bit.

I had to point out to Madison the sad fact that the van's too small for the run of any type of ferret, even the vulnerable, abandoned kind. Plus health and safety etcetera. She stood at the caravan window, looking forlorn, surrounded by those hissing animals jerking on their leads.

After Madison left I started cutting up some onions. 'Listen, Brad,' I said. 'You can't just bugger off to uni without a word to Claire. You need to ask her out, have a chat, sort it all out with her about the baby. She can't stay on forever with those Hustle rellos. The baby needs a father.'

He stopped wiping out the microwave, turned and looked at me. 'Mum. I have to tell you something.'

'I'm fully briefed on chimps, Bradley. What we need to talk about is you. And your responsibilities.'

'Jesus. Will you just sit down and listen for once?'

Right then. I sat down on the wooden stool.

'You know how Dad kind-of, ah...remember when he went to Perth?'

Well, yes. That was years ago. What did Piero going to Perth have to do with anything?

'That time when he went over for Auntie Vanni's wedding? Twenty years ago?'

'Yeah, he went for the weekend. What's this got to do with anything?'

'He met Claire's mother while he was in Perth.'

I felt cold suddenly.

'I won't be asking Claire out, Mum, since she's my sister.'

A quiet afternoon, apart from all the calls to my mobile.

I sent Brad out to Hustle. 'Need more potatoes. Urgently,' I said.

He looked at the two twenty-kilo bags of spuds in the corner, then at my face. I pushed his car keys into his hand and shoved him out the door.

Each time my phone rang, I saw it was the same number. Sophia's. I didn't answer.

I cleaned every surface in that old van. Shining shelves,

shining windows. I cleaned every knife, cutting board and egg lifter. I cut potatoes and made enough chips to feed eight Homicide units. Maybe the ABC team as well.

A voice at the window. 'Cass.' Vern.

'Sophia called.'

'Yep.' I started peeling another potato.

'You need to get up to the hospital.'

Claire was propped up in the bed, face flushed. Sophia was sitting in a brutally upright chair, beside the bed, Brad next to her. Piero's three older brothers stood in a military-style row behind them, arms folded.

I took the chair on the other side.

Sophia held a tiny baby wrapped in pink, one hand smoothing up and down its pink back.

'*Cara.*' Sophia looked at me, her eyes too shiny. Her hand still moved across the baby's back. Those hands had once been olive-brown and tanned. Now they were papery and rustled as she moved.

'Congratulations Claire,' I smiled. Tried to. 'She's beautiful.'

'Brad came over,' said Sophia. 'You have to understand, Cassie, I couldn't tell you.' Had Sophia shrunk since I'd seen her last, a few days ago? Her skin looked loose, like it might flap in the wind.

I folded my arms. 'Course not. I was only his wife. Told everyone else, though, didn't you?' I glanced at the row of brothers. They looked at their feet.

Sophia bit her lip. 'Not me.'

'Well, who then?'

She shrugged. 'Does it really matter now?'

'What a good laugh you all had.' It didn't feel like it

was me who was talking. The real me was somewhere else, watching. 'For twenty years. Poor old Cass. A living cliché.'

Sophia coughed. Tony the middle brother surged forward, taking the baby, holding a glass up to Sophia's mouth. 'Mum. Drink. Don't upset yourself.' He scowled at me.

She took a tiny sip. 'It wasn't like that, *cara*. We would not laugh at you. Everyone love you. Except one or two possibly…Anyway, I didn't want you hurt.'

A pause.

'Look, come over Monday for coffee. Claire be home by then.'

I looked at Claire, at Tony, at his brothers. A row of nods.

'I make biscotti. You like my biscotti. I'm teaching Claire. She learn quickly.'

'Got a bit on at the minute.'

'The thing is Claire, she could do with a little bit help right now.'

I looked at the baby, looked at Claire, at the baby's pointy head. I remembered my life after Dean was born. That wonderful cushion with the keyhole-shaped opening. Hardly being able to go outside, not in a Rusty Bore summer with a tiny baby's skin. Claire gave me a tired lopsided smile.

'And you always say, Cassie,' Sophia's eyes were moist, 'you always tell me you would have like a daughter.'

Sophia's almond biscotti are famous for good reason. As is her ability to hold a family together, regardless of its dim-witted blunders.

*

When I got back to the van there was a letter waiting. From Terry. They let them send out letters, apparently, and don't cut out half the words like I'd expected. He's on remand, expecting to serve a minimum of four years.

He'd scribbled at the end: *Any chance of that takeaway place by the sea someday? I'll wait for you if you can wait for me.*

I folded up the letter. In the circumstances it didn't seem like that generous an offer. Still, maybe it meant Terry wasn't just using me like Dean had said. I sighed and stared off into a shop-by-the-sea middle distance. I shoved the letter in my pocket.

I'll write back, maybe. When I'm ready. Four years is a long time, and I could be anywhere by then.

Author's note

I would like to swear categorically that there is no such place as Rusty Bore. Furthermore, this book does not contain any real people, dogs or ferrets.

But if, like me, you'd quite like it if Rusty Bore did exist, you could try turning off the Calder Highway somewhere north of Wycheproof. You never know what you might find. Please let me know if you do find Cass, I'd love to know if she's real.

I'd also like to thank a number of real people for their support: Euan Mitchell, Nick Gadd, the novel work-shopping groups at Box Hill TAFE, Eileen Hamer, Michael Kurland, Peter Garland, Selga and Sarah Langley and Evelyn and Bill Williams.

Special thanks are also due to the folks at Text, particularly Penny Hueston, Michael Heyward and Mandy Brett.

To Small But Big, aka Nicki Reed, thanks for never letting go.

And to Ross, thanks for never once telling me to quit. In fact, it could be argued this is all your fault.